HOLLI JO MONROE

The Imagined Attachment

The Bath Schoolmates Book 1

BRILLIG PRESS

First published by Brillig Press 2022

This novel is entirely a work of fiction. The names, characters and incidents portrayed in it are the work of the author's imagination. Any resemblance to actual persons, living or dead, events or localities is entirely coincidental.

First edition

ISBN: 978-1-958270-02-8

This book was professionally typeset on Reedsy.
Find out more at reedsy.com

To all those who believed in me. Even when I stopped believing in myself.

Contents

FULL-COLOR MAP AVAILABLE ON HOLLIJOMONROE.COM

iv

Chapter One

August 1818

Dear Elaine,

Please indulge your old teacher the presumption of this note. I wished to give you some parting wisdom. I suspect you will have more than the usual difficulties adjusting to your new life in the country.

Returning to the place of one's youth can be trying. You are no longer a girl of eleven and things will be different in a woman's eyes. Time is needed to reacquaint yourself with the countryside and the people. Trust that in time things will improve and you will feel at home again. Until then, please rely upon me as a confidant.

Given the recent actions of our Miss Penelope, I must also advise you to be sensible in matters of the heart. You cannot help being thrown into the company of the Ashburns. You quite know my feelings about your Mr. Ashburn and I will not repeat them as it would require several pages. I will say only that two and twenty is too old to indulge in a schoolgirl fancy and there are far better things on which to fix your hopes. Set your sights on other worthy goals. All of us need an occupation to achieve true happiness.

I need hardly encourage you to be cheerful or patient. I know your nature far too well to suppose you need such guidance. However, if you find yourself in need of

1

respite, you are always welcome at Pembray House. It has been my great pleasure to be your teacher, employer, and friend.

I look forward to our correspondence. Until then, I remain,

Affectionately,
Honoria Piper

As Elaine Brooke reread Mrs. Piper's note, she leaned against the comforting old oak tree. Dappled shadows danced over the words while wood doves cooed their sympathy; Elaine was insensible to both. Her old headmistress had been correct. Her return home was trying. It had only been a week, but the paper was already showing signs of wear from many readings.

"Perkins, there you are." Mama's voice drifted over the lawn from the kitchen.

Elaine pressed herself tighter against the tree as she listened to her mother and their only female servant.

"You may take the donkey cart to Oakbury. I am too fatigued to go anywhere today."

"Very good, madam," Perkins said. "Will Miss Brooke be needing anything in town?"

"No, she will not."

Elaine cringed at the terseness in her mother's voice. There were things Elaine wanted—books, ink, new gloves, ribbon—but no money for them. Last night, Mama had lectured on the need to reduce her correspondence, claiming the cost of post would land them in the poor house. It was an exaggeration; their funds were meager, but the Ashburns would never evict them from Ryder Lodge. However, if old gloves and ribbons were the price for maintaining ties to her former life in Bath, she would gladly pay it.

At the age of eleven, Elaine had arrived at Mrs. Piper's Seminary for Young Ladies secure in the knowledge that she would always prefer the woods and fields of her country home. Now, at twenty-two, she found herself daily wishing to be back at Pembray House with her friends. Their letters would be a great comfort. Mrs. Piper's note, with its assurance of a welcome in

Bath, had already eased her transition.

Elaine was trying to follow the letter's advice by practicing patience, but after arguing again with Mama last night, she realized exercise and time on her own was needed. In Bath, she had enjoyed long walks or exploring Sydney Gardens. She hoped reacquainting herself with the secret and most cherished places of her youth would make her feel more at home.

With her half-boots, bonnet, and shawl, she had strolled into the garden but only made it to the old oak tree before consulting the letter once again. As she stored the paper in her reticule, she studied Ryder Lodge. The red brick and climbing ivy seemed smaller after years at Pembray House, but what the lodge lacked in size, it made up for in prospect.

Set back from the main village road, a lane of stately trees marked the path to the tidy building. Behind the home, flower beds surrounded the stretch of lawn along a stone wall. The grass was interrupted only by the ancient oak tree. To the east, a tiny bit of woodland, to the west, a kitchen garden. At the far end, on the other side of the wall, ran a cheerfully flowing brook with a quaint wooden bridge leading to lush green woods. The trees marked the edge of the venerable park of Ryder Hall, home of the Ashburns.

Elaine pushed off the tree and stepped into the bright late afternoon sunshine. Grass brushed her ankles as she crossed to the low stone wall. The gate groaned when she pulled it open as if protesting her chosen path. When she crossed the bridge, something loosened in her chest as childhood memories rushed in. It had been eleven years since she had left for school and seven years since she had been in the neighborhood. Elaine imagined she could see her younger self laughing and running. She had been happy here as a child.

She would learn to be happy again.

A breeze sighed through the branches and she heard the echo of Papa's voice as he told her stories of King Arthur. The flash of a rabbit's tail reminded her of setting traps for fairies and catching a poor bunny instead. Daniel had helped her set it free. Glancing up at the trees, she could almost see Daniel standing there, urging her to join him. She could hardly think of her childhood without finding him there.

Daniel Ashburn, the second son of Sir Thomas Ashburn, had become her friend when he found her crying in the woods the day after they buried Papa.

"Are you all right, Miss Brooke?" He had asked softly.

Embarrassed. she had straightened and wiped her tears.

"Master Ashburn." She executed an awkward curtsey. Mama had stressed the importance of being deferential to their august neighbors.

He stuck his tongue out in disgust. "You can call me Daniel."

Despite herself, her mouth turned up. "I'm Elaine."

"I am sorry about your father."

The words brought fresh tears to her eyes. Showing a sensitivity beyond his ten years, Daniel had patiently hugged her and listened to her fears of being without Papa. And when she ceased, with a boyish grin he offered to show her how to catch frogs. Even at seven years old she had been affected by his easy manner.

His friendship was a lifeboat that had rescued her from a sea of grief. He taught her to climb trees and sword fight. He brought her books from the Ashburn library and happily shared his tutor's lessons. He willingly played along with her flights of fancy, taking on the role of Sinbad the Sailor or a Knight of the Round Table with gusto.

Three years later, he left for school and broke her heart. She had mended it with the dream that they would reunite and marry one day. A foolish, schoolgirl fancy that had proven hard to discard.

As the years passed, Daniel's positive attributes grew in her mind. Though Mama assured her that he had a rake's reputation, Elaine did not believe it. She, his intimate friend, knew his character better than the petty gossips. The less Elaine saw of him, the more she could imagine him a perfect paragon.

The last time she saw Daniel was at the annual Twelfth Night ball at Ryder Hall. She was fifteen, and her four years of schooling in Bath had made her more interested in the dancing than the children's games. Elaine had crept outside. Shivering, she watched through the stained-glass window. Her eyes followed Daniel about the ballroom. Newly nineteen, the boy was now truly a man. He was charming, handsome, and already an accomplished flirt. In her fancies he was always a mirror of that night.

For a year, she had dreamed of attending the Twelfth Night ball and captivating Daniel. He would spend the whole night at her side and propose under the full moon. But that year, and every year after, Mama had come to Bath for Christmas with her friend. Elaine had never danced with Daniel or attended another Twelfth Night ball at Ryder Hall.

This year she might attend the ball but was unsure who her partners would be when she had no fortune to attract them. Mrs. Piper's assumption that she would see Daniel now that she was home was unfounded. He was rarely seen at Ryder Hall and unlikely to choose her. The mere half-mile of pleasant woodland that separated their houses might as well be an ocean.

Of course, that had not stopped Elaine from imagining a meeting with him.

He would meet her eye across the street in Oakbury and rush to her side, heedless of the carts and horses between them. He would pass her pew at church and halt at the sight of her, causing the whole neighborhood to crane their necks and whisper. Her imagination did not lack for scenarios. Often, she dreamed that she would captivate him with her beauty and sophistication. Unlike the men she had met in Bath, Daniel would forget about her lack of dowry and court her.

In such pleasant imaginings, Elaine wandered the woods. Thus distracted, she did not notice the large, low-hanging branch until it caught at her loosely-tied bonnet.

"Oh!" she exclaimed as she was pulled back toward the tree. She reached up and tried to untangle the hat. Silently she cursed Penelope for insisting on the complex trimming. When she couldn't get it free, she untied the bonnet and stepped forward, leaving it hanging from the branch. She blew away the hair that had pulled from her simple coiffure and began the now easier task of freeing her captured property.

As it came away in her hand, she gave a cry of victory. A deep voice chuckled behind her, and she spun around. Stunned, Elaine stood as if carved of marble. In all her imaginings, she had never thought to meet

Daniel like this.

He was broader, slightly taller, his hair a darker shade of brown, but his eyes were still a piercing blue, and there was no mistaking that smile. He was dressed fashionably in an expertly tailored gray-blue coat that complimented his eyes and olive coloring, but his cravat was haphazard and his boots scuffed.

Elaine was self-conscious of her plain muslin gown, worn green scarf, and bare head. His eyes flicked to the bonnet in her hand and he smiled. He met her gaze again; she saw approval there. She knew her freckles were standing out against her reddened cheeks as her body warmed all over.

"I do beg your pardon," he said in a baritone so different from the voice she remembered. "You've quite stunned me to silence."

She returned his grin. "Ah, and to silence you is quite the feat."

His mouth quirked as he raised his eyebrows. "You profess to know me quite well. Yet we are not acquainted? Are you perhaps a wood nymph sent to steal my heart?"

Her amusement grew. Did Daniel truly not recognize her, or was he referencing their old games? They had often pretended the woods were full of fantastical creatures.

"I am very much human."

"So not magical?"

"Sadly no."

"But you do know me?"

"I know you, Mr. Ashburn." His brow furrowed. "The eligible younger brother of Sir Phillip Ashburn, fond of racing, dancing, cards, and young women and the despair of matchmakers and scheming mamas alike."

She was being pert but couldn't help it. Long years separated them but to her, they were still intimates.

Daniel looked baffled but grinned at her description of him. "You must know me by reputation. For surely I have not forgotten being introduced to one so lovely."

The riot in her stomach was unexpected. Her fancies had not prepared her for such a reaction to his compliment. His eyes gleamed with mischief.

6

He was aware of the effect of such praise. Mama called him an incorrigible flirt. Elaine was not of the mind to discourage him.

"Mr. Ashburn, are you implying that I would talk to a man not of my acquaintance?"

She placed a hand on her chest in mock shock. Her aim was true and Daniel seemed momentarily stymied before cocking his head.

"I would never malign you. The fault is all mine." He gave a deep bow and smiled playfully. "Anyone can see you are far too genteel to talk in a lane with a stranger. You must forgive my abominable memory and give me leave to accompany you while I try to recall our first meeting."

He offered his arm, and Elaine took it without thinking. Giddiness overtook her. Caught up in the moment, she didn't consider what might happen when he discovered her identity.

"I will not require you to remember our first meeting." She thought that might prove sobering. "My name alone will suffice."

They began to move along the path toward Ryder Hall.

"Only your name?" He hummed and tapped his chin as if in deep thought. "Well, that should not be so difficult given what I know."

"And what do you know?"

"I know that you must be here for the house party."

Elaine frowned. The Ashburns were throwing a house party? That was unusual. Sir Phillip, unmarried and only twenty-nine, was inclined to live quietly with his mother at Ryder Hall. Though a good landlord and a steady neighborhood leader, Elaine had always been a little afraid of him.

"I see I have hit upon the truth," Daniel said when she did not immediately reply.

"Have you?"

"Since the party is not large, all that remains is a simple process of elimination."

"And do you know the guest list?"

She was sure he didn't. Daniel had never been one for details. Though she was four years younger, he had always left the particulars to Elaine. When he had wanted a picnic at the ruins of the Old Priory, Elaine had been the one to create a plan, charm Cook to provide food, and devise a way to transport it.

"I can easily get the list," he said.

"But that will do you no good since I am not a guest at Ryder Hall."

"Not a guest?" He stopped and turned toward her. She submitted to his inspection. Her cheeks grew warm again as his bright blue eyes met hers. He was sure to remember her now.

"There is something about you—" He shook his head.

Disappointment flooded her, dousing the fire he had lit. He had filled her dreams all these years, even inspired her to become an accomplished young woman, but he had not thought of her at all.

"You must be a recent addition to the neighborhood. I am sure I know every pretty girl in the parish." He grinned down at her.

Even the pleasure of being called pretty could not soothe the pain of his lack of recognition. Was she so changed?

They exited the shade of the trees, and Elaine pretended to be absorbed in the view. Before them lay a long lawn and Ryder Hall glowing in the afternoon light. The baronetcy was old and well respected, but the house and grounds conformed to modern sensibilities. Its white walls, columns, and large portico coupled with the formal gardens and serpentine design of the park spoke of the taste and income of the Ashburn family.

With her three hundred pounds, hand-me-down dress, and little beauty, Elaine was uncomfortably aware that she did not belong in such a house or on the arm of Mr. Daniel Ashburn. He was meant for a woman of great wealth, from an old titled family, well known for her accomplishments and beauty.

Of course, Elaine always told herself that her daydreams would never come true, but as he struggled to identify her, she saw the full extent of her folly.

She had harbored a secret hope that Daniel felt as she did. That hope had been buried so deep she hadn't even realized it was still there. No wonder Mrs. Piper had encouraged her to be sensible. For all her polish and refinement, she was still, at heart, a silly girl.

How could she bear to remain in his company? She no longer wanted him to know her identity. She turned to Daniel, ready to make her excuses and depart. But his eyes were fixed on an approaching rider.

Elaine followed his gaze and recognized Sir Phillip Ashburn. Her heart dropped. The baronet, master of all the eye could see, did not look happy as he rode straight for them.

"Here comes my keeper to take me to task." Bitterness tinged Daniel's voice. "But perhaps you are fortunate enough not to be acquainted with my brother?"

Daniel turned to her, clearly intent on ignoring Sir Phillip. Elaine tried to focus on the blue of his eyes instead of the skittering of her heart. Sir Phillip always made her unaccountably nervous.

"He is a nice fellow but practically a hermit and a tremendous bore. Of course, he has the title so nobody ever dares speak ill of him."

"You dare."

"I am quite brave."

Despite herself, Elaine smirked. She had always thought bravery was Daniel's best quality. Sir Phillip was practically upon them, still frowning as he slowed his horse. She wished she had put her bonnet back on. What must he be thinking? She began to pull her arm from Daniel's but he held it in place.

"Never fear. I shall protect you."

He patted her hand and then turned to face his brother.

The family resemblance was strong between them. Their eyes were a similar blue, though Sir Phillip's surely never danced with merriment. Where Daniel was dark-haired, Sir Phillip was fair. His jaw was more pronounced, his skin more weathered from time outdoors. One might call him handsome, though it was hard to see it as he glared down at them from the back of his horse.

"Daniel, you are supposed to be greeting our guests, not gallivanting about the countryside." Phillip dismounted as his brother scoffed.

"I am hardly about the countryside if I am in view of the hall. And you would not have me leave a young lady alone?"

"I think she is more than capable of walking the home woods on her own."
Though Elaine agreed with Sir Phillip, his dismissive tone still hurt.

"Your rudeness astounds me." Daniel's outrage seemed disproportionate, but it appeared to awaken Sir Phillip to his duty.

Turning from his brother, he offered a respectful bow. "Miss Brooke, please allow me to apologize. I am sure my brother is quite right to assume you are helpless."

Elaine's mouth went dry as she curtsied. How had he known her identity when Daniel hadn't? She did not know how to answer his sarcasm.

"Miss Brooke?"

She winced at the incredulity in Daniel's voice.

"How is your health? And your mother?" Sir Phillip asked as if his brother hadn't spoken.

"Excellent, I thank you."

"Miss Elaine Brooke?" Daniel spluttered.

Her entire face burned as she turned to him. He was staring with abashed wonder. Gone were the admiration and the compliments. Now that he knew her identity, he would likely never flirt with her again.

"Miss Elaine Brooke of Ryder Lodge?"

She nodded and looked away only to catch Sir Phillip eyeing his brother with a disapproving frown.

Explaining would expose her foolishness. She took a step backwards. "I should return home."

Daniel took a step forward and raised his hand, as if he would object.

Taking another step back, she rushed to avert his protest.

"I have no need of an escort. I know my way very well."

She curtsied, wished them a good day, and fled into the safety of the woods.

Chapter Two

S ir Phillip Ashburn observed his brother as Miss Brooke disappeared into the trees. There was something in the calf-struck way Daniel stared after the young lady that warned of trouble. Only home an afternoon and already he was creating problems. Problems Phillip would have to solve, for Daniel could not be relied upon.

What would the Talbots think if they saw him with Miss Brooke?

"Daniel." Phillip's horse tossed her head at the low growl of his voice.

"What?" Daniel turned around.

"Miss Brooke is not to be trifled with."

"Phillip, do you really think so little of me?"

"What I think is irrelevant." Phillip gestured to the hall. "Miss Talbot and her parents arrived an hour ago. Instead of welcoming them properly you forced Mother to make excuses for your absence. It was fortuitous that I was the one sent to fetch you. Imagine the talk if a servant had found you squiring around our pretty neighbor."

Daniel grinned. "She is pretty, though not in the usual way. When did that happen?"

"Daniel."

"I really must thank you, Phillip, for forcing me to attend this house party. For too long, I have been denied the pleasure of renewing the acquaintance of my pretty childhood friend."

"For once, be serious."

"Why? You are quite serious enough for the both of us." Daniel pretended indifference as he pulled at his cuffs.

Phillip clamped his mouth shut. He would not have this argument again. Were all brothers this maddening or just his? Among his tenants, acquaintances, and friends, Phillip was known for an even temper and mastery of his emotions. But Daniel, through long practice, knew precisely how to raise his ire.

"And there you go, proving my point with your sullen frown and disapproving air." Daniel's bright blue eyes fairly twinkled. "I think you quite frightened Elaine away."

"*Miss* Brooke can do very well for herself, and in any case she is not your concern. Miss Talbot is the young lady who you should be escorting about the grounds."

"Yes, of course, Miss Talbot." Daniel sighed as if the thought of escorting the beautiful and rich Frederica Talbot were a chore rather than a privilege that many an impoverished bachelor would relish.

In London, Daniel had seemed keen on gaining Miss Talbot's favor, and Phillip had rejoiced. The Talbots' recent elevation to the gentry was of no matter; they were respectable and Miss Talbot a good match for his wayward brother. But at the end of the Season, there had been no engagement. Phillip was forced to take the matter in hand to ensure that the opportunity didn't slip from Daniel's grasp. All would be for naught if Daniel went running after an impoverished tenant.

Phillip decided to play on his brother's competitive nature. "If you do not wish to entertain Miss Talbot, I will gladly take on the task."

Daniel stood a bit straighter. "There is no need to threaten torture on the poor girl."

"Torture? Perhaps she will find me far better company."

"Perish the thought." Daniel stuck out his hand for the reins. "I will ride your horse back. After all, the Talbots are my particular friends and I have deprived them of my company long enough."

Phillip handed over the reins, trying not to smile.

"If you think that best."

"I do. But not because I am jealous. I merely wish to save our guests from your sour company." Daniel swung into the saddle and gave a mock salute before turning and riding toward the house at a fast gallop.

Phillip frowned after him, pretending that the parting shot had not found its mark. Unlike Daniel and their mother, Phillip had never been able to speak easily in company. With practice he had learned to carry on the required sorts of meaningless conversations, but he had not the charm of his brother nor the grace of their mother. Phillip preferred conversations with his tenants or at his clubs, conversations of substance and importance about things he cared about. How many of those conversations would he have in the coming days?

For a moment, Phillip considered turning around and losing himself in the woods, hiding there as Daniel had done, but banished the thought just as quick. He was master of the hall and host to the arriving guests. He would not shirk his duty, even if he were ill-suited to the task. With long, measured strides, he walked toward the house.

He was almost in the shadow of the walls when he caught sight of guests arriving. The late afternoon sun made the faded gilt work sparkle as the carriage trundled down the lane toward the hall. Phillip smiled at the familiar sight. At least he would have his old school friend Richard Farthing and his charming wife to help him through the next few weeks. He turned his steps to greet them at the front of the house. Servants swarmed around the stopped carriage. The footman opened the door, and Richard Farthing climbed out, a characteristic smile on his wide face.

"Ashburn, one moment. "

Farthing turned to help his wife out of the carriage. Formal greetings followed.

Mrs. Jane Farthing was sturdily built with gray blue eyes and a perpetual smile. In character and temperament, she was the perfect companion to the amiable Richard. Phillip often thought that if Richard, a stout man of little fortune and a crooked nose and close-set eyes, could find a match, there was hope for anyone.

Phillip escorted his guests from the carriage to the grand circular staircase that led to the front entrance. The stairs rose above the rusticated basement to the portico. Four large columns supported an impressive triangular pediment that reached two stories high.

Ryder Hall was the pride and folly of Phillip's grandfather. The idealistic baronet had returned from his Grand Tour and rejected the old Tudor mansion that had always served the family. At great expense, the new hall had been built as a model of the Palladian style.

Adhering to the rules of proportion, the solid square of the main house was balanced by the smaller wings flanking it. A single story corridor connected them. Tall rectangular windows marched over the façade, regular as soldiers. The roof was shallow-pitched, the chimneys almost hidden.

It was beautiful and elegant, but had cost a fortune. The estate was still weighed down by the expense. It was all done in the name of recreating pure classical architecture. Phillip could not say how accurate the design was. He had never had the luxury of a Grand Tour. At nineteen, he was running the estate, not running about the continent.

"I see the guests have already run you out of the house," Richard said. There was none of the usual talk of road conditions and weather with him. Of all people, Farthing understood Phillip's aversion to house parties, especially those held in his own home.

Phillip quirked his mouth. "Not quite; I was retrieving my brother from the grounds."

"And how is the Prodigal? Still costing you a fortune?"

Mrs. Farthing slapped playfully at her husband. "Must you say that so loud?"

"Would saying it quietly change the truth?" Farthing whispered.

Phillip smiled. "My brother is as he ever was."

"By which you mean charming but dissipated."

Phillip made no reply. There was no need for words when Farthing knew Phillip's long standing frustrations. He had spent his whole life worrying over Daniel. Shortly after Phillip became baronet, the reports from Daniel's school had been cause for concern. Mother had insisted it was merely Daniel's grief and he would soon come round. But years passed and Daniel continued to be ungovernable.

He had refused to settle on a profession. Farthing had offered to help set him up in the law, but Daniel had been uninterested, just as he was uninterested in the church, the militia, or working for the government. Phillip's connections would have smoothed any path, but Daniel had chosen to gamble at clubs, flirt in ballrooms, and flit about the country with his friends. The family coffers paid for this profligate lifestyle. Phillip hoped marriage would change his brother or at least remove the burden of funding him.

They came to the heavy oak door and it was immediately opened to reveal the dark paneling and marble floor of the entrance hall. It was Mrs. Farthing's first visit to Ryder Hall and her sharp eyes took in everything.

"You have a lovely home," she said.

"I am pleased it meets with your approval," Phillip said. He gestured to the waiting footman. "Tom will show you to your room. There will be no formal dinner tonight since some guests will be arriving quite late. You can request a tray or anything else you might desire. Tomorrow I will be giving a complete tour to all the guests, but Farthing knows his way around if you wish to explore. When you are ready, Mother will host you in the morning room." Phillip indicated the door on the left where faint voices could be heard.

"And you?" Farthing asked.

"If I am not there, I will be in my study."

Farthing grinned at him. "Of course you will."

Tom took the Farthings away, and Phillip stood alone for a moment in the hall, staring at the morning room door. Was it necessary for him to go in? He had already greeted the Talbots and, with Daniel and Mother, they did not lack for company.

Footsteps drew his attention away. Phillip turned around to see his butler emerging from the center of the house.

"Yes, Lennox?"

"Mr. Eden arrived while you were out. I put him in the study."

"Thank you, Lennox. Please inform Lady Ashburn that the Farthings have arrived."

"Very good, sir." Lennox gave a correct bow.

Phillip was a little ashamed at his eagerness to avoid his guests. He strode across the hall, following the Farthings' footsteps through the empty octagon room. The afternoon sun pouring through the high windows accentuated the yellow wallpaper. He exited through the right door and passed one of the large staircases. Farthing's laugh drifted down and Phillip smiled as he continued past the hidden servant stairs to the door of his study.

"Mr. Eden how good to see you," Phillip said as he entered. The vicar stood from the wingback chair by the unlit fireplace and greeted him. Though older than Phillip, Eden was shorter and rounder, with dark hair and a bulbous nose.

"Sir Phillip, please excuse my untimely arrival. I have just returned from London and had no notion that you were entertaining."

"There was no reason you should know. Please sit." Phillip settled into the chair across from him. "We are having a small house party. Some of the guests you know. Mr. Farthing just arrived with his new wife."

Mr. Eden smiled. "I look forward to renewing our acquaintance. I will endeavor to be brief. I would not want to keep you from your guests."

"I assure you I am in no hurry."

"You are too kind."

Phillip inclined his head at the unfounded compliment. Mr. Eden filled the silence. "I only came to inform you that I was unsuccessful in finding a teacher for the school."

"That is disappointing but expected."

They weren't offering enough money to attract a teacher to move from London, and small Brightworth was not a desirable destination.

"However, I may have a solution for the supplies. A good friend in London has a connection. He thinks we can obtain some supplies second-hand at an excellent price."

Mr. Eden detailed his plan and the amount he thought would be needed.

As usual, the vicar had worked out all the particulars and only needed Phillip's approval. Mr. Eden had received the living at Brightworth village the year before the death of Phillip's father.

At nineteen, Phillip had not been equal to the task of advising the older man, but Mr. Eden had always been careful to show deference. In ten years, their relationship had grown and Mr. Eden now often confided in Phillip. Their mutual respect led to Mr. Eden sharing his unique ideas about education and Phillip offering to help fund a school for the girls of the parish.

"I think that will do very well. Have them charge my accounts," Phillip said when Mr. Eden had finished.

"Excellent. And when we find a teacher, we will be able to start the school immediately."

Phillip did not share his optimism. The price a proper teacher would demand was just out of his reach. With the unexpected expenses Daniel often incurred, Phillip could never be sure he would have the additional funds needed. Once Daniel was married, Phillip would increase the offered salary. But he could not in good conscience promise to pay and house a teacher for a year when he was uncertain if the money would be available.

The easiest solution, of course, was for Mr. Eden to teach the girls, but with his duties at Brightworth and the two curacies he held at nearby parishes, he did not have the time or attention for the job.

His business concluded, Mr. Eden levered himself out of the chair. Phillip rose with him.

"Oh, don't bother, I know the way." Mr. Eden waved him off.

Phillip still accompanied him to the study door and wished him a good day. As Mr. Eden's steps faded away, Phillip sighed. The rear entrance to the morning room was on his right. The Talbots awaited.

Muffled laughter reached him. It seemed he was not missed.

He glanced at his desk and its stack of unanswered correspondence. It would be better to dispense with them now, as he might not have time once all the guests arrived. If he were needed, Mother would send for him.

He plowed through missives from the local landowners about the upcoming harvest. He attended to his responsibilities as magistrate—a poacher, a brawl at the pub, a minor land dispute—all common but all in need of his attention. He was writing instructions to his man of business in London when his mother entered.

Lady Ashburn was of generous personality and proportion. Though her dress and carriage were always elegant, she appreciated sensible people over fashionable ones. Not yet fifty, her age hadn't slowed her and she bore the work and strain of the sudden party with ease.

"I thought I would find you here."

There was no censure in her voice but he was abashed.

"My apologies, Mother."

She waved away his words. "It was only the Talbots who required attention and you had already done your duty to them." She sat gracefully in the wingback chair Mr. Eden had vacated. "Thank you for retrieving Daniel."

"Of course. Did he make himself agreeable?"

"You know he did. Daniel could charm a ship from a pirate." Lady Ashburn smiled fondly and Phillip struggled not to let his resentment show.

"Good, I would hate to think we threw a house party for nothing."

She pursed her lips. "This whole affair was your idea, Phillip. No one forced it on you."

Phillip ground his teeth. The decision to have a house party had been his, but his reasons had everything to do with Daniel. If his brother had come up to the mark and asked Miss Talbot to marry him, there would have been no need to manufacture a way for them to spend more time together. Phillip was throwing the party with the express purpose of getting Daniel married, settled, and out of his hair.

"At least try to enjoy our guests," Mother said. "With such short notice, it was a struggle to find company that adhered to your strictures."

Phillip had been insistent that the party be devoid of any other eligible young women. He could not have Daniel getting distracted by a pretty face. With her brown hair bared to the sun and bright green eyes, Miss Brooke flashed into his mind.

"Yes, of course," Phillip said. "You did a marvelous job. I did not mean to imply. . . . That is, I am just tired."

Mother nodded her forgiveness. "As am I. I confess that I am looking forward to the day that your wife will have the run of such things and I can enjoy the fruits of her labor."

"I am very grateful for all your work." Phillip ignored the pointed hint. His mother had been urging him toward matrimony in the last year, but Phillip couldn't consider his own situation until Daniel was properly settled.

"You know it is no bother." Mother smiled warmly. "Now, we must discuss the Hurst sisters. They sent their regrets. There was a death in the family."

"I am sorry to hear that. I have always found their conversation interesting."

The Hurst sisters, spinsters in their fifties, had perfectly answered Phillip's notion of ideal guests.

"Yes, I will miss them, but the chief difficulty was our uneven numbers."

"If it will help, I can excuse myself from dinner."

"Don't talk nonsense. I have already devised a solution. Mrs. Brooke and her daughter will do nicely to balance the table."

"No." The word was out before Phillip could stop it.

"Why, Phillip, how unkind. You have never objected before when Mrs. Brooke has made up our table. Do you not think her grand enough for the Talbots? I'll remind you that her grandfather was an earl. Her present poverty does not change her gentility."

"It's not that. I would object to the Talbots if they were so high in the instep."

Unlike some recently wealthy families, the Talbots did not put on airs. Phillip rather thought they would be impressed by Mrs. Brooke's distant connection to nobility, even if she had fallen out with her family.

"Then why do you object to one of my oldest friends coming to dinner?"

"I do not object to Mrs. Brooke. It is Miss Brooke who presents an obstacle."

Her eyes lit with understanding. "Little Elaine? She is a dear thing."

"She is not so little anymore." Phillip thought of Miss Brooke's pleasing figure standing beside Daniel. She was far from the slip of a girl that had roamed the estate with dirt on her face.

"But surely you do not think there is a danger Daniel would prefer her? They were as close as siblings when they were younger. I am sure he will look on her as a sister and nothing more."

Phillip scoffed. Daniel's smiles and remarks told a different story. "I think there is every danger that he will pursue her."

Lady Ashburn tilted her head as if considering the possibility. "I know there was some affection on Elaine's side."

"What?"

"Her mother told me. When she was young she fancied Daniel, and used to say she was going to marry him, but I am sure she grew out of it. Such schoolgirl infatuations fade."

"Perhaps," Phillip said.

Even if Miss Brooke no longer nursed a tendre for Daniel, Phillip feared what feelings might be ignited during the party. Unlike Phillip, Daniel had an uncanny ability to capture the hearts of young women.

Mother gave a decisive wave of her hand as if shooing the entire matter out the door. "I cannot believe there is any danger. I know you think your brother is fickle, but I see a real attachment between him and Miss Talbot. That he would throw her over for an old—Don't roll your eyes, it's undignified." Mother shook her head. "Even if I agreed with you, there is nothing to be done. The invitation has been sent and their company secured for every night of the party."

Phillip ran a hand through his hair, then scraped it down his face. Miss Brooke's presence would create trouble. He was sure of it. Daniel would flirt with her. Miss Talbot might become jealous. The already wary Mr. Talbot might object to Daniel's conduct. Miss Brooke could be lured into indiscretion. There was no telling the disasters that would befall the party.

His mother might be content to leave things to chance, but Phillip had a feeling that, as usual, he would have to protect Daniel from his own folly.

Chapter Three

When Elaine reached Ryder Lodge, she had run out of self-recriminations over her behavior, but she could not forget the look of bewilderment on Daniel's face. What did it mean? Was he pleased or upset that he had inadvertently flirted with his childhood friend? Would he speak to her again in the same manner?

She hoped he would.

As soon as she entered the house, Mama called for her, a note of discontent in her voice. Had news of her ill-fated meeting somehow reached her mother? Even in their small parish, Elaine did not think news traveled that quickly.

She entered the drawing room and found Mama sitting at her writing desk. After a few more strokes of her pen, Mama looked up from the page and her mouth turned down in displeasure.

"My dear girl, you are quite flushed. If you insist on tramping about the countryside, at least refrain from removing your bonnet like a hoyden. No man is interested in a young woman who looks like she works in the fields."

"Yes, Mama."

Elaine did not have to feign her contrition. Her lack of bonnet had certainly been noticed by Sir Phillip. Although, Daniel had seemed to approve. She warmed at the memory of his charming smile and sparkling eyes; they were an extraordinary shade of blue. She had long thought them a cornflower blue, but seeing them again she thought they might better be compared to the bluebell.

"Elaine, are you listening?"

The image of Daniel's eyes dissolved. "Sorry Mama, what did you say?"

Mrs. Brooke sighed. "This was precisely what I feared. Lady Ashburn is relying on us to be good company and getting continually lost in daydreams will not do."

Elaine bit back her retort and nodded. Her mother was right, though it pained her to admit it. When she was uninterested, her mind would wander. She needed to spend less time building stories in her head and more time attending to the world around her.

"We will just have to hope for the best." Mama gestured to a creamy piece of paper with an elegant scrawl. "We cannot refuse the invitation and abandon our neighbor in her time of need."

Elaine weighed Mama's displeasure if she asked what she meant against her curiosity to know.

"Invitation?" Her curiosity always won.

"You weren't listening at all." Mama's exasperation was tempered by the small smile that played at the corner of her mouth. "You truly are your father's daughter. I could speak to him for a half hour and he wouldn't hear a word of it. Just look at me with wide eyes when I asked him a question. He was too lost in his own thoughts and stories to attend to anything so mundane as household management."

Her voice took on the mix of melancholy and bitterness that often tinged memories of her late husband. Elaine wanted to ask for more details but knew better than to try. Mama could rarely recall Papa with anything approaching equanimity.

"I am sorry." Elaine wasn't sure if she was apologizing for not listening or being a painful reminder of a lost love.

"I know dear. Now, as I was saying, Lady Ashburn is having a house party and, due to unfortunate circumstances, needs us to attend her dinners for the duration of the event."

Elaine was not sure she had heard correctly. "Lady Ashburn wants us to attend them every evening for the coming weeks?" A thrill ran through her. Multiple nights in Daniel's company? Elaine's thoughts wanted to fly away, but she forced herself to focus on Mama.

"I see you understand the great honor. But I want you to understand the obligation as well. As her guests, it will be our task to be generally pleasing and take what burden we can from Lady Ashburn. All the refinements and accomplishments you acquired in school should serve you well. But you must not be too eager to display and you must attend to the conversations. If there are any eligible men among the party, that would be fortunate indeed, for men are not so thick on the ground here as in Bath."

Elaine tried not to flinch at the mention of her failure. Mama had made no secret of her hope that Elaine would find a husband while away from home.

"But the men do not matter as much as helping Lady Ashburn."

"Yes, Mama."

Mama looked at her carefully. "Good. The Ashburns have always been so kind to us. I do not want Lady Ashburn to regret the invitation."

Left unsaid was how much money would be saved by eating at the hall for so many nights. It would relieve some of the strain Elaine's return had created on Mama's limited resources.

"I will endeavor to be a credit to you," Elaine said.

"I suppose I can ask for nothing more." Mama turned back to her correspondence.

Accepting her dismissal, Elaine turned to leave. She could not stay and keep her expression even. Escaping up the stairs, she waited until her bedroom door was safely closed before letting out a small squeal of pleasure.

Before her stretched nights of opportunity, chances to become better acquainted with Daniel and convince him that she would make a good wife. Elaine was sure that there had been a keen interest in Daniel's eyes. Penelope had always said that only the spark of interest was needed to fan the flames of affection.

Elaine imagined that his interest might be the beginning of a grand passion that would overcome him the more time they spent together. He would seek her out in the drawing room and visit the house so that the neighborhood became abuzz with news of his favor. Her lack of fortune would be nothing in the face of his growing love.

At the thought Elaine sobered, for even in her wild imaginings she could not easily dismiss material concerns. In Bath, she was valued for her lively dancing and engaging conversation, but no man courted her. Charity and Penelope were constantly besieged by admirers while Elaine was merely a penniless friend, dressed above her income. Even with her good nature, Elaine could not easily forget the pain and disappointment of being overlooked.

But surely Daniel would be different. If he truly loved a woman, he would not care how much money she had. Was it so impossible to hope that he would see her true self and wish to marry her? The only way to get an answer was to make Daniel fall in love with her, but how did one do that?

Moving to her dressing table, she opened her small writing cabinet and began to compose a letter to Penelope. Among her friends, Penelope Aston was the expert on love. She was already married, having eloped with the handsome Mr. Aston two years ago. Elaine did not want to follow in Penelope's footsteps—for it had all ended badly—but wanted her hard-won wisdom. Penelope would know how to inspire love in Daniel.

Elaine paused before dipping her pen. Penelope was in Bath now and sure to see Mrs. Piper. Perhaps it was best not to mention Daniel by name? Although, her friend might guess the object of her affection.

On her first day at Mrs. Piper's Seminary for Young Ladies, Elaine had proudly declared that she would marry Daniel Ashburn. Eleven years old and full of nervous excitement, she had hoped to impress her elegant new classmates. They had peppered her with questions and did not laugh or scold her like Mama and Perkins.

Of course, Mrs. Piper had been quite severe when she realized being Mrs. Daniel Ashburn motivated all Elaine's studies. She had lectured on the need to acquire skills and knowledge for themselves alone and not in pursuit of a man. Elaine had eventually come around to Mrs. Piper's way of thinking and was happy she had made the most of her education. But now, knowing Italian would not help her. Elaine needed Penelope to teach her the language of love.

Once the letter to Penelope was sealed, Elaine sighed. She hoped the reply would come swiftly. She reached for the most recent letter from Rosamund.

At school, Rosamund had always said the least, but she was an excellent correspondent. She had been the first to leave school at eighteen, surprising everyone by taking a position as a governess. Her letters were filled with amusing stories of her charges and frustrations with the new land steward who had taken up residence after her employers had left on an extended trip. Elaine was thoroughly entertained as she read. Rosie closed her letter with a suggestion that gave Elaine pause.

I know you have declared you never want to be a governess. I have been fortunate in my position, so don't share your fears about the profession.

But you said you enjoyed helping teach at Mrs. Piper's. Your love of books and learning is infectious. Could you not take in students or be a teacher at a parish school? I don't mean to pry, but I do so wish to see you better occupied. I do not think you fit for trailing about after your mother.

The passage struck Elaine. It echoed what Mrs. Piper had said about occupation being needed to achieve true happiness. She had only been home a week and had often been listless. Perhaps she should talk with Mama about the possibility? Teaching was genteel employment, would provide some additional income, and give Elaine something meaningful to do with her time. Would having such an occupation impress Daniel or remind him of her poverty?

For the rest of the day, Elaine did not give much more thought to the idea. She took turns reliving her conversation with Daniel and rehearsing what she would say when next in his company. Even her dreams were filled with him.

The morning dawned bright and cloudless. Elaine was unable to sit quietly in her room and decided to spend the morning outside. With bonnet and shawl firmly in place, she slipped out the back gate. Instead of going into the woods, she went in the opposite direction and followed the brook's path as it meandered west.

Her destination soon came into view. A mist lay over the fields, but the roofless ruin's white stone stood out despite the plants that climbed its walls. It was all that remained of the once proud priory.

Hundreds of years ago, a community of monks or nuns, Elaine wasn't quite sure which, had owned this land. The church had been surrounded by other buildings, the area a hive of activity. Now only the chapel was left standing and the other structures reduced to rubble outlines. Over the years, their stones had been harvested and spread about the county in roads, walls, and buildings. Though Elaine was sure it once had a proper name, everyone called it the Old Priory.

Growing up, Elaine and Daniel had spent hours there. It had been whatever they needed for their games: a French castle, a ship on the sea, the palace of an Indian raja, the Tower of London. For her, it had always been a place full of magic. Did Daniel have the same fond memories? Did he still visit?

As she approached, her expectations of enchantment were met as the mist gathered around the rising stones. With its empty arched window, the chapel rose out of the mist while the tall cross of the burial grounds and the ragged foundations of the other buildings remained hidden.

In Bath, Elaine had seen a painting by a Mr. Turner that had seemed to capture the beauty and mystery of a ruined abbey in Wales. She had admired it while wishing to revisit the Old Priory. How much better it was to be in a place than to admire a painting.

The scene was so picturesque that Elaine couldn't help but imagine it the setting straight from a gothic novel. Perhaps a wealthy heiress with a harsh and disapproving guardian would come to the Old Priory to cry out her anguish. An impoverished scholar would discover her. His kindness would enchant her, and they would fall in love amongst the stones.

Elaine reached the worn, moss-covered cross that marked the burial grounds. She imagined the coffins and bones beneath the grass and shivered. Even with the sun beginning to burn the mist away, it seemed a lonely place.

It was the place of a tragedy. The heroine murdered, and the hero coming

26

to the priory to mourn her death. Her ghost would call to him, and he would wish to join her so they could wander the graves together. A bird trilled, breaking Elaine's thoughts. She shook her head at her foolishness. This was precisely the kind of daydreaming that would frustrate her mother and cause her friends to laugh.

Just as she turned back towards the chapel, the sun pierced the mist and streamed through the arches of the empty windows. Birdsong erupted all around her, and the whisper of a breeze caressed her face. Her heart burst with the beauty of it.

Mr. Turner could not possibly capture such a moment. If only she had someone to share it with. Her mind conjured Daniel just as her eyes beheld a figure crossing before the windows. It seemed he did still visit the priory. Surely Providence was smiling on them.

Chapter Four

A voice shattered the peace of the Old Priory.

"Daniel!"

Phillip turned toward the caller and frowned at the sight of a smiling Miss Elaine Brooke. What was she doing here? At this time? He half turned back toward the chapel expecting to see his brother striding toward him. But there was nothing but beams of sunlight, green grass, overgrown ivy, and half-tumbled walls. It was as empty as when he arrived.

He turned back to Miss Brooke who had taken a few steps forward and shielded her eyes as she squinted against the sun. It struck him that she had assumed he was Daniel. The bright, free smile on her face confirmed she did not see him.

Had Daniel planned a secret meeting? Was their meeting in the woods planned too? Would he be reduced to monitoring Daniel's activities to prevent such indiscretions?

Phillip saw the moment Miss Brooke realized who he was. She stepped into the shade, dropped her hand, and stopped smiling. Like a rabbit the moment before it ran, the panic in her eyes told Phillip she knew she was caught in impropriety. That she recognized she was doing wrong made him even angrier. To her credit, she continued to approach him despite his glower.

"Sir Phillip." Her body radiated tension as she dropped into a correct curtsy.

He bowed stiffly. "Miss Brooke. I believe you were expecting my brother." As a young baronet, Phillip had learned that it was often useful to pretend to know more about a situation than one did.

"Oh no! That is—I did think. . . but the sun. . . obviously you are not." She paused and took a deep breath. "I did think you were Mr. Ashburn, but I had no expectation of meeting him here."

"You saw a silhouette of a man and naturally assumed it was my brother." Phillip didn't try to hide his sarcasm.

"I did." She would not meet his eyes.

"How very curious. And what, pray, brings a young woman to the Old Priory at this early hour?"

"I was walking." She lifted her chin as if daring him to doubt her.

The audacity rankled. Daniel had induced her to this folly, but she was brazen in her denial. She was either heedless of her reputation or enamored beyond reason. Phillip hoped it was the latter, for then he might be able to warn her.

"I would caution you, Miss Brooke, on the imprudence of unchaperoned excursions."

"I thank you, sir, but I have wandered this country since I was a girl."

"You are no longer a girl." He let his eyes sweep over her for a fraction of a second. She was not dressed fashionably, but there was a charm in her figure and features. There was no trace of the knobby knees and mud-stained cheeks he remembered from her childhood. No, she was an attractive woman now.

"There is nothing improper in my walking. Surely you don't think I am in danger on your own estate?"

"Surely you understand the danger to your reputation."

"My reputation?"

"Please don't insult my intelligence, Miss Brooke, by denying your purpose here. We both know that you were not merely walking."

"I know nothing of the sort." She stood straighter, squaring her shoulders as her cheeks flushed. A smattering of freckles stood out against the red. "And it is impolite of you even to suggest—"

"You would have me believe that you came here, alone, at this hour, with no planned assignation?" Phillip's anger made him abrupt.

"Yes, I would because that is exactly what I am doing. I might as easily assume that you have come here, alone, at this hour, for the express purpose of seducing a. . . a. . . milkmaid."

"That is absurd. I am a gentleman and would never—"

"A true gentleman would never question a young lady's honor."

Phillip was speechless, not because Miss Brooke had interrupted him or because of the fire in her eyes, but because she was right. He was not behaving as a gentleman but as some overbearing master.

"Now, if you will excuse me." Without taking proper leave, Miss Brooke spun on her heel.

He should let her go. But since he had already trespassed the bounds of propriety, he surely had nothing to lose by trying again to make her understand. He ran a hand through his hair and followed after her. His long strides brought him close enough to speak and words came out in an uncharacteristic rush.

"Miss Brooke, you must understand that my brother will not safeguard your reputation. He has no thoughts but for his own pleasure. He could never offer for you; his position is such that—"

Miss Brooke abruptly stopped walking and turned to him. He checked his own stride just before crashing into her. He was close enough to count the freckles on her cheek and catch the flecks of brown in her flashing green eyes.

"Sir Phillip, I thank you for your concern. But since you are neither my guardian nor my brother, I cannot see why you feel the need to provide such unsolicited and unnecessary counsel." Her voice was as frigid and sharp as an icicle.

"I am sorry to be blunt, but I had no choice."

"One can always choose to be kind." Her words were coated in disapproval. "Now, unless you desire to insult me further, I wish you good day."

When she walked away, Phillip had the good sense not to follow. Instead, he watched her straight back and long stride with growing frustration. It was fruitless and beneath his dignity to explain himself further. She would not see reason where Daniel was concerned. Mother was wrong; Miss Brooke's school girl fancy had not dissipated and it was impossible that Daniel saw her as a sister.

Phillip turned and strode back to the chapel, growing angrier with each step. Daniel ruined everything. The Old Priory was his refuge, a place to sort through his thoughts, to be free of expectations. Miss Brooke's arrival had been a boulder tossed into a still pond. The ripples spoiled his peace and sullied his sanctuary. How could he enjoy it now, knowing he might constantly be interrupted by clandestine lovers?

He ignored the charms of the picturesque chapel and went around it to look at the road. He half expected to see Daniel galloping on his horse, but the only horse was his own—tied to a nearby tree and looking at him balefully. Frowning, Phillip glanced at the sun and decided to wait. When Daniel arrived, Phillip would remind him of his honor and forbid him from engaging Miss Brooke in any further schemes. It was one thing to charm an opera singer or a worldly widow, but their naive and penniless neighbor was out of bounds. Miss Brooke would not listen, but Daniel had no choice.

Phillip waited and waited, growing more irate with each passing minute. Could his brother not be on time even for a romantic assignation? If he hadn't run Miss Brooke off, she could have witnessed Daniel's unreliability. Perhaps that might have helped convince her? Phillip entertained the idea that Daniel's fickleness might serve to abolish Miss Brooke's feelings, but he doubted he would be so lucky.

When almost half an hour had passed, Phillip gave up waiting. He needed to meet with Mr. Batty at Priory Farm and talk to a tradesman in Oakbury before returning to the hall. He had no more time to waste on his brother's romantic entanglements. He would just have to talk to Daniel and then do his best to ensure his brother acted properly.

Phillip heaved a sigh and mounted his horse.

* * *

When Phillip returned to the hall two hours later than he had planned, he was instantly engrossed in entertaining his guests and setting up preparations for the shooting that would soon begin. With one activity after another, it was nearly time for dinner before Phillip found a moment to talk with his brother. He needed to change for the meal but wanted to have the conversation before he saw to his own appearance. He made his way to the room that belonged to Daniel but had rarely been used in the last ten years.

He gave a quick knock before calling out. "Daniel, I need to speak with you."

Phillip entered the room and was shocked by the disorder he found there. A stack of papers and books on a writing desk, crinkled balls of paper scattered on the floor, and clothes laying all over the bed.

"Why yes, you can come in, thank you for asking," Daniel said from his position before a small looking glass. He was already in his breeches, shirt, and bright green waistcoat, but his feet were bare and he was holding his cravat.

"Where is your valet?" Phillip asked.

Daniel chuckled as he began to tie his cravat. "Did you come here to ask after my servant arrangements?"

"No."

Phillip paused, considering if it was worth pressing the issue. Daniel's allowance provided for a valet—Phillip would not let his brother go without like so many other bachelors—if he had dismissed his man, then what was he doing with the money? It was a question Phillip wanted answered, but now was not the time.

"No. I wished to speak to you about your conduct with Miss Brooke."

"Miss Brooke? I thought it was Miss Talbot you wanted me to court. Have you changed your mind?" Daniel gave an exaggerated sigh. "I really can't keep up with your shifting plans for who I should marry."

"My plan is only that I want you to marry well. You would be a fool to let Miss Talbot slip through your fingers. And I will not deny that I think marrying Miss Brooke would be a mistake. I do not have the money to support you both."

"And I don't give two figs for your plans." Daniel's voice was uncharacteristically sharp.

Phillip clenched his jaw to stop his own cutting words from bursting out. It would not end well if he lost his temper as he had with Miss Brooke. The silence grew between them as Daniel continued to fuss with his cravat. Finally, Daniel spun from his looking glass and threw up his hands.

"Out with it. The sooner you begin your lecture, the sooner you will be finished and leave me in peace to struggle into my boots."

"I have not come to lecture."

"No? You were not about to tell me that I shouldn't flirt with our pretty neighbor or give her any consequence lest there be dire repercussions?"

It wasn't precisely what Phillip would have said.

"So you admit that your conduct towards Miss Brooke has not been entirely honorable?"

"Blast it, Phillip! What do you take me for? Do you think I seduce every woman I meet? I have barely had a chance to be dishonorable with Miss Brooke." Phillip raised his eyebrows at this turn of phrase. "I mean that there has been nothing but harmless flirtation."

"I think we have different definitions of harmless. If you confine yourself to the occasional smile and pretty phrase, then we have no quarrel. But I will not tolerate any clandestine meetings or promises you have no intention of fulfilling."

"Well, then, for once, I believe we are in agreement. I have too much respect for Elaine to trifle with her affections."

Phillip stared at his brother for a long moment, trying to discern his sincerity but he could detect no lie. At last, he nodded. "Good."

Daniel nodded back. "Good."

Phillip glanced around the room but chose not to say anything further about the disorder. He gave another nod and left. As he made his way to his room, he was still uneasy. Only when he was partway changed did he realize that Daniel had not promised to stay away from Miss Brooke. His brother had only promised not to trifle with her affections.

It was a shame Daniel did not wish to go into the law, for his skill with language made him a perfect candidate. He had managed to avoid Phillip's questions and twist the conversation so as to promise nothing. If Daniel thought his feelings were in earnest, he would continue to pursue Miss Brooke and likely ruin his chances with Miss Talbot.

Phillip sighed. He would have to ensure that Miss Brooke and Daniel remained separate each evening. Though that would still leave Daniel free to see her during the day, it would ensure his partiality was not on display for their guests. Phillip had not thought it possible, but his dread for the upcoming weeks had increased.

Chapter Five

⋙✦⋘

T he late summer sun was only beginning to set as the carriage turned off the village road and made the slight climb toward Ryder Hall. Unlike Mama, Elaine could not enjoy the view or the excellent springs in the Ashburn carriage; she was too busy trying to calm her nerves. All day she had swung from excitement at seeing Daniel to dread at seeing Sir Phillip. Mama's many reminders on all that was due to their hosts had not helped. Elaine was keenly aware that she had offended Sir Phillip that morning. Mama would be speechless if she knew.

Elaine could hardly believe her own temerity, but she did not regret her words. It was improper not to apologize, but Sir Phillip had been abominably uncivil. His implication of a lack of propriety on her part and outright villainy on Daniel's could not go unanswered.

How would she meet the baronet with equanimity? Each time she imagined the evening, it ended in some kind of disaster. Elaine's hopes of catching Daniel's interest were secondary now. She would settle for controlling her anger and her tongue.

The carriage came to a gentle stop and soon, they were ascending the staircase to the entrance. The hall was grander and more imposing than she remembered. Perhaps it was the orange light of the sun setting the white stone on fire or the knowledge that its owner objected so strongly to her entire person.

"Remember," Mrs. Brooke whispered. "Lady Ashburn has extended us a great honor and we must help ensure her house party is a success."

"Yes, Mama," Elaine replied.

The door swung open and they were ushered from the grand entrance hall and into the drawing room. Looking at the elegantly-dressed company from the threshold, she was glad she had worn the yellow silk petticoat. Penelope had insisted she needed a dress in the fabric, and Charity, knowing Elaine could not afford it, had subsequently purchased it. She wished either friend was beside her now as she entered the room filled with strangers.

"Mrs. Brooke, Miss Brooke." Lady Ashburn greeted them with her warm smile and drew them off to the side. "You are both looking very well. I quite adore your hair, Mary, and Miss Elaine, that dress matches your coloring just so."

"Thank you, Lady Ashburn." Elaine was able to smile genuinely.

How had Sir Phillip inherited none of the family charm?

Elaine looked about the room as Mama complimented Lady Ashburn's person, home, and carriage. She was the youngest of the guests by at least a decade. A knot of men gathered on the far side of the room, no doubt talking of the upcoming shooting, and in the center, three middle-aged women sat together, smiling. There was no sign of either Ashburn brother.

"Looking for someone?"

The voice came from just behind her. Her heart skipped before she could turn around.

"Dan—Mr. Ashburn." She blushed and he smiled.

"You were looking for me? I am flattered."

She pursed her lips, trying to hold back her smile. "You, sir, do not need more flattery."

"In point of fact, flattery is in short supply in this house."

"Is that so?"

"Indeed, my brother has not once complimented me on my waistcoat."

The mention of Sir Phillip had a sobering effect and Elaine had to stop herself from looking about for him. No doubt he would be watching and judging her conduct with Daniel while imagining all sorts of lies.

"I see you feel the gravity of such an oversight." Daniel misinterpreted her change in countenance. "But you may feel free to correct it."

He pulled back his blue coat to better display his bottle-green waistcoat with its subtle yellow stripes. His eyes, set off by his coat, sparkled mischievously. She ceased to care what Sir Phillip might think. There was nothing improper about trading silly compliments before dinner.

"It is the finest waistcoat I have ever seen."

"Oh, a high compliment indeed."

"I feel that outrageous flattery is best when one is in short supply."

"Agreed." He inclined his head. "Then allow me to return the favor and say that you look as beautiful as Helen of Troy."

Elaine's mouth went dry. Was he in earnest or just playing a game? "I forgot how outrageous you can be."

His grin was every inch the unrepentant boy she had known. "Is that an attempt at more flattery?"

Before Elaine could reply, Mama touched her arm. She almost started. She had entirely forgotten that anyone else was in the room, let alone that Lady Ashburn and Mama were within arm's reach.

"Mr. Ashburn." Mama's greeting was perfunctory. She turned to Elaine. "Lady Ashburn wants to introduce us to Mr. and Mrs. Farthing."

Elaine gave a look of apology to Daniel as she curtsied. Was that sadness in his eyes at her parting? She hoped he knew she would rather not part with him. Her anxiety had melted in the warmth of his presence and ease of conversation. Now she faced the uncertainty of strangers.

The Farthings had just entered the room and were talking to Lady Ashburn. Mrs. Farthing seemed no more than a few years Elaine's senior. Fair-haired and of a similar height, they both smiled when introduced and Elaine thought they seemed an easy, natural pair. Remembering Mama's admonishments, Elaine threw herself into the conversation and denied herself the chance to think of Daniel or the import of their interaction.

As a reward for her attention, she learned that Mr. Farthing was in the law; they had been married that year and resided primarily in London. While discussing their favorite places in Town, a prickling on her neck pulled Elaine's attention away. She glanced over her shoulder to find Sir Phillip watching her.

He looked every inch the baronet in his fine clothes. He was near the group of men but in an exclusive conversation with a short, portly fellow. Though Sir Phillip wasn't quite frowning, she could feel his disapproval from across the room.

She looked away and tried to focus on what Mr. Farthing was saying about an eventful trip to Vauxhall Gardens, but half her mind was across the room. All her anxiety about meeting with Sir Phillip had returned. She struggled to keep her imagination in check. Would he speak to her before dinner? Would he mention their meeting that morning?

Her answer came quicker than expected.

"Ah, here comes Sir Phillip," Mrs. Farthing said, cutting into her husband's story. The Farthings, Mama, and Elaine all turned expectantly at Sir Phillip's approach. He commanded the room without even trying. Instead of meeting his eye, Elaine concentrated on the shorter man accompanying him. The man's hair was beginning to gray, adding an air of dignity to his finely dressed person. He looked at Elaine in return and she had the uncomfortable feeling of being examined like a horse for sale at Tattersalls.

Sir Phillip and the man greeted the Farthings and then turned to the Brookes.

"Mrs. Brooke, Miss Brooke, may I introduce Mr. Talbot, an acquaintance from London and my house guest?"

"A pleasure to meet you, Mr. Talbot," Mama said.

Elaine parroted her.

"Likewise," Mr. Talbot's voice was deeper than Elaine had expected. They exchanged a few pleasantries about the weather while Elaine did her best not to look at Sir Phillip.

"If you will excuse me," Sir Phillip said. "I must attend my mother."

Their eyes met for a brief moment. She was surprised not to see censure but something almost thoughtful. And then he was gone.

"Sir Phillip tells me you are near neighbors," Mr. Talbot said.

Mama smiled. "Yes, we live in Ryder Lodge."

Mr. Talbot's brow furrowed slightly. "I did not see a lodge when we arrived."

Elaine tried not to wince at the implication that they lived in a gatehouse or gamekeeper's cottage. Surely Mr. Talbot had not meant to imply that they were part of the staff? Mama took it in stride.

"No, Mr. Talbot, you would not have seen it from the village road. It is quite the little hideaway. Previous baronets used it as a hunting lodge when the estate was still a deer park. That was many years ago and the Ashburns have made many modern improvements to the house. One would hardly guess its origins. I do not think there is a more conscientious landowner than Sir Phillip."

While the Farthings agreed and heaped more praise on Sir Phillip, Elaine barely managed to keep smiling. What would they say if they knew of his rude and officious behavior towards her?

The announcement of dinner ended the conversation. Mr. Talbot excused himself to fetch his wife. Elaine couldn't help glancing about the room. Her heart sped up at the idea that Daniel would escort her to dinner.

The party would whisper at the honor being bestowed and speculation about the pretty neighbor would be rampant. But the fledgling dream was dashed when she saw an attractive young woman in an emerald dress on Daniel's arm. Who was she?

Lady Ashburn appeared and hastily introduced two older men, a Mr. Evans and Captain Hart, to escort them. Mama took the arm of the reedy, younger Mr. Evans, leaving Elaine with the commanding Captain Hart.

"Miss Brooke, a true pleasure." Captain Hart had a welcoming smile that softened his height and robust build. His hair had little gray, but his face was weathered; she expected he was a Navy man.

She barely attended the captain's conversation as they moved with the others to the dining room. Rather, her attention was caught by Daniel and the young woman on his arm. They were smiling congenially as they talked, but that told her nothing of the degree of their acquaintance.

Elaine did not think of herself as a jealous person. She had never coveted her friends' gowns or pin money, but her stomach twisted as she watched them. It was one thing to know that Daniel Ashburn flirted and charmed other young women; it was another to watch it.

The dining room was large enough to accommodate double the current guests, but the table had been shortened to keep everyone together. The polished tableware and covered platters gleamed in the sun still pouring through the tall windows. Elaine loved how long the days stretched in summer.

Despite her title, Lady Ashburn preferred informality, so there was no precedence to adhere to. Daniel and his partner sat next to his mother. Elaine ended up on the opposite side, only two chairs away from Sir Phillip. A cruel irony to be near the Ashburn she liked least. When she pulled her attention from Daniel, she caught Captain Hart giving her a bemused look.

"I have not yet been introduced to everyone," she said. "Perhaps you could help me learn their identities?" Elaine tried to hide her naked interest, but Captain Hart appeared not to be fooled.

"The young woman with Mr. Ashburn is Miss Frederica Talbot."

Elaine burned to ask more questions but instead forced herself to ask after the other guests. Though she barely registered what Captain Hart told her, her mind was still firmly on the mystery of Miss Talbot. When all were in the room, they sat. Mr. Talbot had taken the seat next to Elaine and his wife was next to Sir Phillip.

Throughout the first course, Elaine spoke with Captain Hart and did her best to be a good dinner partner. Despite her distraction, she was pulled into his conversation. He was a Navy man, though long retired and currently living in London. He had seen action in the Nile and at Trafalgar and spoke eloquently of his love of Lord Nelson.

Listening to him, Elaine forgot her worries and found herself on the ship's deck, cannons blasting, ships sinking, men in the water. She had seen several paintings of such naval battles, but Captain Hart made the events come to life.

But then the second course came and Elaine was back in the dining room. In the shuffling of platters, Elaine caught Daniel looking at her. He raised his glass and gave her a smile that had her hoping all over again. Foolish heart, she thought and turned her attention to Mr. Talbot.

Mr. Talbot looked perturbed and did not return her smile. Elaine turned back to her plate, unsure how to proceed. "Are you enjoying your ragout?" She asked for lack of anything else to say. The food was a safe topic, for Lady Ashburn kept a good table. Elaine was grateful to be able to eat such rich food for the next few weeks.

"I don't much care for ragout."

"Oh."

Elaine, determined not to look in Daniel's direction, found herself looking at Sir Phillip instead. He was talking easily with Mrs. Talbot, but he raised his eyebrow when he met her eye as if asking why she was looking at him. Elaine didn't know and so looked away.

The room was overly warm. She chewed slowly to forestall her need to talk. All about them, others were conversing amiably and Elaine was sure Mama would notice if she was not properly attending to Mr. Talbot. But she did not have the composure to think of what else to say.

Mr. Talbot saved her the trouble by speaking. "Sir Phillip informs me that you are an old family friend."

"We have lived at the lodge since I was very young."

"Yes, he said you are almost a sister to him and Mr. Ashburn."

Elaine was caught off guard by the sentiment but endeavored to reply evenly. "Sir Phillip is all kindness. I am flattered to be considered in so familiar a light."

"You do not consider yourself a sister to them?" Mr. Talbot pressed.

Elaine could hardly say her true feelings towards the two brothers, so she demurred. "I would never presume so much on the family. I have been at school these many years and the familiarity offered to a child may not extend to the adult."

Mr. Talbot gave a decisive nod. "Just so. That is very sensible of you."

Elaine didn't feel the least bit sensible, but she smiled in reply. Mr. Talbot took charge of the conversation and spoke of his pleasure at being invited to the country and hopes for the shooting.

She endured the agony of this small talk while privately despairing that Daniel might think of her as a sister. The thought was lowering since she had spent so long harboring unsisterly affections. But it was hard to deny that Daniel's interest lay elsewhere when he was sitting and smiling with Miss Talbot.

Tormented with such thoughts, the rest of dinner took an eternity. It was a relief to remove to the drawing room. She needed a chance for quiet reflection before the men joined them.

Elaine did not get even a moment to herself. As soon as she entered the room, Lady Ashburn took her and Mama by their arms and insisted on introducing them to the ladies they did not yet know. The drawing room was a comfortable size, elegant without being overwhelming. It was filled with several groupings of fine furniture and painted a cheerful blue.

They moved first to Miss Wilson and Mrs. Cooper, who were already sitting with Mrs. Farthing. The two sisters looked to be at least forty and were very alike with mousy brown hair and sharp features. Though they were seated, it was easy to see that Mrs. Cooper was the taller of the two and a good deal plumper.

They exchanged pleasantries and spoke of their expectations for the party. Elaine found them intelligent but formed no other impression. Next, Lady Ashburn took Elaine and Mama to a window where Mrs. and Miss Talbot stood in conversation.

She wondered if Miss Talbot was enduring some kind of lecture on her behavior, for her eyes were cast down as she listened. Despite herself, Elaine was sympathetic to the other young woman. At their approach, the mother and daughter ceased talking and turned to greet them with twin smiles.

Miss Talbot's pleasure appeared genuine while Mrs. Talbot's smile didn't quite meet her eyes. They were both beautiful women with even features, heart-shaped faces, and white blonde hair, but Miss Talbot's open expression gave her unique appeal. Elaine grudgingly understood why Daniel seemed drawn to her.

Once the introductions were made, Miss Talbot was the first to speak.

"Miss Brooke, I was about to take a turn about the room. Would you like to join me?"

Elaine wished to refuse. She looked at Mama, hoping to be told to stay. But her hopes were dashed when Mama nodded.

"Of course, Miss Talbot," Elaine said.

Miss Talbot's smile was all charm as she linked arms with Elaine. They passed in front of the tall windows that faced the front lawn. The green grass sloped downward to the small lake that glittered in the last rays of the sun. Elaine wished they might walk outside instead.

After a few steps, Miss Talbot spoke. "I am so glad to have another young person make up our party." It was said sincerely, but Elaine doubted her words. Would not Miss Talbot prefer no competition for Daniel's attention?

"I was honored to be invited," Elaine said. She could not return the sentiment.

After a few more steps in silence, Miss Talbot spoke again. "I quite like your dress. The color is quite handsome and the muslin very fine."

"Thank you."

"Mama says good Indian muslin is the only proper kind of muslin."

"I have heard that said."

If Miss Talbot had been any other person, Elaine might have explained that her friend Mary Gilbert was from India and gifted her the muslin. But Elaine's pride would not allow her to admit to being a charity case to this elegant, fashionable woman.

"Your hair is quite lovely." Miss Talbot spoke again when Elaine didn't take up the subject of muslins. Elaine put a hand to her hair. Perkins was not capable of doing anything but the simplest of styles.

"You are too kind."

"No, truly, the color quite captures the firelight."

Elaine's brown hair did have glints of red, but it was strange that Miss Talbot had noticed. Their entire conversation was stilted and strange, with the other young woman constantly saying "quite" and complimenting everything she saw. They had made a complete circuit of the room, returning to the windows, but Miss Talbot showed no desire to join the other ladies, so they continued to walk.

"Have you been to London?" Miss Talbot asked.

"I have visited on occasion."

"How strange that I never encountered you on any of my visits to Ashburn House."

"I was at the mercy of friends who are not acquainted with the Ashburns." Elaine was unable to keep a coldness from her voice.

Miss Talbot was either naively sincere or the most cunning young woman Elaine had ever met. She was able to both show a more significant association with the Ashburns and get Elaine to admit her dependence on her friends. Had all her compliments been meant as insults? Before Elaine could puzzle it out, the drawing room door opened and the men arrived.

When Daniel appeared with Mr. Farthing, his gaze swept the room and landed on the two young women. Instead of the smile Elaine expected, his mouth twisted briefly into a frown. Miss Talbot gave a slight scoff and when Elaine looked, her lips were pursed. What a strange interaction. Stranger still, after such an exchange, Daniel was approaching them.

"Miss Talbot, Miss Brooke, I see you have been introduced," Daniel said. His charming smile was firmly affixed, though it did not reach his eyes.

"Yes," Miss Talbot said. "And Miss Brooke has been good enough to walk about the room with me."

"No doubt you have been telling secrets. Perhaps talking of mutual acquaintances?"

"We were not speaking of you," Miss Talbot answered with a sweet smile that belied the bluntness of her words.

"I did not say you were." Daniel frowned.

"We have been talking about muslins," Elaine rushed into the awkwardness.

"Sharing muslin secrets?" Daniel gave her a mischievous grin. "How mysterious."

"The mysteries of a lady's muslin are carefully guarded," Elaine replied.

"But, Miss Brooke, you forget that I am excellent at ferreting out secrets."

"Oh, I remember."

A thrill ran through her at his knowing look.

Did he recall all the secrets they had shared? Was he reminded of all they had once meant to each other? Surely Miss Talbot's perfect skin and large fortune could not compare to their longstanding bond?

Hope stirred in her breast. Her anxiety about Sir Phillip's censorious opinions and Miss Talbot's perfect eligibility evaporated in the warmth of Daniel's smile. Sir Phillip was wrong. Daniel was not trifling with her. There was no mistaking the light of interest in his eyes.

If they could only spend time alone together, Elaine was sure he would come to love her as she loved him.

Chapter Six

A s the men left the dining room to join the women, Phillip stopped Mr. Talbot and attempted to repair the damage Daniel had done with his behavior and incautious words. Mr. Talbot had asked Daniel about his future plans. True to form, Daniel had given a flippant answer.

"My present plan is to enjoy the wonderful company of this party."

While many had chuckled, Mr. Talbot was not amused. Phillip caught his attention as the men filed out of the room.

"Mr. Talbot, you should know my brother has many interests and aptitude for most professions. It has made it difficult for him to settle on one."

"Is he so fickle?" Talbot asked.

"Not fickle. He hesitates only because once committed, he won't falter in his course no matter the obstacles."

Talbot gave a huff but made no further comment.

Phillip knew little of Mr. Talbot, but he seemed a cautious and suspicious man. Perhaps that was the result of having to protect a pretty daughter with a hefty dowry. The man was obviously wary of Daniel. A complication Phillip hoped to overcome.

Before dinner, Phillip had assured Mr. Talbot that Miss Brooke was merely a childhood friend, but the man had seemed unconvinced. Phillip didn't blame him. It was clear there was affection between Daniel and Miss Brooke with their warm smiles and easy manner.

But Daniel could not marry their poor neighbor. For many reasons, it would be a disastrous connection. No, his brother must marry Miss Frederica Talbot. It was Daniel's best chance at a good life. And Phillip's best chance to finally be free.

Phillip and Mr. Talbot entered the drawing room behind the other men. Phillip surveyed the room and caught Mother's eye. Following her gaze, Phillip saw Daniel speaking with Miss Talbot and Miss Brooke in the far corner. Miss Talbot looked decidedly unsure as Daniel and Miss Brooke smiled at each other.

Holding back a sigh, Phillip crossed the room.

"Miss Brooke," He broke into the conversation. Her smile disappeared, but he was undeterred by her disapproval. Phillip didn't like the situation any more than she did. He had to extract her from Daniel's presence. "My mother asked that I fetch you."

"You do a lot of fetching these days," Daniel murmured so low that Phillip decided to ignore him.

"Thank you, Sir Phillip. I will go to her directly." Miss Brooke smiled goodbye to the other two.

Wordlessly Phillip fell into step beside her.

"I do not need your escort, sir," Miss Brooke said sharply.

"And yet you have it."

Phillip pasted on a smile as they approached Mother and Mrs. Brooke. They were seated together near the large fireplace.

"Elaine, there you are," Mrs. Brooke said. "I was just telling Lady Ashburn how I despair of you being able to stand the dullness of the country."

"Now Mama, Lady Ashburn will misunderstand you." Miss Brooke gave a fond look. "I am quite content to be home. Indeed, I had forgotten the many charms of the countryside."

"True; you could not go on such long walks in town," Mrs. Brooke said.

"No doubt Miss Brooke enjoys the independence such walks afford." Phillip was unable to stop himself from adding.

"Independence is indeed something to be valued," Miss Brooke returned. "But what I most enjoy is the seclusion. Even when walking in a park, one is never truly alone in Bath or London."

"Perhaps especially when walking in Hyde Park," Lady Ashburn said. "When I am in Town, I miss the peace of the country. But then when I am in the country, I miss the entertainments of Town. It seems, like most people, I am doomed to always want what I don't have."

Everyone smiled and agreed with this sentiment.

"Now, if you will excuse me, I must see to the arrangement of the card tables." Mother stood.

Mrs. Brooke followed suit. "Allow me to help you by encouraging people to play."

"Thank you, Mary."

The two ladies left Phillip and Miss Brooke standing together. She narrowed her eyes at him before looking back towards Daniel. Had she seen through his ruse? Would she fly back to Daniel's side? There was nothing for it but to attempt conversation.

"Did you prefer London or Bath?"

The innocuous question seemed to catch her unawares as she dragged her gaze back to him.

"I—I enjoyed them both."

"What did you most enjoy?" He prodded.

She took a deep breath. "Many things. Sir Phillip, I thank you for your interest, but I do not want to keep you from your guests." She smiled tightly.

"You are one of my guests and thus have an equal claim on my attention."

"You aren't interested in my attention."

"You rate yourself so low?"

Her brows knit together. It was a small triumph to deter her. It helped to take away the sting of rejection. He was not as charming or fashionable as his brother, but he did have a title, an estate, and a steady income. For many, those things were rated higher than charm. Yet Miss Brooke did not seem to care. Not that he wanted Miss Brooke's approbation; he had proven that at the priory. He only needed her to stay away from Daniel.

Instead of answering his question, she looked at him carefully, as if trying to see the inner workings of his mind.

"Lady Ashburn left so quickly I was unable to ask her what she needed," she said. "Perhaps, Sir Phillip, you could tell me why you were sent to retrieve me?"

Phillip affected a bland expression. "I do not know, Miss Brooke."

"I imagine neither does Lady Ashburn." She raised an eyebrow.

Strangely, he enjoyed her boldness. His lips twitched, a smile struggling to emerge. Miss Brooke noticed and frowned, which made his desire to smile grow. Around them, the room was filling with guests forming groups for cards.

"Do you wish to play a game?" he asked.

"I thought we were already playing."

"Pardon?"

"Yes, you should beg my pardon, but of course never will."

The bitterness in her voice caught him off guard. Her boldness was suddenly less amusing. He could not pretend to misunderstand her. "If you are speaking of this morning, then let us change the topic." He tried to contain his mounting frustration. "Nothing good can be said on that subject."

Phillip had determined to ignore their disastrous meeting at the Old Priory. Why could she not do the same?

Miss Brooke's cheeks flushed slightly but he could not tell if she was angry or embarrassed. "My mother needs me," she said curtly and spun away.

The lie was obvious. Mrs. Brooke wasn't even looking in their direction. The impudence stirred Phillip's anger, but he was glad she had left. What would his guests have thought if their disagreement had escalated?

He shook his head. It seemed Daniel wasn't the only person capable of getting under his skin.

Miss Brooke went to her mother's side. They spoke briefly and then Mrs. Brooke gestured to a table. Phillip was happy to see Miss Brooke sit down with Miss Wilson, Mrs. Cooper, and Mr. Poole. Daniel was safely partnered with Miss Talbot playing against Mother and Captain Hart. At least now

Phillip would be able to relax.

The even numbers of their party allowed everyone to join a game, and it seemed everyone intended to play. That meant Phillip could not sit out and hide behind his newspaper. Farthing waved him over to a table where he was settling his wife.

"Enjoying your first night as host?" Farthing asked.

"Not quite the word I would use."

Farthing chuckled. "Now, now, this is a fine assembly. I have yet to have an uninteresting conversation."

"I am pleased to hear it." Phillip settled into his chair. If he could not enjoy the party, at least the Farthings would.

"Miss Brooke is very charming," Mrs. Farthing said.

"Oh yes, I wonder that you never mentioned her before," Farthing added with an arch look.

Phillip pretended not to notice his friend's insinuation. "I confess I do not know her well. She has been away at Bath for many years."

What had his friend noticed that evening? Had he seen Miss Brooke's annoyance at his intervention? Had he marked her interactions with Daniel? Having an eye for detail made Farthing a good lawyer and his judgment made him an excellent friend.

Phillip considered asking Farthing for advice on this delicate matter. Unlike his father, Phillip was not wise enough to decide everything alone. But consulting Farthing meant having to describe his shameful behavior that morning. It was also possible Farthing would completely misunderstand Phillip's objections and try to encourage him to court Miss Brooke. No, he would handle this matter himself.

Reaching for the cards, Phillip determined to enjoy the rest of the evening. Daniel and Miss Brooke would not have another chance to interact, being at separate tables. The evening passed without further incident.

Once all the guests had retired for the night, Phillip went to his study and sank into a chair beside the small fire. Lady Ashburn arrived soon after.

"That was an excellent start," she said as she slipped into the opposite chair.

"Yes, well done, Mother."

She sighed. "You are too kind to say it, but I must admit that you were right about inviting the Brookes."

"You have changed your opinion on the matter?"

"I believe there is cause for concern. Daniel greeted her informally and she was very encouraging. It might just be a friendship, but. . . " Mother trailed away and contemplated the fire for a moment. Phillip was convinced that there was danger where Miss Brooke and Daniel were concerned, but he could not give his reasons without sharing his conversations with Miss Brooke.

"I think Mr. Talbot sees more than friendship." Phillip conveyed what had been said.

Mother frowned. "The man has every right to protect his daughter, but such excessive paranoia does not make for a good father-in-law."

"You want Daniel to throw over Miss Talbot and pursue Miss Brooke instead?"

"There is no need to be sarcastic. And, truthfully, I have no objection to Elaine Brooke. She is a kind, intelligent girl from a good family. If Daniel truly cared for her, I would be happy to call her daughter."

"And the scandal from him breaking with Miss Talbot?"

"There is no agreement between them. Just because everyone expects them to marry does not mean they must. I don't wish either of my sons to feel forced in their choice of partner."

"So you have said many times," he said.

Phillip's parents' marriage had not been their choice. While they had enjoyed respect, there had not been love. That Mother wanted him to have what she didn't was understandable, but material concerns could not be set aside entirely.

"I am not trying to force Daniel into marriage," Phillip said slowly. "But if he chooses Miss Brooke, what will they live on? Her fortune is paltry and his spending uncontrolled."

"It would be difficult indeed if they had no income, but your brother is capable. A wife would provide the incentive Daniel needs to find his way."

Phillip scoffed. A tiger didn't change its stripes.

Mother gave him a long-suffering look. "You are too severe on Daniel. I think if he applied himself, he would be successful."

"And if he doesn't? If he never applies himself, never finds a profession?"

"Then we will support them."

"Of course."

"Now, Phillip, don't be distressed. The estate has prospered under your hand and the crops will be better this year. I know it can be a burden being head of the family, but you are intelligent and resourceful." Mother reached out and patted his knee.

Phillip wanted to point out how unfair it was that his life must be in service to his brother's. That he would have to continue to be a careful steward and forgo his own ambitions so Daniel could be profligate.

He said nothing. Mother continued.

"This is all conjecture. Daniel might offer for Miss Talbot tomorrow. He still seems quite taken by her. We may be misinterpreting the degree of his interest in Miss Brooke."

Phillip contemplated telling Mother about that morning but didn't want to worry her further or explain his ungentlemanly behavior.

"Perhaps you are right," he said. "But Daniel's degree of interest may be immaterial if Mr. Talbot finds him unsuitable. If he continues to flirt with Miss Brooke, I am sure he will ruin his chance. If Daniel is to succeed with Miss Talbot, he must be kept from falling for Miss Brooke."

Mother shook her head. "Since you have never been in love, I will excuse such nonsense. You can't control how people feel. It would be foolhardy to try. This is your brother's choice and the consequences will be his to live with."

She was wrong—the consequences would not just impact Daniel—but she was also correct. Phillip was head of the family and so it was his responsibility to ensure Daniel married Miss Talbot. If that meant keeping him from dallying with Miss Brooke, then that was what he would do. If it meant convincing her that Daniel was the wrong choice, he would do that too.

Phillip would not apologize for doing what was best for all concerned. Someday they would understand.

Chapter Seven

E laine passed a fitful night. Her two provoking conversations with Sir Phillip would have been enough to keep her awake, but she also had Daniel's actions and the beautiful Miss Talbot to consider. Her imagination spun stories that melted into dreams. She awoke cross, though she could not quite remember what her dreams contained.

When she sat down at the breakfast table, she was still unsettled.

"Elaine, did you not sleep well?" Mama asked when she glanced up from her food.

For a brief moment, Elaine contemplated unburdening herself, but her mother didn't wait for a response before launching into a litany about the importance of proper rest. Elaine listened as she buttered her toast and, when her mother was finished, voiced her agreement. She did not say that wanting restful sleep and getting it were two different things.

"I am not hungry." Mama changed topics. "Lady Ashburn keeps such a generous table. I daresay I won't need to eat a full breakfast while dining there. I assure you I feel the honor she has done us by her invitation. Such a kindness."

Mama's gratitude grated. Unwillingly, Elaine heard Sir Phillip asking if she rated herself low.

"Lady Ashburn is kind," Elaine said. "But her invitation is certainly a credit to you, Mama."

"It is generous of you to say so." Mama smiled. "Her other guests are certainly to be admired. Mr. Evans has a very high position in government and was most genial during dinner. I am glad you were paired with Captain Hart, as he is a particular and old friend of Lady Ashburn."

"I enjoyed his conversation."

"And what of Mr. Talbot? He seemed pleased with you."

Elaine took a bite of toast to avoid answering. Her conversation with Mr. Talbot had been the source of some of her confusion. His assertion that the Ashburns saw her as a sister had plagued her during the night. She told herself the words were Sir Phillip's and Daniel's feelings towards her might be very different but with little effect.

"Mr. Evans said the Talbots are as rich as Croesus and Miss Talbot has a dowry of forty-thousand. He seemed of the opinion that she is to become Mrs. Ashburn."

The toast stuck in Elaine's throat as she swallowed thickly. Beautiful, rich, and seemingly kind, it was no wonder Daniel appeared to prefer Miss Talbot. And no wonder that Mr. Evans would form such an opinion.

"Perhaps Mr. Evans is mistaken." Her voice came out rough and she reached for her tea.

"Perhaps. But the Talbots being invited to Ryder Hall must mean there is more than just a passing flirtation between them."

"Or there might be affection between Miss Talbot and Sir Phillip."

Mama seemed to consider the idea. "I did not mark any interest between them. However, Miss Talbot would be wise to try and capture Sir Phillip. He would make a much better husband."

"She might not think having a title the most important qualification for a husband."

"It is not the title that makes Sir Phillip superior to his brother. Mr. Ashburn is vain, inconstant, and irresponsible."

"Mama, that is unkind."

"But true. He has no profession. Mrs. Leigh sees him in London and says he is always charming some new young woman. Just last year, it seemed he was courting three separate girls only to offer for none of them."

Elaine had heard such stories from her mother before and had always thought them nothing but neighborhood gossip. But now, Sir Phillip's warning rang in her head. Was she wrong about Daniel? He was charming and no doubt many women fell in love with him. But was he fickle or callous of others' feelings? That did not match the Daniel she knew.

"I am glad Mr. Ashburn has never trespassed upon you." Mama broke into her thoughts.

"Of course not, Mama. He sees me as a sister." Mama did not seem to notice the hint of petulance tingeing her words. Elaine stood. "I will write some letters before it is time for callers."

Mama excused her and Elaine fled to her room. She did not even glance at her desk but sank onto the bed. Did Daniel care for Miss Talbot? Did Miss Talbot care for him? No one watching them last night would think them indifferent acquaintances. But then anyone watching Elaine with Daniel might have thought the same. Might he care for her as more than a sister?

It was not fair. Elaine had known and loved Daniel for most of her life. Miss Talbot, with her forty thousand, was acquainted only with the smooth, charming façade. Elaine knew the real man beneath it. If only Daniel could see how well she understood him, he would surely prefer her. Wouldn't he?

It was all a muddle.

Elaine hoped Penelope had received her letter and would write soon. She sorely needed her friend's insight into men.

With a sigh, she rose and dressed for the day in a simple gown. She attempted to distract herself by rereading *The Sylph*. It was an ill-advised choice since the story revolved around a heroine's childhood neighbor being secretly in love with her.

When Perkins came and told her she was needed in the drawing room, Elaine followed quickly. It was too early for callers, so she didn't bother to fix her hair or check her appearance, an oversight she immediately regretted upon entering the room.

Daniel stood beside the fireplace in his riding costume, his high boots and tousled hair giving him a dashing air. Why had he come at this hour? She glanced at her mother, but her tight smile held no clues.

Elaine's heartbeat picked up as she stumbled through her greeting. She tried to smooth her rumpled gown but could do nothing about the hair that had escaped her braid. His eyes sparkled as he bowed and Elaine wondered if he was amused by her appearance or merely happy to see her.

"Mr. Ashburn was out for his morning ride and thought to stop," Mama said.

"I wanted to invite you," Daniel added.

"Invite me?" Elaine blinked.

"I thought you might want to join me on my ride."

Elaine's heart leapt.

"I thanked Mr. Ashburn but told him we have no horse."

"Oh." Elaine's heart plummeted.

"I thought of that," Daniel said. "I brought a gentle mare for you to ride. And a groom, of course."

This was no whim but a well-planned invitation. He had thought through all the difficulties. It would have been perfect if Elaine could ride. She was reluctant to reject her chance to spend time with Daniel, but he would know the moment she tried to mount.

"I thank you, sir. That was very thoughtful." Elaine smiled to soften the blow. "But I am afraid that I have never learned to ride."

Daniel's eyebrows rose, but he was too well-bred to voice his astonishment. She did not blame him for his assumption. No doubt all the ladies he courted had been tutored in riding from a young age. Miss Talbot was probably a very accomplished rider.

"As I said, Mr. Ashburn, my daughter is no horsewoman." Mama's smile had an edge to it Elaine had never seen. Was it her dislike of Daniel or the idea of Elaine riding? Perhaps both?

Daniel responded with a smile as if her mother's disapproval were a challenge.

"Miss Brooke would no doubt learn quickly if given the chance. Would you allow me to give her a lesson?"

Warmth filled Elaine. Surely Mama could not refuse such a gallant request? Was it not a mark of affection for Daniel to forgo his own pleasure and spend the morning teaching her?

She was suddenly glad she had not taken apart the riding habit Charity had given her. Since she did not ride, she had planned to repurpose the fabric. But now she could impress Daniel instead. Elaine didn't consider how ill-fitting the garment would be—Charity was taller and broader—such practicalities were swept away by the flood of her imagination.

Elaine conjured the image of Daniel gently instructing her. Perhaps he would touch her waist, or leg, to position her properly. She might fall and he would lift her up, their faces coming close. . .

Her daydream was interrupted by the sound of carriage wheels in the lane. Mama already had her first caller of the day. Now she would undoubtedly agree or risk the whole neighborhood speculating over Daniel's early visit.

"Mama, please."

"The horse is very well behaved, and we will stay in your lane so you might watch her progress," Daniel added.

"You see, it will be quite safe," Elaine said.

"No harm will come to your daughter; I will make her safety my utmost priority." Daniel put his hand solemnly over his heart.

But before Mama could answer, there was a knock on the door and the rumble of a male voice. Perkins came in and announced their caller.

"Sir Phillip Ashburn, madam."

At the name, Elaine's eyes flew to Daniel. From his frown and the tightness around his eyes, it seemed that he neither expected nor welcomed his brother. Elaine's sentiments were the same.

Sir Phillip appeared. His clothes were impeccable and his face as handsome and inscrutable as ever. His icy blue eyes swept over the room in quick judgment. Elaine could not tell if he liked what he saw or found it wanting; his expression was infuriatingly neutral. He acknowledged his brother stiffly before turning to greet Mama.

"Sir Phillip, this is an honor."

Elaine winced at how pleased and welcoming her mother sounded. The difference would not be lost on Daniel.

58

"Thank you for receiving me, Mrs. Brooke. I know it is far too early for callers." Sir Phillip gave a pointed look to his brother. Daniel's eyes danced as they met Elaine's. His lips twitched as if he wished to add some remark, but instead, settled on sharing a speaking look with her.

"Oh, you are all that is goodness," Mama said. "As you can see, we are quite at our leisure."

"You are kind, but I don't wish to intrude. I have merely come to collect Miss Brooke for our tour of the neighborhood. I see my brother has anticipated me."

Sir Phillip gave no outward sign, but Elaine suspected he was upset with Daniel.

"Collect Elaine?" Mama looked between the two men.

Elaine could guess her thoughts. To have an Ashburn in her drawing room was an honor, but to have both brothers there seemingly vying for her daughter's company was farcical. Elaine was equally confused.

"Yes," Sir Phillip said. "My brother no doubt neglected to explain that several of our guests wished for a tour of the surrounding country. We thought that Miss Brooke would enjoy the excursion." He smiled. In a few words, Sir Phillip had changed Daniel's offer of an intimate morning into nothing more than a group outing.

Mama nodded, plainly relieved to have an explanation.

"Yes, of course, that is, he did not say, but what a lovely idea. How good of you to think of her."

"It is unfortunate that Miss Brooke cannot ride," Daniel said smugly.

"Yes, very unfortunate that the groom and horse will not be needed. But, as planned, I brought the gig so there should be no difficulties."

Sir Phillip's reply was even, but that only proved he was accomplished at falsehoods. She doubted there had been a plan between the brothers. Just as last night Lady Ashburn had not asked for her company. Did the man always lie with such impunity when it suited him?

"Who else is in your party?" Mama asked.

"Mr. and Mrs. Farthing, Miss Wilson, Mrs. Cooper, and Miss Talbot will all be accompanying us. They are waiting at the top of the lane. They did not wish to overwhelm you at this hour."

"How thoughtful," Daniel muttered.

Sir Phillip ignored the comment. "Our plans include visiting Oakbury, so I would be happy to collect anything you might require."

Elaine's hopes for time with Daniel dissolved as Mama thanked Sir Phillip for his thoughtfulness. She had not accepted Sir Phillip's invitation, but he was not a man to be refused, at least not in front of her mother. Elaine would always prefer Daniel to Sir Phillip, but there was little chance Mama would allow her to have a riding lesson now.

Daniel seemed of the same mind as he gave her a shrug. Unaccountably, Elaine was angry with him for giving in so easily to his brother. Did Sir Phillip dictate every aspect of his life?

"I will fetch my things," Elaine said with all the equanimity she could muster. She escaped to her room, where she collected her spencer, bonnet, and gloves. She took a few moments to restore her hair to good order. As she readied herself, she contemplated telling Sir Phillip that she would much rather spend the morning with Daniel.

She could see the baronet turning red with frustration at her obstinacy and imagine the sharp barbs he would say. It was not hard to envision since she had already defied him twice. Elaine frowned at her reflection. She really must try and keep hold of her temper. Sir Phillip did not need further cause to think ill of her.

Mama appeared in her doorway. "It was very kind of Sir Phillip to invite you. Please do not return his kindness with ingratitude or impropriety."

Elaine looked up from pulling on her gloves. Did Mama know her thoughts?

"It would be foolish to offend a baronet in favor of his dissolute brother."

"Mama, Daniel is—" At the stern look she amended. "I mean, Mr. Ashburn is not—"

"I do not wish to discuss it. You are no longer a girl and Mr. Ashburn is no boy. You are too old for this childish fancy." Mama adjusted Elaine's bonnet. "Now go. Sir Phillip is waiting outside."

"Yes, Mama."

Elaine trudged down the stairs, her mother's words ringing in her ears. Did Mama object to Daniel because she thought he was trifling with Elaine? If he showed actual partiality, would she still object?

Perhaps they were destined for a love like Romeo and Juliet, with family and friends arrayed against them? Elaine did not find the idea appealing. It had not ended well in the play. She shook away the thought as she exited the house.

Sir Phillip and Daniel turned to her with contrasting expressions. Daniel, sitting atop his horse, smiled while his brother looked annoyed.

"Ah, Miss Brooke. Please tell my brother how unfashionable this gig is."

Sir Phillip scoffed. "A gig is perfectly proper."

"And is imminently practical since it requires only one horse." Daniel shook his head as if despairing of his brother's choices. "I assure you, Miss Brooke, that when I take you for a ride, it will be in my phaeton."

Elaine, aware that Mama was likely listening, replied carefully. "I am sure the mode of transport is not as important as the company."

Daniel grinned. "A very astute observation. Don't you agree, Phillip?"

Sir Phillip didn't reply, but a muscle flexed on his cheek. Daniel chuckled and tipped his hat before turning his horse down the lane.

Elaine watched him, delaying the moment when she would have to face Sir Phillip. Phaeton, gig, or barouche, no type of carriage would change the fact that she was to spend the afternoon beside a man she did not like.

She could see clearly how they would sit in awkward silence or exchange more unkind words. Daniel might take pity on her and ride beside them. She imagined laughing with Daniel while Sir Phillip fumed beside her and gave a small smile at the thought. She emerged from her imagination to find Sir Phillip analyzing her with his cold stare. How long had he been watching her?

"Are you ready, Miss Brooke?"

"Quite ready." Elaine gave him a polite smile. Mrs. Piper had always insisted they practice a polite, neutral smile. She claimed it was the single most valuable skill for a young lady. Elaine was now grateful for the training.

Wordlessly, Sir Phillip acted in place of a footman and handed her into the gig. His movements were sure and his hand engulfed her own. It was the work of a moment and she was settling herself on the padded bench. The gig was well-worn, but like everything the Ashburns owned, it was well made and well maintained. It was certainly better than the donkey cart Mama kept.

The gig rocked as Sir Phillip climbed in beside her. In the confined space, his leg brushed hers before they both drew away. Elaine revised her earlier assessment; surely a larger carriage would be preferable when one did not care for their company.

Sir Phillip urged the horse into motion and soon they were under the dappled shade of the stately trees that lined the lane. She had hoped to spend the morning in this lane with Daniel, but Sir Phillip had ensured that would not happen.

Had Sir Phillip known Daniel was at the lodge and set out to disrupt his plans? She would have thought the baronet had more pressing concerns, but his earlier behavior had shown him to be meddlesome. Whatever the reason, she was now with Sir Phillip and under strict instructions to behave.

Mrs. Piper had praised her patient and cheerful nature and she would display it now. At school, Miss Minerva had taught her the art of conversation. She was not always the best student, and she often faltered when conversing with dull people, but she was determined to rise to the challenge of being polite to Sir Phillip. She sought a neutral topic and was pleased when one readily came to mind.

Yes, she would impress him with her propriety and excellent conversation.

"It was clever of you to learn that I do not ride. Who told you?" Elaine asked.

"No one told me. It was a logical assumption for anyone who took the time to think about it." His flat tone implied that Daniel should have made the same assumption. She hated that he was right.

"I think, Sir Phillip, you are rather in the habit of assuming things." The words came out more challenging than she intended.

"My assumptions tend to be correct."

"How lucky for you." Elaine paused and looked at the trees as she searched for composure. Sir Phillip had made some outrageous assumptions at the Old Priory. She turned back to him. "Yet I know of at least one instance where you were utterly mistaken."

He glanced at her with a disapproving frown. "I won't pretend to misunderstand you. You speak of the other morning. I will admit to being wrong in particulars, but I was correct in essentials. And so, though delivered ill, I will not apologize for my words. Not that you have heeded my advice."

Elaine clamped her lips against a snarl of frustration. How could she endure an entire morning with this man? He felt no remorse for his insults and was reiterating his imagined authority over her. Mama didn't want her to offend the exalted owner of Ryder Hall, but that was impossible unless she didn't speak at all. Elaine swallowed her words. It would serve Sir Phillip right to sit in silence the entire morning.

She looked ahead. They had almost reached the end of the lane where the rest of the party waited.

Mr. Farthing and his wife were in a smart landau, its top open to the bright sunshine. Mrs. Farthing was sitting close to her husband, their hands entwined. Miss Wilson and Mrs. Cooper sat across from them. Elaine envied them, but not for the plush padded seats. She wished for a long bench to separate herself from her companion.

In front of the landau, Miss Talbot sat on a beautiful gray horse in a becoming red habit. Daniel had brought his horse next to hers and they were smiling as they conversed. Perched on their horses, they looked as much a couple as the Farthings.

Jealousy filled Elaine. Daniel had come to the lodge to spend time with her, not Miss Talbot. She should be the one talking and riding with Daniel. It did not matter that she couldn't ride. She was meant to be smiling and laughing and it was all Sir Phillip's fault.

As they arrived, the group greeted them.

"We are so gratified you could join us, Miss Brooke," Mrs. Farthing said with pleasing enthusiasm.

"Yes," Miss Talbot added. "I am so glad you came."

Elaine thanked them, trying to match their smiles. Miss Talbot seemed as genuine in her enthusiasm as Mrs. Farthing, but it did not give Elaine the same pleasure. She was still unsure of Miss Talbot's sincerity.

"Well, let us not waste the sunshine," Daniel said. He urged his horse forward as if to lead out the party.

"We are going past Beechhurst first," Sir Phillip said.

Daniel gave a casual nod as if that was the obvious route choice, though he couldn't have known his brother's plan to travel clockwise. Ahead the road split into three different directions and they could easily circle the neighborhood by continuing straight instead of turning left toward Beechhurst.

If only Daniel would defy him. Sir Phillip should not always get his way.

Miss Talbot urged her horse beside Daniel's and he gave her a welcoming smile. Perhaps he did not wish to defy his brother? He might be happy with the new arrangement. Now that he had Miss Talbot for company, her vision of Daniel riding beside the gig and laughing seemed unlikely.

She would be stuck in silence with Sir Phillip. If only it would rain and drive them all inside. But the sky was a glorious blue, marked by only a few puffy clouds.

For the first time in her life, Elaine cursed the good weather.

Chapter Eight

As the gig rolled down the lane, the sun shone bright, its heat tempered by a gentle breeze. Sometime in the night, it had drizzled and left the morning air fresh and earthy with little dust. One could never enjoy such air in London. Mother had praised London and the country equally, but Phillip was of a different mind.

Miss Brooke was silent beside him, her attention not on the fields or the nearby house but fixed on Daniel and Miss Talbot. Moving faster than the carriages, they rode at the front of the company, engrossed in a lively conversation. Phillip could not be happier with this turn of events, but Miss Brooke was frowning.

Good. Let her see Daniel's fickle nature. Perhaps the evidence of her own eyes would persuade her to listen to his advice. It would be much easier if Miss Brooke would just see sense and reject Daniel. Then Phillip would not have to stoop to instructing Lennox to inform him of Daniel's activities or rearrange his entire day to interfere with Daniel's plans. It had worked this morning, and Phillip could only congratulate himself on his scheme of a neighborhood tour, but he could not spend every day watching Daniel like a nursemaid. The sooner Miss Brooke quit being intractable and saw reason, the better.

They came to the lane leading to Beechhurst and Phillip stopped the gig to tell the party about the house. The Leighs had been in the parish for generations, but Beechhurst, despite its grand name, was built only twenty years ago with money made in cotton by Mrs. Leigh's late husband. It was a fine house with a good prospect and extensive grounds.

Phillip liked the building but did not much care for Mrs. Leigh. They had little in common. When the widow wasn't spreading gossip, she was talking about her sons, naval officers who were rarely in residence, or her married daughters in London. The woman took maternal pride too far.

Phillip said none of this and instead pointed out the more refined features of the house and grounds. The Farthings were politely interested and Miss Wilson peppered him with questions about the woodland behind the house and the flowers in the front. The woman was interested in botany, among other things, and he did his best to satisfy her curiosity before they continued.

Miss Brooke kept silent, though she doubtless could have contributed. Mrs. Leigh was a particular friend of Mrs. Brooke. Her eyes, and likely her mind, seemed fixed on Daniel and Miss Talbot. The pair had continued their ride, seemingly oblivious that the rest of the party had stopped. As usual, Daniel was thinking of nothing but himself; he didn't know the planned route but expected everyone to follow him.

Phillip hoped Miss Brooke had noticed his brother's selfishness. But it was hard to tell what the young lady was thinking since she continued to be silent. Usually Phillip would not mind being spared useless conversation, but he grew weary of her watching Daniel.

They were almost to Rough Oak Farm when he broke the silence.

"Perhaps, Miss Brooke, you might wish to comment on the countryside?"

She blinked and turned to him as if coming out of deep thought. "And what comment would you wish me to make?"

"Whatever you please."

"If we were consulting my pleasure, I would be allowed to stay silent."

Before Phillip could make a reply to this impertinence, she sighed and gave a slight shake of her head.

"Apologies, that was ill-considered. Of course, we should talk about the countryside." She turned to look out at the ripening fields as if searching for an appropriate comment. "It is quite beautiful," she said.

Her banal remark was disappointing; better not to talk than endure such blather.

"Yes, quite," he said.

She turned to him. "You don't find it beautiful?"

"I do not deny that it is beautiful. I find nothing so beautiful as this part of England. But it is so much more than merely pleasing to the eye. Surely you must see the hard work and ingenuity that has gone into what you see, how Mr. Smith has enlarged his north field and has implemented a crop rotation instead of letting that one lie fallow." Phillip gestured to the field beside them, green with clover. "Do you not observe how the crops are near harvest and likely to produce well? Can you not see what that means for Smith's family and the many others who will eat and grow prosperous from it?" Phillip paused; he had slipped into a lecturing tone.

Perhaps silence was best.

Nothing but the sound of the wheels and the clip of the horses was heard for a long moment.

"You are quite right." Miss Brooke surprised him with her agreement. "I have been so long in Bath that I forgot that the land is not just for looking at."

Her admission disarmed him. This land was his home, sanctuary, and responsibility, but she had not been in residence for a long time. Phillip well-remembered his return following the death of his father and his struggle to reacquaint himself with life in the country.

"Returning home after a long absence can be disconcerting. Everything seems both familiar and different at the same time," he said.

"How well you express the feeling." Miss Brooke seemed surprised that he had feelings at all, let alone ones that might be in harmony with her own. He glanced from the road and found her green eyes trained on him in curiosity. They were quite pretty eyes.

He looked away.

Miss Brooke turned her attention to the countryside and at length spoke.

"Once I could navigate these lanes by starlight, but it has been years since I have wandered them. Much has changed." Her tone was contemplative as if she were thinking over all the changes in the neighborhood. He hoped she would count the changes in Daniel in her tally.

"I would be happy to talk of any changes you notice," he said. "This corner of the country is one of the few subjects on which I can confidently say I have mastered."

She gave a small laugh. "I am sure you believe yourself master of many things."

Before Phillip could ask the meaning of her comment, the turn in the lane brought Rough Oak Farm into view.

"What a great change," Miss Brooke exclaimed. "Rough Oak always had a derelict air about it. It is perfectly charming now."

"Four years ago, Mr. Gregory Smith took on the lease and he has done a great deal to it."

The tidy, well-maintained farmhouse and outbuildings were a testament to Mr. Smith's economy and Mrs. Smith's pride in her home. It made Phillip smile. He liked the Smiths. They were good tenants and amiable neighbors. As if conjured by his thoughts, Mr. Smith came around the corner of the house as they approached.

"Sir Phillip," he hailed.

Phillip stopped the gig and waited for his approach. With permission, Phillip introduced Mr. Smith to Miss Brooke. She was effusive in her praise of the farm and Smith was all proper modesty. As they spoke, the landau drew near. Phillip waved them on, thinking to follow right behind, but Smith engaged him on a question about the harvest and it was many minutes before their business was concluded.

Mr. Smith excused himself with a tug of his forelock. Hoping to catch up quickly to the others, Phillip urged the horse to a faster pace.

"I had no notion that farming could be so interesting," Miss Brooke said.

"Are you mocking me, Miss Brooke?" Phillip turned a wary eye on her.

"No, I am in earnest." She smiled at his disbelief. "You mentioned before that one of the fields was left to lie fallow. Can you explain what you meant?"

Phillip was surprised but pleased by her question. Most women did not find a discussion of crops diverting, but it was a subject he could talk on at length. His explanation was forestalled as Daniel came around the turn in the lane at a fast gallop.

Phillip was momentarily anxious at the thought of some calamity, but his worry dissipated when he saw the grin on his brother's face. Daniel was riding recklessly for enjoyment because if he injured himself, he was the only one that would suffer. Phillip had not indulged in such behavior since he became the baronet. If some accident befell him, it would have wide-ranging consequences.

Miss Brooke fiddled with the ribbons of her bonnet as Daniel slowed his horse.

"Phillip, I cannot believe you left your guests to get lost while you discussed seed yields or some such with a farmer."

Daniel's horse circled around them and came up beside the gig. Phillip didn't bother explaining himself; Daniel would only mock him further.

"I am sure our guests are fine. Farthing is acquainted with the area."

Phillip did not say that unlike Daniel, Farthing had asked about the planned route. Richard had accompanied Phillip often enough to know that he rarely moved about the country without having to stop and address the concerns of his neighbors and tenants.

"Ah," Daniel grinned. "But did you wish them to go to the London road or to turn down the track to Oakbury, or perhaps take the early turning through the woods to Meecham Park?" Daniel shot a conspiratorial look to Miss Brooke. "Help my brother see how remiss he was in his duty."

"On the contrary," Miss Brooke said coldly. "Sir Phillip would have been remiss if he had not stopped to address Mr. Smith's concerns."

Phillip fought the urge to look at her in amazement. Had she just taken his part against Daniel?

Daniel chuckled uneasily. "Very true, Miss Brooke. You have neatly caught me." He looked to Phillip. "In any case, you are right. Farthing was informed of your intentions and I have only come to tell you that they decided to avoid the traffic of the London road and take the lane through Meecham

Woods."

"Thank you. But you might have saved yourself the trouble as I would have taken the shorter route in any case," Phillip said.

"But then I would have been deprived of the opportunity to converse with Miss Brooke."

"I think, Mr. Ashburn, that it was not me but the opportunity to gallop that drew you away."

"Cannot both reasons be true? Though I confess, one inducement was much stronger than the other."

The corners of Miss Brooke's lips turned up as she shook her head.

"You will not ask me which was the stronger?"

"I dare not, for fear of learning that I compare unfavorably to a fast gallop on a horse."

Daniel patted his mount. "It is a very, very fine horse."

Miss Brooke laughed and Phillip saw that whatever had caused her initial coldness had melted before the warmth of Daniel's charm. Phillip envied Daniel's remarkable ability to please. His brother had drawn a smile and laugh from Miss Brooke in mere seconds while he had not achieved as much in a half hour. It had happened so quickly. Their conversation flowed too rapidly for Phillip to participate.

"Now come, Miss Brooke," Daniel said. "I have sorely neglected you. No doubt my brother has been an ill replacement."

"Your brother can hear every word you say," Phillip interjected.

"Apologies, Phillip. I only meant that Miss Brooke can have little interest in conversations about farming."

"And why would I not be interested?" Miss Brooke asked.

"Because it is a boring subject, ill-suited for the ears of a lady. I think Miss Talbot would fall asleep if I tried to speak of such things."

"Indeed?" Miss Brooke flushed. "Pray tell, what subjects does a true lady show interest in?"

Could Daniel hear the frustration in Miss Brooke's voice? Phillip wasn't sure if it was being compared to Miss Talbot or the implication that she was not a lady, but Miss Brooke was clearly upset.

"I did not say a lady could not be interested in farming. I only thought that you would not be interested in such things." Daniel tried to correct his error.

"Are you now an expert on my interests?"

Phillip couldn't help enjoying the exchange. It was nice to have someone else on the receiving end of Miss Brooke's sharp tongue. He didn't try to hide his smirk as Daniel fumbled for a response.

"Oh look, Meecham Woods." Daniel gestured to the turn ahead where the lane narrowed and disappeared into the trees. "We will have to continue this conversation another time. You will excuse me while I take another opportunity to gallop."

Daniel urged his horse forward, leaving Phillip and Miss Brooke alone once more.

She sat stiffly beside him, her arms folded and lips pursed. While Phillip was happy she had quarreled with Daniel, it left him in an awkward position. Should he continue their conversation or attempt to address his brother's comments and flight? He chose to remain silent. The clomp of hooves and birdsong surrounded them as they turned into the trees.

Meecham Woods was a small expanse of old forest that bordered the Covington's estate. It separated the house and grounds from the traffic of the London road less than a half-mile away. The ancient oak and ash trees had been there since the land was a royal hunting ground, and they crowded together as they reached their boughs to the sky.

Irregular beams of light pierced the canopy, illuminating the forest floor where a handful of flowers brightened the gloom. Phillip always found himself thinking of the history the trees had witnessed. Had King Charles II once leaned against them to catch his breath in the middle of a hunt?

Phillip wondered what Miss Wilson had made of the woods. Perhaps Farthing had answered her questions.

Miss Brooke sighed and a glance proved that she was out of temper. Phillip was frustrated that Daniel's unthinking words had wounded her. Perhaps silence was not the best course.

"My brother treats everything as a jest and does not think before he speaks."

Instead of being soothed, Miss Brooke seemed offended. "That is unjust. Your brother has an easy character and speaks his mind. It is not his fault that I found the content of his speech to be upsetting."

"Yes, his implication that you have unladylike interests is entirely your fault."

"He did not mean to offend. He only pointed out that talking about farming is not a normal topic of conversation and he is right."

Phillip could not believe his ears. "Are you determined to always find good in him?"

"Are you determined to always find fault?"

Their eyes locked and he found nothing to admire in the challenging spark of her gaze. Phillip was sure that if he poured out every grievance against his brother, laid bare his every fault, that Miss Brooke would dismiss them all. She could not see sense where Daniel was concerned.

"I think we should stick to discussing the countryside," he declared and turned his eyes back to the lane.

"How lovely to find something we can agree on," Miss Brooke murmured but said no more.

A few long moments brought a break in the trees and a view of Meecham Park. Then they turned out of the woods and came upon their waiting party. Unconscious of the hurt and discord he had sown, Daniel was grinning beside Miss Talbot.

Phillip gave his apologies for the delay.

"Do not trouble yourself," Mrs. Farthing said. "Mr. Ashburn was kind enough to tell us about Meecham Park."

Phillip hoped Daniel had confined his comments to the house and not spoken openly about their neighbors. Phillip liked Mr. Covington and his eldest son but could not abide the mother and unmarried daughter. Much of this dislike was because Mrs. Covington seemed to think her daughter should marry an Ashburn and was very single-minded in promoting a match each time they met. Reluctance to be in company with Mrs. and Miss Covington was one of the few things Daniel and Phillip agreed on.

"And Miss Wilson," Mrs. Farthing continued, "was so kind as to inform us about the trees and plants. So you see, we have been entertained in your absence."

Phillip appreciated Mrs. Farthing's assurances. "That is good to hear. We are quite lucky Miss Wilson is so well informed. A keen, curious mind is a wonderful attribute in a companion."

"I am glad to find company that appreciates the subject of horticulture." Miss Wilson, closer in age to his mother, smiled like a schoolgirl praised for her work.

Phillip did not look at Miss Brooke as they continued their journey north toward Brightworth village. In silence, they rode to the Old Manor House where his ancestors had lived for generations before Phillip's grandfather had built the current modern estate.

When they pulled away from the Old Manor, Miss Brooke ventured to ask again about fallow fields. Phillip accepted the renewal of their conversation without comment.

The subject of farming proved to be fertile and they rarely strayed from it as they took their circuitous route through the neighborhood. From Brightworth village, they turned north to admire the prospect of Ryder Hall from across the manmade lake. The lake was another feature added by his grandfather. Though Phillip was aware of the cost of such beauty, he never tired of it.

It was only after they had traveled north of the hall and turned west toward Ashford that they exhausted the subject of crops and land improvements. Fortunately, they were once again surrounded by woodland and Phillip easily fell into explaining how such land was managed and hunted.

Contrary to Daniel's predictions, Miss Brooke was not bored and asked several insightful questions. Despite her attention occasionally wandering to Daniel and Miss Talbot and the need to repeat himself when she did not listen, Phillip was pleased with her conversation. It was, he reflected, their first true conversation. Despite being close neighbors, the difference in their age and her long absence at school had prevented them from being properly acquainted.

When they passed through the hamlet of Ashford and turned south toward Oakbury, Daniel turned his horse and came back to the gig. Miss Brooke shifted beside him and Phillip did not have to look to know that all her attention was focused on his brother. Daniel smiled at her before addressing Phillip.

"Miss Talbot would like to gallop. I thought we might take advantage of the road and meet you in Oakbury."

"I think that would be nice for Miss Talbot, but you must keep to the road," Phillip said. He wanted an engagement, not a scandal.

"Do not worry; we shall not stray." Daniel grinned and took a hasty leave. He barely paused beside Miss Talbot before they both galloped away.

Once again, Daniel left silence in his wake. Miss Brooke seemed to retreat into her own thoughts. Could she see now that Daniel was fickle? Did she understand that Miss Talbot was to be his wife? Phillip doubted it. That was too sensible a conclusion.

As if to emphasize how foolish Miss Brooke could be, the ruins of the Old Priory came into view. She gave a small sigh that Phillip couldn't interpret.

The overgrown and tumbled-down walls seemed to loom over them as they approached. The shadows and his memories of the other morning pressed upon him. When they were almost beside the priory, he slowed the gig and pulled it off the lane. The landau stopped beside them.

Mrs. Farthing spoke as soon as they were close. "What a delightful folly! It is so perfectly situated."

"I am glad you like it," Phillip said. "But it is no folly. Those are the remains of a priory."

Mrs. Cooper and Miss Wilson brightened. "A real priory?" Mrs. Cooper asked. "I would enjoy hearing of its history."

"I would love to explore it properly," Miss Wilson added.

"And I simply must paint it," Mrs. Farthing said.

Farthing laughed. "It seems, Ashburn, we should make a proper visit."

"I expected as much," Phillip said. "I have planned an excursion to the ruins for my guests. I hope you will all join me."

The invitation was met with universal approval and after a few more minutes of admiring the ruins, they continued on toward Oakbury.

"I am sure your guests will enjoy visiting the Old Priory," Miss Brooke said.

"Yes, I believe they will."

"I think I will never tire of the sight of those old walls."

"How lucky that you can walk to them whenever you wish." Phillip tried to keep his voice even. He had no desire to renew their previous fruitless arguments, not after reaching an uneasy truce.

"Yes, I am very fortunate to be able to walk to the ruins." Miss Brooke mimicked his tone.

There was silence between them. Any more words on the subject might spring a trap.

He considered what to say next. The subject of the priory seemed fraught with difficulties and no other suitable topic came to mind. He began to feel a familiar uneasiness as he groped for something to say. Did Daniel ever struggle to say the right thing? No, Daniel never thought before he spoke or acted. Perhaps that was what Miss Brooke admired about him.

The longer Phillip remained silent, the more he felt the need to say something interesting when he spoke. He urged his horse faster. The sooner they arrived in Oakbury, the sooner he could be relieved of making conversation.

Chapter Nine

E laine had always thought of Oakbury as a bustling market town, but as the gig made its way down the high street, she was struck by how small it seemed. She had grown accustomed to multiple shops and streets full of shoppers living in Bath. Her time in London had introduced her to enormous warehouses of goods and the press of numerous people. At first it had excited Elaine, but soon she had tired of the noise, smells, and crowds. Oakbury, with its handful of shops and smattering of pedestrians and vehicles, was precisely the right size.

When the gig stopped in front of Hartley's booksellers, Elaine tried not to breathe a sigh of relief. While the morning had contained several pleasant surprises—Sir Phillip was not the worst conversationalist she had encountered—it was still far from her hopes. Sir Phillip's overbearing manner, pompous confidence, and judgmental silences were trying enough without the added pain of watching Daniel.

Miss Talbot was an excellent horsewoman and an excellent conversationalist, judging by Daniel's attentiveness. When Daniel was with her, it was as if Elaine did not exist. Watching them had been torture, but speaking to him had been worse.

Daniel thought her unladylike. He found Miss Talbot the superior woman. Elaine had never imagined how her heart would drop and her stomach twist as she was found wanting.

When Daniel and Miss Talbot had galloped ahead, Elaine had been seized by the image of them strolling through Oakbury. Everywhere they walked, the gossips' heads would turn and everyone would assume that Mr. Daniel Ashburn had at last been tamed. Every dinner table in the county would be filled with talk of the unknown and fashionable young woman. Speculation of their engagement would be rampant.

As Sir Phillip climbed down from the carriage, Elaine searched for Miss Talbot's charming horse or Daniel's striking form among the small stretch of shops, but neither were to be seen. Where were they?

Sir Phillip's cough pulled her eyes from the street, and she looked down to see him with his hand outstretched. After a moment of hesitation, she took his hand. When her feet touched the ground, she was too close to Sir Phillip. Sitting beside him, she had almost forgotten how imposing he could be when staring down at her.

She took a step back.

"Where might I escort you, Miss Brooke?" he asked.

He seemed all solicitude now that they might have an audience. But he had been silent since the Old Priory since he had pointedly not invited her to visit the ruins with his guests.

"I don't need an escort."

The words came out sharper than she intended. She winced. Why could she not curb her tongue with him? A real lady would not say such things to a baronet.

The retort hung between them as the Farthings approached.

"Mrs. Cooper and Miss Wilson have their own errands." Mr. Farthing gestured to the two ladies as they entered the booksellers.

"Sir Phillip, I am going to steal Miss Brooke." Mrs. Farthing took Elaine's arm. "You have had her to yourself all morning."

"And you are with me, Ashburn." Mr. Farthing clapped Sir Phillip on the back. "You promised the sight of a capital gun."

Neither Sir Phillip nor Elaine made any protests and were separated without further words between them.

"Now, Miss Brooke." Mrs. Farthing's blue eyes twinkled. "I am determined that we will be good friends."

Elaine smiled. "I would like that very much."

Though only a few years apart in age, Mrs. Farthing was her superior in station and experience. She at least did not find Elaine unladylike. Mrs. Farthing was slightly shorter and broader than Elaine but exuded a natural grace. Her features were not quite regular, but one hardly noticed since her constant smile made her countenance pleasing.

"If we are to be friends, I must ask, do you paint?"

"I paint tolerably well," Elaine said.

"That is no answer at all, for all young women, be they great proficient or beginner, are taught to reply thus. Now speak candidly."

"My ability is barely above middling."

"But do you enjoy it? Skill is not as important as the enjoyment of putting paint to canvas."

Elaine considered her reply. She wanted Mrs. Farthing's approval, but a friendship could not be built on lies.

"I do not dislike painting, but it does not absorb me. I get lost in my thoughts only to discover that my companion has finished while I have been gathering wool."

Mrs. Farthing's perpetual smile warmed. "That is quite a particular problem."

"And do you paint, Mrs. Farthing?"

"Tolerably well." She gave a sly smile.

Elaine laughed.

"In truth, I am no great talent, but I love to commit a scene to canvas. My husband is very indulgent and will happily sit beside me all afternoon while I paint. But here, where there is shooting and Sir Phillip, I hate to keep him from his own pleasures. I had hoped we could paint together. Pray, do you know if Miss Talbot paints?"

"I do not." Elaine tried to temper her disappointment. It was likely that Miss Talbot did paint and Mrs. Farthing would vastly prefer her company.

"Here is the haberdashers." Elaine nodded toward Dawson's as they approached the shop.

"Then let us go in."

Thankfully the talk now turned to ribbons, bonnets, and fabric. Mrs. Farthing seemed to enjoy fashion as much as painting. They spoke at length on the latest styles, trimming bonnets, and the value of a matching reticule. Elaine could not afford the newest fashions and only had two reticules but enjoyed the discussion. They passed the next half-hour happily.

In the midst of helping Mrs. Farthing choose between a blue and green ribbon, Elaine's happiness dissolved when the door opened to admit Daniel and Miss Talbot. They both looked flushed and pleased as they approached.

"At last, we have found your hiding place," Daniel said as if he genuinely had been looking for her.

"Our hiding place?" Elaine couldn't stop her frown.

"Please don't be upset with Mr. Ashburn," Miss Talbot said. "It was such a lovely day and he obliged my fancy."

This speech did not soothe Elaine's feelings.

"You cannot blame me either," Daniel said. "A good host should not deny his guest the pleasure of a hard ride, especially when they are an accomplished horsewoman."

Daniel's approving smile was a knife to Elaine's heart. Perhaps he wanted a wife that could ride? Was he glad he hadn't spent the morning teaching a novice?

"I blame neither of you, for you have come just in time," Mrs. Farthing said. "I need your opinions on these ribbons."

As Miss Talbot's and Daniel's opinions were consulted, Elaine found herself extraneous to the conversation. With the fashionable Miss Talbot there, Mrs. Farthing would have no use for her thoughts. She had no desire to be where she was not wanted.

"Apologies, but I need to run an errand for my mother," Elaine said as soon as there was a break in the conversation.

"I shall accompany you," Daniel said.

Elaine hated that her heart was thrilled at his simple offer. She tried not to imagine that he had been wishing for the chance to talk with her alone and told herself that he was only being considerate as they took their leave and exited the shop. When she took his offered arm, she ignored the thought of gossips speaking her name with Daniel's.

She was so focused on controlling her hopes that she forgot to speak.

"Where is your errand?" Daniel asked after they had walked past several shops.

Since she had no true errand, Elaine settled on the first shop that came to mind.

"Hartley's."

"The booksellers?" Daniel's eyebrows rose.

"Yes."

He chuckled as he stopped and turned them around to retrace their steps. Her cheeks heated. Neither spoke about their change in course.

When they entered the shop, they were met by the pleasant smell of leather, glue, and paper. Elaine took a deep breath. The smell of books always reminded her of her father and the hours spent in his study as a child. The study was bare now, all the books long sold to help pay the bills. She understood the necessity; one could not eat paper, but Elaine often wished for the warm, full shelves of her childhood.

"Are you quite all right?" Daniel asked.

"Perfectly fine." Elaine smiled to add weight to her assurance.

They stepped more fully into the shop. Books lined the walls, along with two freestanding shelves in the center of the room. On the right, the shopkeeper was at the counter, deep in conversation with Miss Wilson and Mrs. Cooper. Elaine smiled at the two sisters and the three brown-wrapped books Miss Wilson held.

Elaine could not afford any of the fine leather volumes on display—just one would cost two years of her pin money—but she enjoyed pulling them from the shelf, her fingers dancing over the leather, admiring the illustrations, and turning the pages. She wandered to a set of black leather books. Daniel trailed after.

"Are you fond of reading?" He asked.

"Quite fond." How did he not know that about her?

Daniel raised an eyebrow.

"You are surprised?"

"I never imagined the lively and playful girl I knew would turn bookish."

"But doth not the appetite alter? A man loves the meat in his youth that he cannot endure in his age."

"I suppose that is possible," Daniel said.

"That was a quote. From Shakespeare, Benedick says it when. . . never mind." Elaine shook her head. "Perhaps I am bookish," she muttered.

Daniel looked as if he were holding back a laugh.

Did it make her a bluestocking to quote Shakespeare? Did Daniel think it an unladylike interest? She had quoted favorite lines with her friends so often she had come to think it normal. Elaine pulled a book from the shelf in an effort to hide her nerves.

"It is so odd," Daniel said. Elaine looked up to see his too blue eyes studying her. "We share so much history that I feel as if I know all about you. Yet in many ways, we are strangers."

"Yes." Elaine hated how true his words were.

"It is not the normal progression of an acquaintance."

Another Shakespeare quote was on the tip of Elaine's tongue when the shopkeeper arrived beside them.

"Might I help you?" He asked. His deep-set eyes traveled between them as he rested his hands on his vast belly.

Elaine had not intended to come to Hartley's, but it had reminded her that her reading material was limited.

"Yes," Elaine said. "I was hoping to join the circulating library. Might I see your catalog?"

"Of course." The man bowed slightly before going to his counter and returning with a slim pamphlet. Elaine thanked him as she took it.

"I will be at the desk when you are ready," the shopkeeper said. As he walked away, Elaine opened the catalog and began to read through the titles.

The small number of available volumes surprised her. She had not expected Hartley's to have the inventory of the libraries in Bath or London, but it still seemed very small. Her heart sank further when she saw the price of a subscription.

She did not have a guinea to spare. In the past, she had been fortunate to have friends like Charity and Penelope who let her borrow books with their subscription. But her friends were far away and she had only her own meager funds. She might save her shillings or talk with her mother about the purchase, though that would risk a lecture about frivolous spending. If only she had a small income of her own.

"Find anything you like?" Daniel asked

Elaine closed the pamphlet and shrugged. "I don't think I will subscribe."

Daniel plucked the pamphlet from her and scanned the titles. He hummed thoughtfully. "I understand not being interested in Milton or Smollett's *History of England*, but what woman can resist *Belinda* or *Waverley*?"

"I have already read both."

"Ah, I see the problem. You are a voracious reader and have exhausted this entire list."

Elaine took back the pamphlet. "I am not so great a reader."

"Not the whole list then, only all the novels."

Despite herself, Elaine smiled at Daniel's teasing tone.

"You do not protest your love of novels," Daniel said.

With anyone else, she might have demurred, but she could not resist the mischievous glint in his eyes. "I confess I love novels above all others."

"An excellent vice." He looked both ways and leaned closer as if imparting a great secret. "I also prefer novels."

"Of course you prefer novels." Sir Phillip's deep disapproving voice broke the spell Daniel had cast.

They turned as one to see him standing behind them. Elaine pulled away from Daniel as if she had been scalded. She felt like a child caught by Cook as she and Daniel tried to sneak pastries.

"There you are." Daniel made it sound as if they had been looking for Sir Phillip and not whispering in corners.

"And here you are, both of you."

"No need to thank me for rescuing Miss Brooke from your neglect."

"I did not neglect—"

Daniel made a tsking sound over his brother's protest. "When a gentleman brings a woman into a market town, they should escort them to the shops and admire anything they choose to purchase. Surely you know that. Frankly, I am amazed that you abandoned her after being so eager for Miss Brooke's company this morning."

Though Daniel spoke lightly, there was an edge of resentment in his tone. Was he upset at not getting to spend time with her or just that his plans were thwarted? Elaine wanted to believe the former.

"I did not abandon her," Sir Phillip said with barely disguised frustration. "I left her with Mrs. Farthing, a respectable chaperone. I would like to know why you separated them?"

Elaine hated the implication in Sir Phillip's voice.

"We were talking of novels," Elaine attempted to forestall whatever retort Daniel might have ready. "Do you read novels, Sir Phillip?"

The question was ill-considered. Sir Phillip was more likely to lecture her on the evils of reading novels than confess to enjoying them.

"I do not," he said flatly.

"My brother can't be bothered to do anything even remotely enjoyable."

Elaine was at a loss. "I am sure that is not true."

"No, Miss Brooke," Sir Phillip said. "It is true. I prefer to concern myself with practicalities and leave the daydreaming to those with ample leisure time."

"Yes, it would not do to have dreams," Daniel said.

Sir Phillip fixed his brother with a stern look. A muscle in his jaw twitched, then he turned to her. "Miss Brooke, if your business in town is concluded, I need to return to the hall."

Daniel replied for her. "I'm afraid Miss Brooke has yet to pick a book. And to be certain she gets the right one, she will need to look over the entire shop."

Sir Phillip did not even look at Daniel. "The gig is outside. I will attend you whenever you are ready."

The hostility between the brothers was palpable. If she went with Sir Phillip directly, it would give him a point in the battle between brothers. If she stayed with Daniel and looked over books, she would award a victory to her childhood friend. Elaine did not like either option.

"Thank you, Sir Phillip. I will be with you presently."

He nodded and stiffly took his leave. When he was gone, Elaine turned to Daniel and fixed him with a chiding look.

"What?" He asked.

"There was no need to antagonize him so."

Daniel shrugged. "What else can I do?"

"What do you mean?"

Daniel sighed and turned to the bookshelf. Idly he danced his fingers along the spines. "I am the dependent younger brother. Phillip's word is law; we both know it. He wanted you to come on his tour, and so you are here. He wants you to leave now and expects to be obeyed. It is just the way of the world. But he can't tell me what to say or who I will—"

Daniel gave her a sheepish smile. Elaine wished desperately to know what he was going to say. But he shook his head instead. "I know it must seem childish, but I oppose him where I can. It has become our way."

"It wasn't always that way between you." Elaine could vividly remember how much Daniel had idolized his older brother. Thanks to Daniel's stories, Elaine had thought Phillip Ashburn larger than life long before she ever met him.

"Yes, well, things change."

The gulf of years stretched between them and she did not know how to bridge it. As Daniel had said, in many ways they were strangers.

"Now, let us take as long as possible and look over every book." Daniel's melancholy seemed to disappear and his charming smile returned. How much did Daniel hide behind that smile?

Elaine glanced out the window to where Sir Phillip stood beside his gig, watching them with hard eyes. She had no stomach for pretending merriment under the baronet's watchful gaze. What was the point of looking through books she could not borrow?

"I think it would be better if I go."

Daniel's face fell. "If you go now, he wins."

"It's not a contest," Elaine said.

"Allow me to escort you." Daniel offered his arm.

It was hardly necessary and would likely result in more hard words between the brothers, but Elaine could not refuse. She took his arm. It was the least she could do to soften the blow. She had no desire to be in the middle of the brothers' conflict, but it seemed unavoidable.

Once outside, Daniel waved off Sir Phillip. "I will assist her into the gig."

There was a thrill in holding Daniel's hand as he helped her up. In contrast to Sir Phillip's perfunctory help, Daniel was solicitous. Her whole body was alive at the contact, her mind racing. Thus distracted, she slipped on the step when the gig rocked with Sir Phillip's weight. Daniel reached for her waist and steadied her. Elaine was warm all over but she didn't know if it was from embarrassment or excitement. The touch was too fleeting to be sure.

Once she was settled in the seat, Daniel smiled up at her. She had been forgiven.

"I will endeavor to make up for your disappointing morning by ensuring you have an entertaining evening."

Sir Phillip scoffed. Elaine ignored him.

"Thank you."

Daniel's smile turned mischievous. "Dinner cannot come soon enough."

Before Elaine could respond, Sir Phillip snapped the reins and the gig began to move. Daniel stepped back, smiling even wider.

Any joy Elaine might have felt at Daniel's declaration was tempered by doubt. Did he really wish to see her or merely to annoy his brother? This question led to others. She could not help but rethink all her interactions with the brothers. Did Daniel care for her at all? Or was she just a pawn in his game with Sir Phillip?

Chapter Ten

As they drove through the streets of Oakbury, Phillip tried to regain some measure of calm. It was difficult when one of the objects of his frustration sat beside him. He had rearranged his morning to prevent Daniel from spending time with Miss Brooke, only to discover them together at Hartley's. It was infuriating.

Worse, Daniel took him to task for not escorting Miss Brooke properly and called the morning a disappointment. How lowering. To think he had been enjoying his conversation with Miss Brooke while she had merely tolerated it. No doubt she had been counting the minutes until she could be free of him.

They left Oakbury on the well-traveled eastern road to Brightworth. No doubt she was upset that he had cut short her pleasure. But he had responsibilities at the hall and he would not leave her with Daniel.

They did not speak and he was glad Ryder Lodge was not far. He kept the horse at a brisk pace. Soon he was turning down the tree-lined lane that led to the lodge and slowed the horse. Miss Brooke shifted in her seat, her body just grazing his. Perhaps Daniel was right about the gig being too small.

He glanced at her but she was staring straight ahead. She shifted again and then spoke. "I must thank you, Sir Phillip."

"I do not require your thanks." Phillip was proud of his even voice and demeanor.

"Regardless, I appreciated seeing the country and learning about the crops and woodlands."

She sounded sincere but Phillip was not fooled. "Daniel would say that my conversation pleased only my pride and vanity."

"And you think he is correct?"

"I won't venture to speculate if you were pleased with my conversation. But I don't deny that I take pride in my holdings and speaking of them. But my brother believes it is the ownership alone that I care for. To look at the land and claim it as mine is not enough for me. The source of my pride is the work that makes it prosper."

"And you can certainly be proud of that work. A compliment on the estate is a compliment to you and your effort. I truly was interested in all I learned."

Warmth bloomed in his chest. Ridiculous to care what Miss Brooke thought.

"But there is nothing wrong with having other interests," she added.

Phillip's grip tightened on the reins. "I am kept very busy by my responsibilities."

"But you must have room in your days for music, reading, exercise, or other things you enjoy."

"I do not."

"That is a shame. My life would be empty without at least some entertainments."

Phillip did not trust himself to reply. Miss Brooke would never understand.

They had reached the end of the lane and he pulled the horse to a halt in front of the lodge. He waited for a brief moment before remembering that the Brookes had no footman. Holding back a sigh, Phillip climbed down from the gig, walked quickly around the carriage, and thrust his hand out to assist her.

"You could at least try to enjoy your life," Miss Brooke said as she took his hand.

How dare she judge him. She knew nothing of how he had struggled to live up to his father's legacy, the expectations of his neighbors, or the demands on his funds.

His resolution crumbled. When her feet hit the ground, words burst forth like a dam breaking.

"Miss Brooke, I would thank you not to pass judgment. Life is not one of your novels. I have responsibilities and cannot afford to be a fashionable man of leisure, traipsing about London with no thought but how to please myself."

"You are speaking of your brother."

"Yes, my brother is a sterling example of that species of dandy."

"You are wrong. He thinks of more than leisure."

Phillip bristled at her bold declaration. He leaned forward. "You do not know Daniel as I do."

"No." Miss Brooke did not shrink before him. Her chin high, gaze direct, she spoke. "But in some ways, I might know him better." She tugged her hand from his grasp, unaware he was still clasping it. He looked down and then back into her flashing eyes. The words would not be stopped.

"Daniel never thinks seriously and wastes his days in frivolities. I can't enjoy my life because he refuses to take responsibility or choose a profession. I—"

Phillip broke off. She looked at him, her eyes wide and curious now, but he should not be speaking so, especially not to Miss Brooke. He found his control and swallowed back the self-pitying words.

"Good day, Miss Brooke."

He bowed and didn't wait for a reply.

He fumed all the way back to the hall.

* * *

Once home, Phillip sequestered himself in his study. After ensuring all was in order for the shooting, he spoke with his land manager about Mr. Smith's concerns. Then he caught up on his never-ending correspondence. All these tasks were made more difficult by his distraction. He did not think he had a brooding temperament but he kept replaying his conversations with Miss Brooke.

She wanted him to enjoy himself! How could he possibly enjoy himself when there was so much to do? How had she managed to get him to speak so openly? What must she think of him? Should he beg her pardon for his rash words and loss of composure? Or was it good that he had spoken openly about Daniel's faults? It was clear the young woman was blind to Daniel's true nature. Perhaps his blunt words would help her finally see?

When Phillip went to dress for dinner, he did not have any firm answers to his questions, just a lingering sense of apprehension for the upcoming evening. It had been a disaster of a morning and he had little hope dinner would be better.

He would prefer to stay far away from Miss Brooke—she had an uncanny ability to rile him—but his preferences didn't matter. Daniel had promised to entertain her and so Phillip would need to intervene. He could not consult his own feelings or find enjoyment this evening.

This was not a new circumstance where Daniel was concerned. And yet, it seemed to chafe more than usual. Still, he would do his duty. Unlike Daniel, Phillip understood what was at stake.

As Phillip left his room, he came upon Daniel in the corridor.

Daniel looked over Phillip's evening clothes. "Your valet does an excellent job with the material he has."

"Thank you for the compliment. I'll tell him you approve," Phillip replied as they reached the stairs.

"To be clear, I complimented your valet, not your person."

"Yes, very clever." Phillip was already tired of their verbal dance. It was going to be a long night. He let Daniel take the stairs faster, hoping to avoid further conversation, but Daniel paused on the landing.

"Tell me, Phillip," Daniel said when he was two steps from the bottom. "What are your intentions towards Miss Brooke?"

Phillip nearly missed the last step. "My what?"

"Your intentions. You went to considerable effort to spend the morning with her. In fact, I would wager you knew of my plans and actively sought to keep me from spending time with our neighbor." Daniel gave a knowing smile. "So I can only conclude that you wished to keep Miss Brooke to yourself. Am I wrong?"

"Are you acting as her father or her brother?" Phillip asked, echoing his conversation with Miss Brooke. He pushed past Daniel and headed for the drawing room.

"I am asking as your brother," Daniel said as he fell into step beside him. "And as your brother, I should caution you on raising hopes in the young lady."

Phillip held back a snort. "Trust me. Miss Brooke perfectly understands my position."

"Does she? And pray, what is it?"

Phillip wondered if Daniel was jealous or merely lashing out for Phillip's interference that morning. If he was genuinely interested in Miss Brooke, would that make Daniel more or less likely to pursue her? Phillip didn't know.

They paused outside the drawing room which was already occupied by several guests. Daniel leaned close and whispered. "I ask only that you don't steal her away for more boring conversation. I promised an entertaining evening and would hate to disappoint our guests."

Daniel escaped through the door and left Phillip to stew on his words.

It was true that some might see him escorting Miss Brooke as a sign of partiality. Heaven knew the neighborhood needed little encouragement to speculate on his marriage. Miss Brooke was young, pretty, and—as she proved through her conversation that morning—uncommonly intelligent. But while the neighborhood gossips might assume she was overjoyed by his attention, Phillip was certain that she had no hopes in his direction. The young woman wanted to become Mrs. Ashburn, not Lady Ashburn.

Despite Phillip's trepidation, dinner went smoothly. His mother arranged the seating so cleverly that nobody seemed to realize they had been managed. Daniel escorted Mrs. Cooper but was seated across from Miss Talbot. Miss Brooke was escorted again by Captain Hart and seated near Lady Ashburn, where she appeared happily engaged. Phillip did not witness a single shared look between her and Daniel, though the young lady almost caught him in his scrutiny once or twice.

When the ladies had retired and the brandy had been passed around, Phillip discussed the planned shooting to general acclaim. Daniel seemed as enthusiastic as the rest. Phillip was gratified by Mr. Talbot's look of approval. He would make sure Mr. Talbot and Daniel were thrown together while shooting. Daniel was an excellent sportsman and would appear to advantage. And as long as Daniel was shooting with Mr. Talbot, he could not sneak away to see Miss Brooke. The shooting had bought Phillip a day or two of peace.

This triumph was fleeting, for as soon as they entered the drawing room, Daniel went straight to where Miss Brooke sat with Mrs. Farthing and Miss Talbot. Phillip resisted following. He reasoned that Daniel's eagerness could as easily be for Miss Talbot's company. Besides, Jane Farthing was there to temper the conversation. He might go and speak with Miss Wilson or join Mr. Evans and Mr. Poole and talk about their new guns.

But Phillip did neither of those things. Instead, he watched Daniel and the women in lively conversation. Wherever Daniel went, there was lively conversation. Miss Brooke's eyes were inviting and her smile seemed brighter as she spoke to his brother. It was all too clear that she cared for him. No doubt others could see it too.

What had Daniel just said to make her laugh?

"If I didn't know you better, I might think you were upset."

Phillip started at Farthing's voice. How long had his friend been beside him?

"I am not upset," Phillip said as he turned his attention to Richard.

Farthing smiled sardonically. "Of course not. Only you looked quite serious just now." Farthing tipped his head toward Daniel. "Is The Prodigal not behaving?"

"Does he ever?"

Farthing chuckled. "Good point. Shall we go ensure he is not scandalizing my wife?"

Phillip allowed Farthing to lead the way across the room and was surprised that instead of dread, he was eager to join the conversation. Farthing opted to stand behind his wife, leaving Phillip to sit in the second armchair next to Daniel.

"Sir Phillip," Miss Talbot sat between Mrs. Farthing and Miss Brooke. She greeted him with her usual grace. "You shall help us discern the truth of the story."

"What story?" Phillip glanced about the group. Daniel and Miss Brooke both looked like children with a secret.

"The story of Miss Brooke saving me from being trampled to death," Daniel said.

Miss Brooke shook her head. "It was not so dire."

"So you claim," Daniel replied.

"You see the muddle we are in?" Miss Talbot said with a fond smile.

"I am trying to see."

Miss Talbot tried to explain. "Mr. Ashburn told me that Miss Brooke saved him from a charging bull when they were children. But Miss Brooke claims that she did little more than help him understand the danger."

"Helping Mr. Ashburn see his own folly would still be a great feat," Farthing said. His wife swatted his arm discreetly. Phillip silently agreed with his friend.

"Miss Brooke is being modest," Daniel pointedly ignored Farthing's comment. "I am positive that without her intervention, I would have been injured, perhaps killed."

"An exaggeration," Miss Brooke said with barely suppressed mirth.

"I don't exaggerate." Daniel's affront was comical and earned him smiles and chuckles.

"I think we must all listen to Miss Brooke's version of the story and then decide," Mrs. Farthing said.

There were nods all around.

Daniel inclined his head. "I will bow to the opinion of this august body. But I reserve the right to correct Miss Brooke when she makes an error."

All eyes turned to Miss Brooke. Despite himself, Phillip wanted to hear the story. He had been away at school when the two of them had run rampant about the estate. Mother's letters had been full of tales about little Elaine and Daniel, but he could not recall a story about a bull. How many childhood stories were known only to Miss Brooke and his brother?

Miss Brooke's tongue darted out to wet her lips, the only sign of nervousness before she began her story.

"It was a long time ago, but as I remember it, Priory Farm had a new young bull. Mr. Ashburn and I went to see it. It seems silly now, but I was quite excited by it all, no doubt because Mr. Ashburn had made it seem like a grand adventure." She smiled at Daniel. "But when we got to the paddock, I was disappointed. It was just a yearling and it barely looked at us."

"Now, that is not true," Daniel interrupted. "It was a great ginger brute. Perfectly terrifying in its size."

Miss Brooke raised her eyebrows. "That is not how I remember it."

"Your memory is faulty."

"Mr. Ashburn, let her tell the story," Miss Talbot scolded. Daniel sighed but kept silent.

"I declared that the bull was not in the least frightening and expressed a wish to do something else. Then Mr. Ashburn jumped into the paddock. He proclaimed he was going to fight the animal."

"Fight it?" Farthing chuckled.

Phillip was not so amused. He could easily see his young, brash brother trying to prove his bravery by imagining himself a Spaniard in an arena facing an angry bull.

"As he approached, the bull began to display signs of anger and I called out telling him to come back but he must not have heard me."

"I heard you. I just didn't listen because my plan was to dodge the bull when it charged," Daniel added.

"Oh dear," Mrs. Farthing said.

"Not a very good plan," Mr. Farthing put in.

"Yes, well, I was a child," Daniel muttered.

Miss Brooke continued. "I jumped off the fence and went after him. The bull was kicking up dirt and I was sure it would charge at any moment."

"How did you know when it would charge?" Miss Talbot asked.

Miss Brooke gave a half smile. "My father explained it to me once. He was always teaching me those kinds of things. I guess it was fortunate that I remembered."

"Very fortunate," Phillip murmured. What might have happened if she had not known what to do? Would Daniel have been gored or trampled all because of his bravado? Phillip shuddered at the thought of his scrawny little brother, broken and bloody.

"When I got to Daniel, I grabbed his hand." She closed her eyes as if transported back to that moment. "When he turned, the bull began to run toward us. I screamed and the bull slowed a little."

"It was a very formidable scream," Daniel said. "I admit that when I turned and saw the bull, I was terrified and tried to run. But Elaine wouldn't let me."

Miss Brooke colored. "I knew that running was the worst thing to do and that we had to back away slowly and move to the side."

"And that's what we did, even as the bull kept coming and all I wanted to do was run. She kept her head."

"I screamed several times."

"I am sure anyone would have screamed in that circumstance," Mrs. Farthing said.

"I know I would," Farthing said. Everyone smiled.

"As I recall," Daniel said. "After it was over, you had the presence of mind to scold me and hit me a few times for good measure."

"You deserved it," Miss Brooke replied.

"You did," Phillip agreed.

"I think you were both courageous." Miss Talbot patted Miss Brooke's arm. "Mr. Ashburn did not exaggerate in the slightest. You clearly saved his life."

"At the time it felt that way, but now that I am older, I think the bull was only trying to intimidate us."

Phillip shook his head. "I know a bit more about the animals and I assure you it was a narrow escape. My brother is fortunate you were there to save him from himself. I think everyone will agree with Miss Talbot that you were uncommonly brave and saved Daniel's life."

Miss Brooke looked away, her cheeks red as everyone murmured their agreement.

"You see, Miss Brooke," Daniel said, "everyone agrees that you are braver and smarter than I."

Miss Brooke practically glowed from Daniel's praise as everyone laughed at his self-deprecation.

"Excuse me." Lady Ashburn's voice rose above the dull murmur of conversations. All eyes turned to where she stood beside the fireplace. "For your enjoyment, I have asked Daniel to read to us this evening."

Daniel rose with alacrity. "I hope you will enjoy my poor offering."

He took his leave and moved to Mother's side.

"Mr. Ashburn is a fine reader," Miss Talbot said. "Do not you agree, Miss Brooke?"

"I have not had the pleasure of hearing Mr. Ashburn read," Miss Brooke replied.

"Truly? But how could that be?"

"My brother and Miss Brooke have not been in each other's company for many years," Phillip explained smoothly.

"Oh," Miss Talbot said.

Phillip thought Miss Talbot's shoulders relaxed slightly. Though no one had remarked upon it, Daniel and Miss Brooke had used each other's Christian names. Phillip did not think Miss Talbot was so caught up in the story that she missed that detail. Hopefully knowing of the long gap in their acquaintance would soothe Miss Talbot's worries.

Daniel took a seat near a candelabra in the center of the room and opened a book. He thumbed the pages a few times before pausing and beginning to read.

"I wandered lonely as a cloud. . ."

He did indeed read well. His voice was rich and he imbued the words with weight and light in appropriate measure. Phillip was a little surprised at the choice of poetry. He did not think Daniel enjoyed Wordsworth. A glance around the room showed that everyone was listening and enjoying the performance.

It was hard not to be jealous of such ability to give pleasure. Mother never asked Phillip to read. His reading always came out stiff and stilted when he didn't like the passage or too hurried and incoherent when he did.

As Daniel read about the joy of daffodils, Phillip looked particularly at Miss Talbot and Miss Brooke. Both seemed to hang on every word, enraptured by the poem or the reader. Were both young women in love with Daniel? Were both destined to have their hearts broken when he chose neither of them? Phillip hoped that for Miss Talbot that would not be the case. But neither did he wish for Miss Brooke to be injured.

As if sensing his thought, Miss Brooke's eyes shifted towards him. Phillip quickly looked away.

The light applause caught him by surprise. He hadn't realized Daniel had finished the poem. He clapped along with the rest and when Miss Brooke caught his eye again, he didn't look away. She frowned, the light in her eyes dimming before Miss Talbot drew her attention away by whispering in her ear.

What was she thinking? Why did he cause her to frown while Daniel made her smile? Though Phillip wasn't charming, he was still a man of stature with an estate and title. Many women would smile at him regardless of their personal feelings, but not Miss Brooke.

She had a mixture of impertinence and bravery he had not encountered before. She was no longer a child standing before a charging bull, but she was still brave. In some ways, speaking her mind was even more commendable. Phillip didn't always like what she said, but he admired her the courage they required.

That morning she had accused him of making assumptions, being unjust to Daniel, and not enjoying life. There were undoubtedly more criticisms that she had not yet voiced. Did Miss Brooke see Phillip as a charging bull, a terrifying animal she must stand up against to protect Daniel? It seemed clear now that Miss Brooke felt that Daniel needed protection from him.

Daniel's concerns about his intentions were ill-placed. Miss Brooke saw Phillip as a heartless, dull, officious, older brother, far from desiring his company. And as Daniel began another poem, Phillip was surprised to realize that he wished to change her mind.

Chapter Eleven

⁓ ◦◦◦ ⁓

The little parish church in Brightworth village was notable for its stained glass, dry interior, and kindly vicar. In every other way it was unremarkable, and yet to Elaine, it was the loveliest of churches. Bath Abbey, St. Paul's Cathedral, and St. George's in Mayfair were all much grander but forbidding and uncomfortable. The Brightworth church with its worn pews and familiar faces was where she belonged.

As she listened to Mr. Eden expound upon the principle of loving one's neighbor, Elaine found herself struggling to find love for more than a few of her fellow congregants. The Ashburns and Talbots sat together in the family pew. Daniel and Miss Talbot were positioned near the aisle and Elaine could not help but look at them. Occasionally Daniel would turn his head to say something to Miss Talbot and Elaine would feel a stab in the vicinity of her heart. They made a charming couple.

Elaine was not alone in watching them. When the Ashburns had arrived with their guests, there was a general turning of heads and whispered conversations. The neighborhood's interest in Miss Talbot had grown over the last few days, no doubt fueled by Mrs. Leigh spreading whatever stories Mama had told her of their dinners at Ryder Hall.

The other guests had also generated some interest. More than one older widow cast a speculative eye at Captain Hart as he escorted Miss Wilson and Mrs. Cooper to a pew. Mr. and Mrs. Farthing had courteously joined the Brookes and the other men had found solo seats. The already full church seemed almost bursting.

It was a pity that the neighborhood's curiosity superseded Mr. Eden's excellent sermon. As if he sensed that everyone was eager to be at liberty, he kept his remarks short.

As they stood to leave, Elaine saw the Farthings share a smile and nod. They seemed to have a secret method of communication. Elaine had seen similar looks between her teacher Miss Minerva and Mr. Henry before they married. Was it something people in love did? Would she ever have someone who understood her so? All her attempts to communicate lately had gone awry.

The parishioners spilled into the churchyard, their eyes watching the newcomers with varying degrees of subtlety.

The Brookes and Farthings were some of the last to exit. Mr. Eden stood just outside the door, speaking pleasantly to everyone as they left. The vicar was a middle-aged man of average height, dark hair, and a genial smile. The regularity of his features was disturbed by the squashed nature of his nose. He took his responsibility as a clergyman with just the right amount of seriousness, so it was easy to like him.

The Farthings praised his sermon highly.

"Thank you," Mr. Eden said with a modest dip of his head. "I am gratified to know at least someone was listening."

"For shame, Mr. Eden," Mama said. "Of course people were listening. You have such a lovely voice."

"Perhaps they heard my voice, but I am not sure the content of my sermon penetrated their minds."

Mrs. Farthing laughed. "'Tis true, our party seems to have distracted many."

"I am sure the novelty will wear off by next week," Mr. Farthing offered.

Mr. Eden smiled. "I see you are unfamiliar with the nature of a small parish church. I rather think the interest will increase and I will be forced to cancel the sermon altogether."

"No sermon at church? Now that would be irregular," Elaine said.

"But perhaps preferable to some." Mr. Eden's smile proved he was not upset about the prospect. Everyone assured him that they should prefer a sermon and in turn, he assured them he would do his best. As the others took their leave, Mr. Eden detained her.

"Miss Brooke, I just had a rather interesting conversation with Miss Wilson."

"Really?" Most conversations with Miss Wilson were interesting. She was a wealth of information and opinions.

"We were discussing schools and she mentioned you might be interested in teaching."

Elaine was a little taken aback. She had mentioned to Miss Wilson her desire to find some useful employment only the night before. They had talked about teaching as a possibility but Elaine had not asked her to look for opportunities. Still, teaching at the parish school would be an excellent solution to her problem, providing both income and purpose.

"I am interested in teaching, but I was not aware of a parish school," Elaine replied.

"At present there is not, but Sir Phillip has been anxious to establish one. "

"He has?" Elaine was not able to hide her surprise.

Mr. Eden smiled. "Indeed. Sir Phillip is most anxious for the good of the parish and he understands the value of education. Unfortunately, my additional duties have prevented me from being the teacher."

"Yes, I see."

"If you will permit me, I will talk to Sir Phillip about giving you the position."

Elaine wondered what the baronet would say to the idea. She had endured his censorious looks for three evenings. His opinion of her was not high.

"You have not even asked about my experience teaching," she said.

"Having gone to school yourself, I dare say you understand the basic principles." Mr. Eden's easy smile was contagious.

"I do, but I also occasionally instructed the younger girls when I was at Mrs. Piper's Seminary."

"Miss Wilson did say as much. I will be sure to tell Sir Phillip. I can make no promises, but I think he will agree."

Elaine could not share his confidence but thanked him and went in search of her mother. She was surprised that Sir Phillip wanted to fund a school. She had sat in many drawing rooms where the prevailing opinion was against educating the poorer classes. That he might share her opinion—that everyone could benefit from being able to read, write, and do sums—was disconcerting.

"Miss Brooke!"

Elaine turned to see Miss Covington approaching. She steeled herself for the encounter.

Miss Margaret Covington was delicately pretty with dark hair, fair skin, and a bonnet that cost more than Elaine's current ensemble. Their age was the only thing they had in common. Elaine had known Miss Covington since they were girls and had disliked her for almost as long. As children, Miss Covington had turned up her nose at Elaine's games. As adults, Miss Covington barely acknowledged Elaine's existence.

The Covingtons owned Meecham Park and could afford a governess, the latest fashions, and a house in London where they spent the Season. They must have recently returned to the neighborhood, for Elaine had not thought them home when they had driven by Meecham Park on their tour. Although, at the time, she had been distracted by her frustration with Sir Phillip.

"I hardly recognized you! It has been an age," Miss Covington exclaimed.

Elaine chose not to mention the numerous times she had ignored Elaine when their paths crossed in Bath.

"I have not been much in the neighborhood these last few years," Elaine said.

"Yes, so dreadful you had to be packed away to that awful school." Miss Covington wrinkled her nose.

"I assure you I enjoyed my time in Bath. Mrs. Piper employed the best masters and my schoolfellows were all that was good-natured and refined."

"Of course, dear." Miss Covington's condescending smile was grating. "I am sure you were quite at home with that sort."

"I was. They have become my lifelong friends." Any of Mrs. Piper's students were worth ten Miss Covingtons.

"How fortunate. I am sure you will have need of such friends in your later years, for it seems your hope to find a husband close to home has been thwarted."

Elaine flushed. "You are mistaken."

"Am I?" Miss Covington gave a false, tinkling laugh. "My apologies, but when we were younger, you were adamant."

"Things change," Elaine said.

Of course Miss Covington would use her childish declarations against her. Did the entire neighborhood still think of her as the little girl who proclaimed she would be Mrs. Ashburn?

"Of course, dear. Come, let us greet Miss Talbot." Miss Covington took Elaine's arm and began to steer her toward where Lady Ashburn and her party stood beside the gate.

"Are you acquainted?"

"We have met several times in Town."

Elaine didn't push for further information. It made sense that two rich and elegant young women knew each other. Miss Covington must have had many opportunities to interact with the Ashburn family both in London and at home. Likely she knew them all much better than Elaine. Proving her assumption, Miss Covington greeted Lady Ashburn and Sir Phillip with familiarity before turning to Miss Talbot with a too-wide smile.

"Miss Talbot, it is so wonderful to see you in my little corner of England. You must come and call on us."

"Thank you, Miss Covington." Miss Talbot was all kindness and smiles. "I hope that my obligations to my hosts will allow for a renewal of our acquaintance."

Elaine refused to feel slighted that she had not been invited to call. It was not like she particularly wanted to form a connection with Miss Covington, but to have Miss Talbot favored still stung. Just like Sir Phillip not asking her to join the excursion to the Old Priory. It was difficult to be excluded.

102

Elaine looked away and caught Sir Phillip watching her again. In the evenings whenever she saw his look, she was sure he was finding fault, but now, in the brightness of the sun, his gaze seemed full of pity. When their eyes met, he raised his eyebrows almost like Daniel when he meant mischief. Then he quickly shifted his attention to Miss Covington.

"Sir Phillip, you must accompany Miss Talbot when she visits Meecham Park. I am in need of lively young society." Miss Covington's voice was sickly sweet and she smiled invitingly.

"Miss Covington, I believe your carriage is waiting," Sir Phillip said.

It was an innocuous comment, but when said in that short, authoritative way, it had the effect of ending the conversation. For once, Elaine appreciated his domineering nature.

Miss Covington's smile expanded instead of falling. "Thank you, Sir Phillip. I would not want to be left behind. Imagine the indignity of having to walk home."

Elaine ignored the barb.

How did Miss Covington know that Elaine was walking home? As usual, Mrs. Leigh had conveyed Elaine and Mama to church in her carriage. And as usual, Elaine had told them she would walk to the lodge. The older ladies could gossip without her and she appreciated the warm sunshine and exercise after sitting in the pews. But now, Miss Covington had turned her choice into a symbol of her poverty.

"I am very fond of a Sunday walk," Lady Ashburn said with only the slightest twitch of her lips.

"As am I," Miss Talbot added.

Elaine smiled, grateful for the two women.

"It is providential, Miss Covington," Sir Phillip spoke with false concern. "that you have a carriage so that you might not test your limited stamina with the journey."

Miss Covington's smile faltered. Had Sir Phillip complimented or slighted her? Elaine wasn't sure, but she appreciated watching the haughty young woman flounder.

"Yes, well. . . Thank you." Miss Covington made her goodbyes and departed for her carriage. Elaine was not sorry to see her go.

"Do you intend to walk today, Miss Brooke?" Miss Talbot asked.

"Yes, I was going to walk home," Elaine said.

"Then we should all walk together," Daniel spoke from behind.

Miss Talbot and Elaine turned as one to see him grinning. Elaine wondered if he had been waiting for Miss Covington to depart before joining their group. He had never liked her when they were children, but then, they weren't children anymore. He might enjoy flirting with Miss Covington and find her all that was charming.

"If you are both ready, we shall ramble far and wide this afternoon." Daniel spread his arm to indicate the whole countryside.

Elaine couldn't muster any enthusiasm for the scheme. In her mind, she saw plainly how Daniel and Miss Talbot would walk together. She would straggle behind and enter into the conversation only sporadically. The scenario seemed more likely than the reverse. She dared not hope Daniel would give her more attention than Miss Talbot.

"Oh, Mr. Ashburn, that is a very kind offer, but there is no need," Miss Talbot said. "Miss Brooke and I will do very well together. You should continue to the hall and attend to your affairs."

Daniel looked between them as if he would protest.

"Let them alone," Lady Ashburn said. "Young women need to have the chance to exchange confidences."

"That is exactly what I am afraid of," Daniel said with an exaggerated frown. "I am not sure I should allow you to spend too much time together."

Miss Talbot arched her brow. "I don't recall needing your permission."

Elaine found herself fighting a smile and when she looked at Sir Phillip, he seemed to be doing the same. Elaine had not seen this side of Miss Talbot. Clearly, she was a woman used to getting her way and in this case, Elaine did not mind one bit.

Miss Talbot arranged everything with her parents and the ladies soon set off together down the lane.

* * *

104

The bright day might have been too warm for a walk but for the gentle breeze fluttering the ribbons on their bonnets. They spent the first steps sharing observations on the village and passing carriages.

Since the destination of the ramble had changed, Elaine chose a path heading north, planning to overshoot Ryder Hall and then wind back west following the brook. Miss Talbot expressed no curiosity at their direction but exclaimed over the beauty of the countryside.

Sir Phillip's lecture on how the land was more than just pleasing to the eye came back to Elaine. She smiled at the memory. She couldn't look at the fields around her and not think of his crops and land management lessons.

She didn't share her thoughts with Miss Talbot. Her eyes might glaze over as Daniel had claimed. Instead, they talked of the ripeness of the fields and the charming woods that marked the edge of the park surrounding Ryder Hall. When they at last exhausted their environment, Miss Talbot deftly changed the subject.

"I understand you attended school in Bath."

"I did. Mrs. Piper's Seminary."

"I have heard that is quite a rigorous institution. How did you find it?"

"Mrs. Piper places a great emphasis on learning more than the usual subjects. My education was quite complete. I can't imagine a better place to be educated."

Elaine tried not to sound defensive, but it was difficult after Miss Covington's slights. Miss Talbot seemed all that was polite and pleasant but perhaps she was better than Miss Covington at hiding her true nature.

Miss Talbot sighed. "I always wanted to go to school like my brothers, but Mother and Father insisted that I be taught at home. They thought it best and perhaps they were right. They are very attentive to my wellbeing. I suppose you made many friends there?"

Elaine couldn't stop her smile. "Yes, we are as close as sisters."

"How lovely it must be to have confidants you have known for such a considerable time." Something in her voice made Elaine wonder if Miss Talbot had any confidants.

"It is a blessing. Though I confess that we weren't always blissfully happy.

Over the years, we fought and argued and were jealous of each other. Just like siblings, I imagine."

Miss Talbot smiled. "And what would you fight about?"

Without meaning to, Elaine began sharing all about Charity, Penelope, Mary, and Rosamund, the scrapes they encountered as children, their first steps into adulthood, how they had schemed to get their teacher married, and other fond remembrances.

With each story, Elaine became more aware of how much she missed them. The letters were not the same as being together. They could not talk so eagerly that their sentences crashed into each other. She could not dissolve into giggles with or tease a page full of ink.

"You miss them," Miss Talbot said when Elaine drifted into silence.

She nodded. "I do."

"As Wordsworth said, 'there is comfort in the strength of love.'"

Elaine smiled at her quotation from the poems they heard the other night. "A true sentiment. I draw much comfort from their letters and support."

"I envy your friendships. My governess was a kind of friend, but she has moved on to another family. In London, I did try to become acquainted with other young women but it was difficult to move past mere civility."

Elaine could well imagine it would be. With her fairy-like beauty and large fortune, Miss Talbot was unlikely to inspire anything but jealousy in those who wished to compete with her. Had not Elaine done the same thing? She had treated Miss Talbot not as a person of reason and emotion but as an obstacle to being with Daniel.

"Perhaps I am not capable of deep friendships." Miss Talbot sounded wistful as she looked out over the fields.

"I think, Miss Talbot, that the fault lies not in you but in others."

Miss Talbot sighed. "A kind thought. I wish it were true."

"It is true, and I shall prove it to you with my own friendship."

Miss Talbot's answering smile was blinding. "Oh, Miss Brooke! I had so hoped to be your friend. Mr. Ashburn speaks so highly of you and I thought that if ever we met, we would be fast friends."

"Mr. Ashburn speaks of me?" Elaine couldn't help asking.

"Yes, of course. He can hardly tell a childhood story without you being featured."

This knowledge bewildered Elaine. She had thought the story of the charging bull an aberration. She had spent so much time assuming that Daniel did not remember her that it was surprising to think that his friends might have heard of her as often as hers had heard of him. His stories likely did not conclude with a declaration that he would marry her.

Miss Talbot laughed. "You seem surprised."

"It has been years since we were children. I did not think he remembered."

"No doubt he wished you to think he had forgotten. Mr. Ashburn has an uncanny ability to hide his true thoughts and feelings. Before I met him, I thought men were rather simple to understand, but he confounds me."

Elaine smiled. "In that feeling, you are not alone. I find many men to be confusing." She thought of her attempts to parse meaning from Daniel's words or glances over the last couple of days and her equally frustrating conversations with Sir Phillip.

They had come to the stream and the old stone bridge that crossed it.

"If we turn off here, this path follows the water and leads to Ryder Hall. It will be cooler under the trees."

"I am completely in your hands, Miss Brooke."

As children, Elaine and Daniel had fished off the stone bridge, waded in the stream, caught frogs, and floated paper boats. Daniel had even taught her how to swim, though his tutor had put a swift end to the lessons when he found out. As an adult, Elaine blushed at the thought that she had stripped down to her small clothes with impunity.

She considered sharing one of these stories with Miss Talbot but decided against it. She wanted to keep her memories with Daniel to herself.

"Did you miss home when you were at school?" Miss Talbot asked.

Elaine considered the question. "At first, I was very homesick. I missed my mother; she was my only family. My father, you understand, had died years before." Elaine thought it best not to mention how much she had missed Daniel. "But with my friends, I found a new family and eventually settled into my life in Bath. Mrs. Leigh, who lives at Beechhurst, began bringing Mother to Bath with her in the winter so I saw her more often. But that meant I came back here less. It is only since my return that I have realized how much I love this country."

Elaine had always associated her homesickness with missing Daniel, but it was clear to her now that it was the country itself she missed and the longing for a simpler time.

"Bath and London do have their charms," Elaine added. "Tell me, what did you enjoy most about London?"

The conversation turned to a discussion of all there was to see and do in the capital. Elaine was pleased to discover they shared many of the same views. Their conversation flowed as swiftly as the stream they walked beside.

Elaine was surprised to realize that she genuinely liked the heiress. Miss Talbot was good-natured with interesting opinions and a love of stories. It would be easy to grow their acquaintance into a true and deep friendship. The only impediment was their mutual desire to become Mrs. Daniel Ashburn.

Chapter Twelve

fter the prying eyes and many introductions at church, Phillip wanted nothing more than to be left alone for an hour. Once back at the hall, he excused himself and made his way to the library. He paused at the entryway and considered the books lining the walls.

The books, all bound in matching black leather, were the work of generations. His spendthrift grandfather had purchased the bulk of the titles, but Phillip had added to the collection judiciously. He was proud of the collection, even if he rarely opened the books. He didn't have the time to read. Miss Brooke's condemnation from days before came to his mind. Would reading something purely for pleasure count as "enjoying life"?

Instead of sitting in the armchair, Phillip wandered to the shelves. The book of poetry Daniel had read the other night sat on the end of a half-empty shelf as if someone didn't want to lose it among the others. Phillip picked it up and was thumbing through the pages when Daniel entered. Unaccountably embarrassed, Phillip shut the book and pulled it behind his back.

"So, this is where you are hiding." Daniel looked around the room as if expecting someone else to be there.

"I'm not hiding."

"No, of course not. You are doing some significant work." Daniel gestured to the book Phillip had behind his back. "Let me guess, the *Annals of Agriculture?*"

Phillip lifted his chin. "It's important to stay abreast of the latest techniques."

Daniel chuckled as he threw himself into an armchair. "Yes, but would it injure you to read something just for entertainment?"

Did everyone think that he was incapable of leisure? Phillip was half-tempted to tell his brother what the book truly was, but instead, he placed it back on the shelf. He joined Daniel in a matching armchair and reached for the newspaper Lennox had left folded on the side table.

"How can you read the paper on such a glorious day?" Daniel groused. "Let us go for a ride or a walk."

Phillip narrowed his eyes at his brother. "A walk? Perhaps in the direction of the lodge?"

Daniel grinned slyly. "Perhaps."

"And if we happen to run into Miss Talbot and Miss Brooke?"

"Why then, we could all walk together."

In spite of himself, Phillip chuckled. It was clearly bothering Daniel that the two young women had preferred to walk without him. Phillip had rather enjoyed watching Miss Talbot stand up to Daniel. It was surprising that Daniel hadn't tried to charm her to get his way. Phillip had added "knows how to manage Daniel" to his list of Miss Talbot's good qualities.

"I believe Miss Talbot would not be pleased to see us," Phillip said.

At this, Daniel frowned. "If Miss Talbot is not, then Elaine will be. She, at least, is always eager for my company."

Phillip sobered at the comment. "Miss Brooke's company is not the one you should be seeking."

"And why not? She is intelligent, kind, and gently bred. She deserves the pleasure of my company as much as any young woman."

"And if the Talbots should misinterpret your intentions?" Phillip asked, wishing he knew Daniel's intentions.

This thought seemed to sober Daniel. "Talbot doesn't approve of me; he has made that plain enough."

"Mr. Talbot only wants what is best for his daughter."

"Which, of course, is not me."

"I did not say that."

"No, merely implied it."

Phillip held back a sigh. He had not intended to offend his brother, but he needed to make him see how his actions with Miss Brooke were hindering his cause with the Talbots. Phillip had kept careful watch the last few days and, contrary to Daniel's feelings, he thought Mr. Talbot was warming.

"Mr. Talbot puts great stock in his daughter's preference. He knows that she cares for you but little else. You have a reputation as a charmer and idler. You must show him that you are more than that. If Talbot could see the steadiness of your character, he would have no objections."

As Phillip talked, Daniel launched himself from the armchair and stalked to the window. But having started, he would not be deterred and pressed his point.

"But how can he possibly trust you with his daughter and her fortune if he sees marked attentions to Miss Brooke?"

"Marked attentions?" Daniel spun around. "Miss Brooke is an old family friend and a dear acquaintance. Am I not allowed to show affection?"

"Miss Brooke is no longer a child. She is a young woman of considerable beauty and charm, not to mention intelligence."

"You seem very sensible of her charms."

Phillip ignored the insinuation. "But as you well know, she has no material advantages to promote—"

"She is poor." Daniel began pacing back to the armchairs.

"Yes."

It was baldly said but it was the truth. The Brookes had almost no income, they lived on the Ashburns' charity, and Miss Brooke's dowry was barely worth mentioning. One had to be sensible of that reality.

"And one can't possibly marry a poor woman, no matter her other advantages."

Daniel spun around and stalked back to the window. Phillip watched him from the armchair.

"You are twisting my words. No matter how much they love one another, a man and wife must have something to live on. As a man with no profession, you cannot afford to marry for affection alone."

Daniel stopped and crossed his arms like a petulant child. "You tell me nothing I don't already know. But I swear to you, Phillip. I won't marry without affection. You cannot command me to marry where I do not love."

"I would never do that." Phillip was offended that his brother would even suggest such a thing. He was not some tyrant dictating from on high. "I have seen you with Miss Talbot, and I know you care for each other. I would not support the match if I thought you indifferent."

Whatever reply Daniel might have made was interrupted by the arrival of Richard Farthing.

"Hello." Richard paused in the doorway, newspaper in hand. "Am I interrupting?"

Daniel relaxed his posture and managed a half-smile as he moved to the doorway. "Farthing, how fortuitous. Perhaps you can explain to my brother that being mercenary is a bad beginning for a marriage."

"I did not—"

"I am going for a ride." Daniel cut in and then made his bow. He escaped before Phillip could say another word, leaving him with Farthing and his questioning look.

"It's nothing. An old argument."

Phillip tried to wave it away as he gestured Richard to sit. Farthing merely hummed as he settled into the armchair and opened the newspaper, seemingly content to let Phillip stay silent. His friend knew all too well how to manage him.

As Farthing read his paper, Phillip pretended to do the same. He did not see the words before him. He turned over the conversation in his mind.

He could not regret his opinions, only the manner in which he expressed them. He had not meant to make Daniel feel inferior or frame a union with Miss Talbot solely for her fortune. He was not so unfeeling as to want his brother to marry a woman he did not like because she was rich. But neither would he let Daniel think himself in love with Miss Brooke simply because he thought Mr. Talbot would refuse him.

No matter Miss Brooke's many good attributes, if she married Daniel, they would always be dependent on the estate and that would not be good for any of them. Surely he was not mercenary or unfeeling for such sentiments?

Farthing had not yet turned a page when Phillip spoke.

"Is it mercenary to want Daniel to marry a woman with a fortune?"

Farthing lowered the paper. "It could be if he married her for that reason alone. Do you doubt his affection for Miss Talbot?"

"In London, I thought they were perfectly suited. But now. . ." Phillip shook his head.

"Now there is a pretty neighbor to consider."

Phillip looked sharply at his friend, though he should not have been surprised that Richard had accurately discerned the problem.

Richard gave him a sympathetic smile. "Miss Brooke seems a very amiable and kind young woman."

"Indeed, she is also intelligent, witty, outspoken, and courageous." Phillip had seen enough of Miss Brooke to recognize that she had many good qualities. He understood why Daniel was drawn to her. "No doubt she will make some man a good wife."

"Some man?" Farthing raised his eyebrows.

"Daniel does not have the means to marry a woman with so little to her name."

"I seem to remember you repeatedly declaring that you would never marry for money like your parents did. And yet, you would not give your brother the same courtesy."

Phillip sighed. It did sound like hypocrisy when framed that way. Had his worry for Daniel's future caused him to imagine an attachment? He would not order Daniel to marry Miss Talbot but did arranging the house party and interfering with Miss Brooke amount to the same thing?

"I had hoped he would fall in love with someone rich," Phillip muttered.

Richard laughed. "If only love were so biddable an emotion. Jane's dowry was not as big as my father would have liked, but I loved her so completely that I did not care. And though we have to watch our expenses, it is a worthwhile exchange for her as my life companion."

"So you are saying that I should let Daniel court Miss Brooke and damn the consequences?"

"I am saying that if your brother is truly in love with Miss Brooke, he is unlikely to give her up because she is poor. I don't think you would respect him if he did."

Phillip nodded. Farthing shook out his paper and returned to reading while Phillip thought over his words.

Richard was right. When Daniel loved, he loved fiercely. If he truly loved Miss Brooke, there would be no way to keep him from her. But Phillip did not think Daniel or Miss Brooke were in love, yet. They had an affection and ease borne from a long friendship, but was that love? Having never been in love, he could not say for sure, but he thought it only a seed. It was certainly possible for love to grow from such a seed. Was it wrong to stunt the growth or encourage affection to bloom elsewhere?

"Is there another reason why you wish Miss Brooke's affections to be unengaged?" Farthing spoke with studied nonchalance, barely looking up from his paper.

"What other reason could there be?"

Farthing shrugged. "Perhaps a personal interest?"

Phillip ran a hand through his hair. His friend's implication was clear. Daniel had warned him that his interest in Miss Brooke might be misunderstood, but Phillip thought Farthing knew him better than that.

"My only interest in Miss Brooke is her connection to my brother."

Farthing hummed an annoying sound that could mean anything.

"I am not interested in courting her."

"Of course not. Why would you wish to court an intelligent, witty, and courageous young woman?" Farthing's smirk betrayed him as he repeated Phillip's words.

He clenched his jaw, pressing his teeth together in frustration. How had the conversation turned on him? At present, he had no thought of courting anyone. When Daniel was settled, when the estate took less time, then he would search for a wife. He had come to the library to be alone, not to endure his friend's teasing.

Phillip stood. "I think I will go for a walk." He strode to the door, doing his best to look like he wasn't running away. Farthing's deep chuckle echoed behind him.

Once out in the bright sunshine, Phillip headed for the formal gardens. A few turns around their ordered beds would calm his mind and help him forget Farthing's absurd insinuations. The day had grown hot; the cloudless sky highlighted the grass and flowers, making them more colorful. He walked around the back of the hall with its expanse of well-manicured lawn and went through a small stand of trees.

When the formal garden came into view, Phillip was surprised to see his mother and Captain Hart already occupied it. Their backs were to him as they proceeded down the stately flower-lined walk. Phillip's first thought was to go and relieve her of the man's presence. Her duties as hostess did not extend to traipsing about in the heat. Captain Hart should not have imposed on her daily walk.

But no sooner had Phillip made up his mind than his mother laughed. The sound reverberated back and stayed him. He could not remember the last time he had heard his mother laugh with such happy abandon. Clearly, Captain Hart was not an imposition and Mother had no need for his interference. She laughed again, quieter this time but still full of mirth. What was Captain Hart saying? Phillip was half tempted to join them just to know, but it would be an intrusion.

He continued past the formal garden and headed for the path along the stream. Eventually, the water emptied into the lake, but here it rushed beside a shaded track. It was unlikely any of his guests would have discovered the trail. Here he could be alone with his thoughts, just him and the sounds of the rushing water.

The image of Mother and Captain Hart lingered.

Had his mother ever laughed that way with his father? Their match had not been one of affection. Having inherited the debts of his father, Sir Thomas Ashburn had been eager to acquire capital. The Cartwrights had wanted their daughter to be a lady. The marriage satisfied both parties' wishes. Love or happiness hadn't factored into the union.

Though Sir Thomas was a considerate and generous husband—Lady Ashburn always had a liberal allowance—he was not faithful. Mother gave him his heir and spare in short order and with the duty fulfilled, Father felt at liberty to look elsewhere. It was a common enough practice, but Phillip did not want such a marriage.

There was much to admire about Father. His commitment to the estate, his work ethic, keen intellect, and the respect he garnered from his peers and tenants. Much of Phillip's life had been spent trying to emulate these traits and he did not think he quite measured up to Sir Thomas's legacy. But for all this admiration and striving, Phillip had never wanted to emulate his parents' marriage. Yet now, after all these years, he better understood his father's reasons.

Any woman he married would be responsible for two households and her dowry would help to shore up an estate still recovering from his grandfather's debts. His wife would be a partner. He had kept himself guarded to prevent falling in love with someone unequal to the task.

Since the baronetcy had been thrust upon him at nineteen, Mother had been by his side teaching him and managing the house. The very idea of throwing the annual Twelfth Night ball without her was terrifying. He could not declare with the same boldness as Daniel that he would not marry without genuine affection.

Phillip removed his hat and ran a hand through his hair. All this just because he heard Mother laugh? Was he afraid she would leave him? He did not even know if she liked Captain Hart or if the man was interested in remarrying. It was pure fancy. There was no need to think about a wife until he ascertained Mother's mind.

Phillip's thoughts were interrupted by voices on the path ahead. He frowned in the direction of the noise. Who had discovered this trail? Would he never have peace during this blasted party? He considered turning on his heel and striding away before he was seen but a laugh made him pause and in that moment of indecision, he was caught.

Miss Brooke and Miss Talbot appeared through the trees. Miss Brooke spoke with animation, her words carrying over the burbling of the stream. Miss Talbot hung on every word with breathless anticipation.

"Then Mr. Henry walked into the room—" Miss Brooke stopped abruptly as she caught sight of him. "Sir Phillip."

The displeasure in her voice and face were evident, but she quickly masked them as she dropped into a hasty curtsey. Phillip couldn't help but think how different Daniel's welcome would have been.

"Miss Talbot, Miss Brooke, what a surprise." Phillip made his bow. "I had thought you were walking to the lodge?"

"Oh, are we not?" Miss Talbot looked at Miss Brooke in evident confusion.

"No, we are nearer to the hall," Miss Brooke said.

"No matter." Miss Talbot shrugged. She gave Phillip a gracious smile. "You have caught us in the middle of a story. Miss Brooke was just recounting how her teacher fell in love with the music master. She has such a way with description that I was quite taken away. "

The praise brought a blush to Miss Brooke's already flushed cheeks. It was most becoming. Phillip pushed the admiration away. He should not be noticing Miss Brooke's looks.

"Well, I have no desire to disrupt your conversation," he said stiffly. "I will leave you to your walk."

"Please stay," Miss Talbot said. "We would be honored by your company back to the house."

It was a pretty speech, accompanied by an equally pretty smile. Miss Brooke made no objections and so he would turn back. The path was wide enough for them to walk abreast and Phillip found himself sandwiched between the two young ladies.

Miss Talbot took control of the conversation. "Sir Phillip, I must say, I have never seen fields and woods quite so beautiful."

"Thank you. I am glad they meet with your approval."

Miss Brooke made a strangled cough beside him. He cast her a look and she raised her eyebrows. It occurred to him that she might wonder why he had not scolded Miss Talbot for her use of a word that had so offended him on their driving tour. Even if he could have spoken, he had no answer for her. He hardly understood why he expected more from Miss Brooke than the usual pleasantries.

If Miss Talbot noticed their look, her manners were too good to remark on it. "I am looking forward to our visit to the ruins. From Miss Brooke's description they seem quite romantic. Or is the word gothic? I can never remember. In any event, they seem like something out of a novel."

He glanced at Miss Brooke. "Do you find the ruins romantic?"

She flushed. "I only meant to describe how otherworldly and mysterious they feel, as if great things once happened there and might happen again."

How well she described his own feelings about the Old Priory.

"They do have a special quality," he agreed. He turned to Miss Talbot. "You will have to judge for yourself if it be romantic or gothic."

"I look forward to it. Almost as much as I would look forward to the opportunity to dance."

This elicited a small gasp from Miss Brooke. The two girls exchanged a look.

"Now, Miss Brooke, it's too late; I am determined to ask him."

"Then you have greater courage than me," Miss Brooke returned with an arch smile.

Phillip had always thought that young women in competition for a man's affection were meant to be at odds but it seemed that Miss Talbot and Miss Brooke had become fast friends. If they could be friends, perhaps neither of them cared for Daniel? Or one had already bowed out of the competition? But which one? He hoped it was Miss Brooke. He looked between them but there was no way of knowing.

"What do you wish to ask me?" He finally asked.

"Miss Brooke tells me that the Assembly Rooms in Oakbury are quite modern."

"Yes, I understand they are very elegant." Phillip's suspicions were raised.

"She also informed me that there was to be an assembly next week." Miss Talbot gave a coy look that somehow seemed both practiced and spontaneous.

"I see. And no doubt you wish to attend the assembly? I am not your father to dictate your social calendar."

"But we would not wish to go without you, Sir Phillip. I am sure many of your guests would enjoy the chance to dance."

It was well done. Phillip could hardly refuse when presented in this way. He did not enjoy attending the assemblies; too many mothers put forth their daughters for his perusal, too many eyes judging how he danced and with whom he danced. He usually avoided them, but now he had no choice.

"Naturally, we shall all go if that is your wish." He spoke with as much grace as he could muster.

Miss Talbot gave her effusive thanks and shot Miss Brooke a triumphant smile. He had been thoroughly managed, and he did not like it one bit. Miss Talbot was trouble and Phillip was only too glad to leave her to Daniel.

"Oh, dear." Miss Talbot stopped walking.

"Are you well?" Miss Brooke asked as they both stopped and turned.

"It is only my boot. I need to retie my lace. Do not wait for me. I will be along shortly." She waved them away and Phillip had to fight to keep back his frown. Yes, Miss Talbot was very managing. He did not think for a moment there was anything wrong with her bootlace.

Perhaps she was a very clever competitor? In trying to throw him together with Miss Brooke, she saw a way to eliminate her rival. Or perhaps she was in league with Farthing? He was certain Miss Brooke did not wish to be left alone with him. He glanced at her. Her forehead was furrowed in thought. No, she was not in on this scheme.

They were only a few steps away from Miss Talbot when Miss Brooke spoke in a low tone.

"I did not tell her about the assemblies in the hopes that she would devise a way to attend."

Phillip gave a noncommittal hum, his best imitation of Farthing.

"Truly, I did not. We were only talking of the amusements of the neighborhood and I happened to mention the assemblies."

"And you see my lack of attendance as more evidence of my inability to enjoy my life. So I shall tell you, madam, that there is nothing enjoyable about the assembly in Oakbury."

When she didn't respond, he glanced at her. She bit her lip and her shoulders shook.

"You are laughing at me?"

"I am trying not to laugh. I had never thought to see you so discomfited by the thought of a few hours in a ballroom."

"It is not dancing but being on display that I dislike." Frustration made him honest.

Instead of continuing to tease, Miss Brooke seemed to pause and think. It was several steps before she spoke again. "I had not considered that aspect. If you truly despise it, I am sorry that you have been maneuvered into attending."

Her apology caught him unawares. He had expected to be told that a baronet should be accustomed to being on display. But for once, Miss Brooke was not judging him harshly. She seemed genuinely distressed at the situation.

He leaned toward her and dropped his voice to a whisper. "Don't worry. I plan to turn my ankle before the dreaded day."

She turned to him with wide eyes. "Sir Phillip, is that a jest?"

He smirked.

Her shock dissolved into a smile and he found himself chuckling. When they weren't at odds, Phillip found he quite liked Miss Brooke's conversation. The assembly might not be so terrible if he danced a set with her. She was probably a lovely and spirited dancer. Should he shock her again by asking for a dance now?

He glanced back to see Miss Talbot following them discreetly. Her satisfied smile made Phillip realize he had almost fallen into a neat trap. Getting him to ask for a set had likely been Miss Talbot's goal all along.

They stepped from the shade of the trees and the stream rushed on, curving away from the path to eventually swell and spread into the shallow lake. Ryder Hall and the blue sky were reflected in the still water; even from this distance and angle, it created a stunning view. Phillip did not love the expense that his grandfather had incurred in building it, but he appreciated the fruits of the labor.

"What a splendid prospect." Miss Talbot was effusive in her praise. "Let us get closer." She moved toward the lake, outpacing himself and Miss Brooke.

"Perhaps," Miss Brooke said, "Captain Hart will wish to accompany us to the assembly."

Phillip did not understand the comment until he followed her gaze. Mother and the Captain were approaching the house arm in arm. He frowned.

"I am sure Lady Ashburn would appreciate his attendance," she added.

He did not like the dreamy note in Miss Brooke's voice. Though Phillip had entertained similar thoughts, it was not Miss Brooke's place to speculate. Mother was not a character in a play or novel.

"Don't let your fancy run wild, Miss Brooke," he said sternly.

"I am not being fanciful."

"No? You observe them walking together and naturally assume that they are about to read the banns."

"I never said—"

"You did not, but I suspect you were thinking it."

"I forgot that reading minds was one of your talents." She stopped walking and turned to him with hands on her hips.

Miss Talbot was several feet ahead now, but Phillip kept his voice low. "Do you deny that you thought they made a charming couple?"

"And would that be so wrong?"

"To make such speculations with no evidence is unjust."

"I agree. I believe I told you as much at the Old Priory."

"The two situations are very different."

"I suppose they are. For you assumed much worse than a possible inclination."

He held back a sigh. How had they moved so quickly from agreement to argument? Would she forever be reminding him of his folly? In the three days since their disastrous meeting at the ruins, he had come to believe he had been mistaken. There had been no planned assignation. A man of integrity would admit his mistake.

"You must allow me to apologize for my presumption," he said grudgingly.

Miss Brooke stared back, her eyes so wide he could count the flecks of brown.

"I should not have questioned your honor," he added.

"I—I . . . thank you," she murmured.

He nodded.

Feeling foolish, he gestured to where Miss Talbot stood staring out at the lake. They continued to walk. For the first time, the silence between them was congenial.

"You must admit they do make a charming couple," Miss Brooke said.

"I will admit no such thing. I refuse to make speculations based on two people walking together. By that logic, the two of us must be halfway in love."

"Now who is being fanciful! Why the very notion—"

Miss Brooke seemed unable to complete her thought, though Phillip understood her meaning well enough. Miss Brooke had no interest in him.

He only wished Farthing or Miss Talbot could hear her outright astonishment. The two meddlers might have matchmaking in mind, but their efforts would not bear fruit. Miss Brooke barely tolerated him. That he was starting to admire her did not signify anything more.

Chapter Thirteen

When Mrs. Leigh heard the Brookes would be attending the next assembly, she positively insisted on shopping in Oakbury. And so Tuesday Elaine found herself at Dawson's looking for something inexpensive that would breathe new life into her gowns. Over the years, she had become quite adept at using the right accessories to make her sparse wardrobe appear to advantage. But after several nights attending dinner in her two suitable gowns, she had exhausted her shawls, jewelry, ribbons, and lace.

Getting an entirely new dress or petticoat was out of the question. She was not Miss Talbot to have dresses sent from London because her mother declared "nothing they brought with them would suit." Miss Talbot would undoubtedly be the most elegant and sought-after young woman at the assembly.

Elaine was only slightly jealous of Miss Talbot. She was used to being overshadowed by her richer, prettier, and more interesting friends—and Elaine had come to consider Miss Talbot a friend. Like Charity, Miss Talbot wasn't a spoiled heiress, and like Penelope, she had a way of lighting up a conversation. She was modest and proper but not afraid to find the elements of the ridiculous in herself or others.

It was easy to see why Daniel might favor Miss Talbot, though Elaine was not entirely sure they were courting. She was equally confused about his feelings toward herself. After his first attempt, Daniel had not called again at the lodge. Had Sir Phillip forbidden it? Elaine thought it possible and the idea made her angry with both Ashburn men, one for being a tyrant and the other for not defying him.

Elaine had thought Penelope's advice would help, but her letter had arrived with unexpected counsel.

You asked for advice, but I dare not give it. I have learned that I know nothing of love or affection, and all my schemes only serve to hurt those I care for. I will say that if Mr. Ashburn doesn't realize your value, then you are well rid of him. You should not chase after those too stupid to see your worth.

These were not the sentiments of the young woman who had constantly been devising ways to attract a beau. Elaine had been hoping for instruction on how to smile or what to say. But it seemed Penelope's elopement and marriage had taught her to look at love differently. Elaine could not deny that chasing after Daniel had not brought her happiness. It would be nice to be chosen.

"That will never do. We should do something in red."

Mama's scold pulled Elaine from her musings. She looked down and realized she was fingering a bright yellow ribbon.

"Yes, that would look well with the green," Elaine said.

Mama sighed. "I do wish we could afford a new petticoat, but your green one is quite fetching under the white muslin. And though everyone at the hall has seen it, it will be new to those at the assembly."

"Yes, of course." Elaine couldn't say she didn't care for anyone at the assembly. That would only encourage Mama to talk about the eligible men that would be in attendance and the importance of making the right impression on them. Elaine only cared about impressing one man.

Mama called over Mrs. Leigh, and they began debating the merits of ribbon and lace. Elaine nodded along for a while before excusing herself to look at the gloves displayed by the window. As she approached the window, she saw Daniel pass by on the street.

He was alone with an uncharacteristic frown on his face. He seemed so somber she had the inexplicable desire to follow after him and ask after his health.

Their last actual conversation had been days ago in the bookshop. She did not count the meaningless banter and drawing room talks at the hall. Daniel was all smiles and charm but nothing of substance was discussed. Their interactions were hollow, as if she were talking to a character in a play and not a person of flesh and blood.

Her discussions with Sir Phillip were different. Even though their conversations had a tendency to turn contentious, Elaine still enjoyed them. He could be rude and officious, but his words were honest and not some calculated compliment. He was thoughtful and perceptive. He recalled her opinions and words with an exactness that both flattered and annoyed. And, Sir Phillip could be quite humorous at times, which made it harder to be upset with him.

"Do none of these suit?" Mama came up beside her.

"Oh, I have not properly looked."

Mama shook her head. "Too lost in your head to pick a pair of gloves."

"I'm sorry, Mama."

Elaine set her mind more firmly on shopping and had soon picked gloves, lace, and ribbon that she could afford. They eventually made their way to the counter where Mrs. Leigh stood with a small mountain of purchases.

"Now, since this shopping expedition was my scheme, I insist on buying everything," Mrs. Leigh declared.

"That is not necessary," Mama said. "We are perfectly capable of—"

"Of course you are, dear." Mrs. Leigh used soothing tones. "But you forget that I did not give Elaine a birthday gift. You can't deny me the pleasure now."

After a few more protests, Mama relented. Elaine was surprised how similar the exchange was to those she had with her friends when they went shopping. She wondered if Mama felt the same mix of shame and gratitude.

What a dreadful thing it was to be poor and dependent on wealthier friends. Elaine wished again for her own money. She wanted to be the one buying gifts for those she cared about. When she received her salary for teaching, she would buy Mama a new bonnet and become a subscriber to the circulating library. Perhaps she would save up enough for a new dress? Elaine allowed herself to spend the money in her head many times. It did not matter that the position was not yet hers.

When they left Dawson's, Mrs. Leigh's maid took their parcels to the carriage while they continued down the street to the apothecary. They had been there several minutes when Elaine realized the conversation would not be short. She excused herself and told Mama she would wait at Hartley's.

It was not market day, but the street was bustling with coaches, carts, and pedestrians. Elaine amused herself by making up stories about those she passed. After her long absence, she did not recognize many, so it was easy to imagine them in the middle of a grand story.

When she arrived at the bakery, she was brought out of her thoughts by the sight of Daniel conversing with Mrs. and Miss Covington. Elaine had no wish to speak with either woman, but they lay between her and Hartley's, so she squared her shoulders and continued on.

When she was a few steps away, Daniel caught sight of her and his smile widened to something more genuine. "Miss Brooke, how delightful to see you here." He spoke as if they did not see each other every night.

The Covington ladies were less enthusiastic in their greeting. "We were just talking to Mr. Ashburn about the upcoming assembly," Mrs. Covington began in her nasal voice. "It's a pity your mother doesn't have a subscription."

"Fortunately, Miss Brooke will be attending with my party," Daniel said.

"Yes, I am looking forward to it. I understand the assembly rooms are quite elegant."

"How droll you are, Miss Brooke." Miss Covington feigned a smile. "Nobody used to the great houses of London would call Oakbury's assembly rooms elegant."

Elaine returned the smile, keeping back her inappropriate reply while she imagined Miss Covington turning an ankle in her first set.

"Not everyone has your particular sense of taste, Miss Covington." Daniel's reply was all charm and sparkling blue eyes.

Miss Covington's smile grew wider, with no indication she sensed the mockery behind his words. No doubt Miss Covington hoped to dance with Daniel at the assembly. He was not the baronet, but he was handsome, winsome, and currently Sir Phillip's heir. All excellent reasons to secure his favor.

Daniel was welcome to her.

"I must be going." Elaine curtsied.

"If you are heading to Hartley's, I shall accompany you," Daniel said.

Elaine tried not to give a smug look to Miss Covington. It seemed Daniel was not interested in securing a dance. They said their goodbyes to the clearly disappointed Covingtons.

After they had taken a few steps away, Daniel spoke softly. "I must thank you for saving me."

"Saving you?"

"Yes, you saved me. It was not a charging bull, but I assure you that your assistance was invaluable."

"Do be serious."

Daniel made a face, proving that he had no intention of being serious. As he grinned, all Elaine could think of was the sad, pensive look she had glimpsed through the window. If she asked, would he tell her what had troubled him? Or would he put on his mask and make a jest before changing the subject?

The noise of the street dropped away as they entered the bookshop and she was enveloped in the smells she loved. She moved to the back shelves and was only a little surprised when Daniel joined her instead of making his escape. Before he could say anything, she turned to him with determination.

"Is everything quite all right? Are you happy or—?" The questions were too personal but she had to know. "I only ask because I saw you earlier."

"Earlier?"

"On the street, you looked forlorn."

Understanding lightened Daniel's features. "Ah, yes. I was only brooding on the lot of second sons. Dependence on my brother and all that." He waved his hand and gave a half-smile that didn't meet his eyes.

Elaine thought of her own dependence on the largesse of others. What must it be like to have your entire income dependent on another? She thought of Sir Phillip's charges against Daniel—that he was a wastrel with no profession. Perhaps having nothing worthy to occupy his time was the true source of his unhappiness?

"You need not be dependent on Sir Phillip," Elaine said. "You could get a profession of your own."

Daniel grimaced. "You are starting to sound like him."

"I am only saying that if you don't like being beholden to your brother, you should find a way to change your situation. Don't allow yourself to be slowly poisoned with resentment."

"The fastest way to accomplish that aim is to marry an heiress. Is that what you would have me do?"

"No, of course not." Elaine squirmed at the suggestion as an image of Miss Talbot came to her mind. Was he thinking the same thing?

Daniel sighed. "I am sorry, Miss Brooke. I should not have spoken so." His charming smile slid back into place, his mask restored.

"It's not just money you need. You would be happier with some occupation. Spending time doing something you truly enjoy would ease your temper."

"Perhaps you are right."

Having trespassed the bounds of propriety, Elaine fell silent.

"We have a large collection of books at the hall."

Elaine blinked at the change in conversation. "I understand it is a superb library."

"You should come and borrow some books. Indeed, I insist you save your money and avail yourself of every dusty tome."

"That is a generous offer. Thank you."

He shrugged as if it was no matter and took a step back. "You should come today, this afternoon if you would like. I am sure nobody will be there."

"I will."

"Good." He smiled, crooked and genuine. An echo of the boy she once knew.

Daniel took his leave and left the shop. Elaine watched him disappear. Had she agreed to borrow books or arranged a clandestine meeting?

* * *

Later that afternoon, when she arrived at the hall, Elaine confidently told the footman that she knew the way to the library. As her footsteps echoed past the staircase, she was overwhelmed with nerves. Belatedly, she realized how it might look if she was caught wandering the hall alone.

Lady Ashburn and others might accept her story of coming to borrow a book, but Sir Phillip was bound to assume the worst, just as he had at the Old Priory, and this time he would be right. Or at least Elaine thought he would be right. She was still unsure what Daniel had meant by his invitation.

The clatter of footsteps on the stairs startled her. Conjuring a glowering Sir Phillip, Elaine rushed to the library door and practically threw herself inside, with the door closed and her heart skittering in her chest. She was a fool. Surely running about the house was far more suspicious than being found walking sedately.

"Miss Brooke, whatever is the matter?"

Elaine could not contain her gasp of surprise as she whirled to face the speaker. Sir Phillip rose from a black armchair, looking alarmed. She had caught him in an informal moment. He wore a plain blue waistcoat with no jacket and a loose cravat. The effect made him look younger and she recalled that he was not yet thirty.

"I was. . . That is. . . Nothing is the matter," she said, though her heart was hammering.

"You seem quite flushed." His voice was neutral even as his gaze inspected her.

What must he be thinking? What possible reason could she give for bursting in on him in his private library? What would she do if Daniel arrived now?

"It is a warm day, and I. . . well. . ." In a vain attempt to distract him, she gestured to the book in his hand. "What are you reading?"

Instead of answering, Sir Phillip placed the book on the armchair and moved toward her.

"Miss Brooke, if you would please." His voice was stern and Elaine was sure he was about to berate her. For once, she thought she might deserve it. Instead, he approached within a few steps and frowned at her. It occurred to Elaine that he might want to leave the library or perhaps show her out.

She took a step forward at the same time he stepped forward. She moved to the side and so did he. Elaine looked up at him and laughed nervously. He seemed taller this close. The light from the windows caught in his hair and created a halo.

His hands came to her shoulders. Her heart pounded in her ears. Was he about to kiss her? Is this how it happened? Did she want to kiss him?

"Stay," he said in a commanding tone.

He dropped his hands, stepped around her, and moved to the closed door. He opened it, but instead of departing, he turned back around.

Elaine's cheeks heated as much from her wild thoughts of kissing as from the realization that they had been alone in a room with the door closed.

"Apologies, I did not think of the door. That is, I didn't think that being alone with you. . ." She shook her head and turned away.

"I understand that you think nothing of being alone with me, but I have no wish to cast aspersions on your reputation," Sir Phillip said gruffly.

He was right. Elaine knew how quickly a reputation could be ruined; she had seen the misery Penelope's imprudence had caused. Yet she had come with the express desire to be alone with Daniel. Was she so desperate for his attention? It was wrong of him to even suggest a clandestine meeting. Had that been his intent? She still didn't know and now she didn't want to discover the truth.

But she couldn't run away; Sir Phillip blocked the door. If she left now, he was sure to grow suspicious.

"I came to borrow a book," she said hurriedly.

To avoid his piercing gaze, she turned to look about. Long windows flooded the room with light and gave a view of green grass and the woods in the distance. Ceiling height shelves lined the remaining walls, teeming with black leather volumes. Elaine breathed in the smell of books and smiled. Papa would have loved this room.

"This is an impressive collection," she said.

"Thank you." She turned from the books to find Sir Phillip gazing at her. She had noticed him doing that often, though she wasn't quite sure why. Was he looking to censure her? Or monitoring her interactions with Daniel?

He sighed and looked to the window.

"I should go," she said. "I have interrupted your solitude."

"Yes, you have."

Elaine ducked her head at his words.

"But if you leave without a book, then the interruption will be for naught."

She looked up and was surprised by his thoughtful expression. Elaine attempted a smile and hoped that Sir Phillip wouldn't ask who had offered to let her borrow a book. Perhaps he thought her audacious enough to turn up uninvited?

He crossed to a shelf and began to examine titles. With his back to her, she noticed that his collar was not standing up right. It was the most minor imperfection, but she had the strangest desire to go and fix it. Instead of joining him, she walked further into the room.

He turned to her. "If you wish for a novel, they are shelved here."

"I didn't think you would have novels in your library," Elaine said.

"Why should we not have novels?"

"Because you don't approve of them and think them unfit for reading."

Phillip wrinkled his brow. "I gave no such censure."

"You criticized your brother for preferring novels."

"Because he shouldn't be wasting his time with such frivolous things."

"So reading novels is a frivolous waste of time?" His assessment injured Elaine.

"That is not at all what I meant." Sir Phillip ran a hand through his hair, ruffling it in an undignified manner. How had she never noticed that it curled slightly? He took a deep breath. "What are you interested in reading?"

There was no way Elaine would admit to wanting to read a novel now. "I was hoping to learn more about farming."

He frowned. "Farming?"

"Is it so hard to believe that I am interested in agricultural techniques?"

This was technically true. Elaine had been interested in what she had learned from Sir Phillip, even if she didn't want to read a book on the subject.

Sir Phillip didn't answer her question. Instead, he gestured behind her. "There are several volumes on the third shelf."

She nodded and turned to the books. Behind her, she heard Sir Phillip returning to his chair. She looked over the titles: *Observations on Livestock*, *Annals of Agriculture*, *History of the Dishley System*. Had Sir Phillip read all of these? Probably; it was the responsible and intelligent thing for a man of his station. If she picked one, would he then expect her to converse knowledgeably on the subject? She could see the disaster unfolding in the drawing room.

He would ask her a question and she would respond incorrectly, proving she hadn't read the book. He would frown in disapproval and change the topic, lecture her for not being attentive, or chuckle and make a joke. Elaine had seen so many different sides to Sir Phillip in the last week that she could not settle on a reaction, even in her daydream.

A throat cleared behind her and she nearly jumped as she came out of her imagination and turned around to see Sir Phillip standing a respectful distance away. He held a book in front of him like a shield. She reached for it and after a moment of hesitation, he thrust it into her hands. She glanced down at the title: *Le Morte D'Arthur*.

She smiled and traced the embossed words with her fingers.

"This is one of my favorites," she breathed as tears sprang to her eyes. She didn't look up for fear Sir Phillip would see. Her father had adored his copy and often told her the stories of King Arthur. "An excellent choice, sir, and a lovely edition, but I have my own copy." Elaine had refused to let Mama sell it. The volume was battered but cherished.

"Good, because I was not attempting to lend the book to you."

Elaine looked up with a knitted brow. Sir Phillip was smiling and she couldn't help but return the gesture.

"Then why did you give it to me?"

"I didn't. You assumed. . ." He stopped and shook his head. "It doesn't matter. I merely wanted to show you that I am capable of enjoying myself."

"This is what you were reading?" She exclaimed.

Sir Phillip's cheeks flushed. "Well, you might be shocked. No doubt you think I am incapable of appreciating it. And I confess that I have not read anything for pleasure in years. A fact I had not realized until your pointed words last week."

It was Elaine's turn to blush. She had been unpardonably direct to him the morning of the tour. She had thought he would harbor an everlasting dislike for her impertinence, but it seemed he had forgiven her and even taken the words to heart.

"I had no notion my words would have such an effect," she said.

"Neither did I, and yet today I decided to heed your suggestion."

"And has reading for entertainment been a sore trial?"

"I can't say as I had barely begun before being interrupted." He flashed an almost boyish grin. Elaine caught her breath.

"Then I apologize again for my untimely arrival. One should not be kept from tales of chivalry."

He chuckled.

She held out the book. As he took it, their gloveless hands brushed and a tingle spread up her arm. Elaine pulled away as if burned. She put both hands behind her back to hide her reaction.

"While in principle I agree with you," Sir Phillip looked down at the book and then up. "I confess it was not an unwelcome interruption."

For the second time that day, Elaine found herself unsure what a man meant. Was Sir Phillip saying he enjoyed her company? She could hardly credit it, and yet he had not been unwelcoming. He hadn't questioned her presence or assumed she was there to meet his brother. The fact that he didn't suspect made her feel worse. What would Sir Phillip think when his brother arrived? She didn't want to know. If Daniel ever showed up, she hoped to be long gone.

"Still, this is your home and I should leave you to your reading." She motioned to the book.

Sir Phillip nodded slowly. "Of course, but you are welcome to stay."

"Thank you, but I really should return home." Elaine dropped a hasty curtsy and fled from the room.

She had come to the hall in hopes of clearing up her confusion about Daniel's actions and feelings. But as she left, all she could think of was Sir Phillip, their conversations, and her surprising reactions to him. He was not the forbidding and pompous older brother she had always assumed. When they weren't at odds, she enjoyed talking to him. That he liked King Arthur was a decided point in his favor. If only she had met that version of Sir Phillip first, how different things might be. As she entered the shade of the woods, she was more confused than ever.

Chapter Fourteen

⁓∘ঌ৹ৎ৹∘⁓

Phillip sipped his drink and half-listened to the gentlemen conversing around the table. It had been another successful dinner full of lively conversation and good food, but Phillip was unsettled. He knew the source of his disquiet but not how to dispel it. He could not stop thinking of Miss Brooke and her unexpected visit to the library that afternoon.

She had often been in his thoughts but always as a problem to be solved. Now the problem was his attraction to her. He could no longer deny the strong pull to her as they stood close or when their hands brushed. Phillip had been attracted to women before, but none of them had been his near neighbor, in love with his brother, or so totally uninterested in him.

"I must say, Ashburn." Farthing pulled him from his abstraction. "The party has been a success."

Phillip tipped his glass in acknowledgment. "I believe all of the credit goes to Lady Ashburn."

"To Lady Ashburn," Farthing said in a raised voice. The toast was repeated around the table. Farthing finished his drink, put down the glass, and regarded Phillip.

"What?" Phillip asked.

"I was just wondering when I might toast the new Lady Ashburn." Farthing gave a slow grin as Phillip rolled his eyes. "I am merely reminding you of

135

your responsibility to produce an heir."

"I have an heir."

Richard scoffed. "The Prodigal doesn't count."

Phillip ignored the comment. He was grateful no one else seemed to be listening to this nonsense. All were deep in their own conversations.

"I didn't take you for one of those men that insist on seeing all their friends before the parson."

"I only want to see you happy and, in my experience, a good wife is a sure way of securing happiness."

"And in my experience, a good wife can be deuced difficult to find."

"You have not been properly looking, or perhaps you are too blind to see her."

Phillip took another drink. What had come over Farthing? He had never cared that Phillip took no interest in the marriage mart. Who was he too blind to see? Miss Brooke came unbidden to his mind and he pushed the thought away. Farthing did not understand the situation. Miss Brooke was not a candidate for Lady Ashburn.

"Farthing, you were fortunate to find a woman eager to accept your hand. Not all of us are so lucky."

His friend chuckled. "Ashburn, you are a baronet, with an estate, a house in town, and a kind and steady character. Any woman would accept your suit."

"I beg to differ with you, my friend."

He could think of at least one woman who would not accept him. Miss Brooke hadn't the slightest romantic interest; she wasn't even sure she enjoyed his company. It didn't matter that with each conversation he found more to admire. She was foolishly attached to Daniel.

He pushed away his glass. He was turning maudlin.

Farthing frowned as Phillip stood. Most of the other gentlemen rose to follow him to the drawing room. Mr. Poole and Mr. Talbot stayed, deep in conversation about canals and investments.

Once in the drawing room, Phillip paused to get his bearings. Miss Brooke was sitting with Miss Wilson talking with animation. He wanted to join them, but he told himself, only because it was likely to be an interesting conversation.

Farthing clapped him on the back. "A woman cannot reject what she does not know is on offer."

"Meaning?" Phillip pretended ignorance.

Farthing leaned closer; Phillip smelled brandy on his breath. "At least try to woo her. She is not indifferent to you."

It was annoying how his heart jumped at those words. Was Farthing just drunk or had he seen some marks of feeling from Miss Brooke? Did he have reason to hope?

"Trust me," Farthing said, "my courtship of Jane was not entirely plain sailing. Learn from my mistakes, friend." He gave a cheeky grin and wink before wandering off to his wife.

Phillip stood in indecision. If Miss Brooke knew of his interest, would it change anything or would he be humiliated? His eyes wandered to where Daniel was talking with Lady Ashburn, Captain Hart, and Miss Talbot.

What would Daniel say? He had cautioned Phillip against raising Miss Brooke's hopes, but surely he would not object if Phillip's intentions were honorable? It mattered little if Miss Brooke did not wish for his attention.

Phillip glanced back around the room and found Miss Brooke looking at him. She quickly averted her eyes, but it was enough to decide him. Phillip made his way to her side.

Miss Wilson greeted him with a smile that softened her sharp features. "Sir Phillip, are you coming to join us?"

"If you will have me." He glanced at Miss Brooke as he sat down and was gratified by her brief smile.

"We were just discussing the life of a single woman," Miss Wilson said.

"A topic I confess I know nothing about, but I am happy to learn."

"Let us talk of something else," Miss Brooke said in a rush.

"I am keen for our visit to the priory," Miss Wilson said.

"As am I," Phillip replied.

"I suppose Miss Brooke you have been all over the ruin. Will you be our guide?" Miss Wilson asked.

"An excellent idea." Phillip would happily let her lead the group. But Miss Brooke did not seem as taken with the idea.

"I do not believe I am going on the excursion," she said slowly and avoided his gaze.

"Oh, that is a pity," Miss Wilson said.

"You will be greatly missed," Phillip added. He had been looking forward to walking the ruins with her and erasing their previous encounter from her memory. She looked at him with a curious expression. An awkward silence grew.

"Literature?" Miss Wilson said, no doubt thinking it a safe, neutral subject.

"On that topic, I believe Miss Brooke has the superior knowledge. She has chided me on my lack of well-rounded reading." Phillip smiled when Miss Brooke gave him a speaking look. "But I am currently rereading *Le Morte D'Arthur.*"

"Really?" Miss Wilson seemed unimpressed. "And what do you think of it?"

"I am enjoying it very much."

"How interesting. The stories always struck me as a lot of running about for nothing."

Miss Brooke looked scandalized. "You do not like King Arthur stories?"

Miss Wilson shrugged. "They lack historical accuracy and narrative cohesion."

"I must confess to a strong bias," Sir Phillip said. "I was quite enamored with King Arthur and knights as a child. Reading them is like sitting down with an old friend."

"Ladies and gentlemen." The conversation halted and they all turned to where Daniel stood. "We have had several nights of cards, music, and conversation. So, I have been commissioned to devise a game." Daniel's eyes swept over the group. Did his smile broaden when he looked at Miss Brooke? "Now I know you would all be happy just playing Poor Kitty."

There were chuckles about the room.

Phillip frowned. The very notion of their guests on their hands and knees while others petted them and called them "poor kitty" was absurd. They weren't adolescents. Next Daniel would suggest Hot Cockles or Snapdragon.

"But instead of a boring old staple, I have invented a new game."

Phillip didn't like the glee in Daniel's voice. Could he have created something worse than Poor Kitty?

"This game is a faster variation on tableaux vivant. We are dispensing with spending all day putting together a scene full of costumes and props and adding an element of competition. Mrs. Brooke," Daniel gestured to the older lady who smiled graciously, "has done us the honor of picking several well-known stories and writing them down on pieces of paper. Those who wish to pose will divide into teams of two. Each team will draw a piece of paper and decide how best to portray their story. For props, you are permitted only the items in the room."

"I thought you said there was an element of competition?" Mrs. Cooper asked.

"Indeed, excellent memory, madam. When the tableau is presented, everyone will write down what story they think is being portrayed. Points are awarded for guessing correctly and by being the team whose pose is most recognizable."

Daniel answered and clarified several other questions until it seemed everyone was satisfied with the rules of the game. An unmistakable current of excitement filled the room and Phillip had to admit Daniel's scheme was sound. Though he did not intend to act out any story himself, Phillip would enjoy watching others.

"If you will excuse me," Miss Wilson said. "I am going to partner with my sister." She rose and left Phillip with Miss Brooke.

"This should be interesting," Phillip said to fill the silence.

"You think it silly and immature," Miss Brooke said.

"I did not say that."

She raised her eyebrows.

"You think me entirely incapable of frivolity?"

"I did not say that."

He shook his head. Why must she think of him as a judgmental elder? Was she right? He had automatically decided he would not participate. Yet he was not even thirty, the game was perfectly harmless and might even be enjoyable with the right person.

"Miss Brooke, will you be my partner?" As soon as he asked the question, he realized how much he wanted her to say yes.

"Are you sure? I do not want you to feel obligated."

"Feel obligated? Didn't you once say I only do what I want?"

She colored. "I never said that. Though I understand you assuming I would speak so boldly."

"Your boldness might be your best quality."

The compliment made her blush deepen and his heart picked up speed. She looked about the room instead of meeting his eyes. Was she hoping Daniel would ask to be her partner? The thought made his stomach sour. He resisted the urge to follow her gaze.

"If you would prefer someone else," he said. He kept his tone light but his heart was heavy.

"No." She brought her attention back to him and smiled. He grew warm in the sun of that smile. "I would enjoy being your partner. And I think I will be able to join the party at the Old Priory."

Mrs. Brooke arrived with a hat full of paper. She looked questioningly between him and her daughter.

"Miss Brooke has agreed to pose with me."

"How very kind of you, Sir Phillip. You honor us with your attention." Mrs. Brooke sounded as if she thought it a great favor. Phillip squirmed. Mrs. Brooke wrote their names together on her scoring sheet before holding out the hat. He drew a small folded piece of paper and she wished them luck before departing.

All about the room, teams of two were looking at their papers and talking in low tones. Phillip unfolded theirs and read quietly.

"Jack and Jill."

"Hmm." Miss Brooke scrunched her forehead in thought, an adorable wrinkle formed between her eyes. "How should we portray that?"

He leaned forward to keep the conversation private. "It seems we should have a hill and a pail of some kind."

She gave him a long-suffering look. "Yes, but which part of the rhyme will be most recognizable? Should they be going up the hill or should Jack have a broken crown?"

Phillip considered the idea. "I think the broken crown could easily be confused with other stories."

Miss Brooke hummed in agreement.

They continued to talk over their plan for a few more minutes. The room filled with murmured conversations as others did the same. Phillip was eager to see what the other poses were. Their own plan was simple, but he thought it would convey their story admirably.

With their plan completed, they were at leisure to talk, but Phillip found himself at a loss. Daniel would have a charming story or compliment, but Phillip couldn't think of anything that would suit. He was saved when Miss Brooke spoke.

"I am surprised that you enjoy King Arthur stories."

He smiled. "Despite opinions to the contrary, I was a boy once. And what boy wouldn't find questing knights entertaining? How did *Le Morte D'Arthur* become your favorite book?"

"My father. . ." A shadow passed over her face just like in the library, then she smiled. "He loved to tell me about the knights of the round table and take me on quests. He even named me for the Elaine of legend."

Phillip wanted to ask which of the many Elaines she was named for, but she had that far-off look he was starting to recognize. She wouldn't hear him if he spoke. He took the opportunity to admire her countenance. After a few moments, she returned from wherever her mind had wandered.

"Sorry, what were you saying?"

He held back his smile. "Nothing."

"Oh."

Feeling bad for embarrassing her, he rushed to fill the silence. "I also went on quests as a child."

She tipped her head. "I can't quite picture you running about the countryside pretending to be a knight."

"I assure you I did. You can't possibly think my brother the only Ashburn to go adventuring? Where do you think he learned it?"

"I guess I never considered."

It was clear she was considering it now and Phillip hoped she might see him in a different light.

Daniel calling everyone to the doorway acting as the stage prevented further conversation. They were given paper and small pencils to write their guesses. Footmen appeared to move chairs and soon the whole party formed a circle facing the doorway. Daniel and Miss Talbot sat beside him.

"Phillip, you're playing?" Daniel asked.

"Of course. Miss Brooke graciously agreed to be my partner."

Daniel grinned. "How very kind. I hope the task has not been too taxing."

"I am happy to be with Sir Phillip," Miss Brooke said primly.

"Happy?" Daniel looked between them and then raised his eyebrows. "Would that be due to the story you get to act out? Is it violent? Romantic?"

Phillip grew hot.

Miss Talbot hushed them as Mrs. Brooke stepped in front of the doorway to address the group. She reiterated the rules and the scoring before calling up the Farthings.

"Everyone close your eyes while the team creates their tableau," Mrs. Brooke instructed.

There were sounds of scraping and whispering from the doorway but Phillip was focused on the slight brush of Miss Brooke's arm. Was she truly pleased to be his partner?

"Open your eyes."

Mrs. Farthing was sitting on a chair with her stocking foot raised. Farthing knelt before her with her slipper in one hand; the other lifted her foot as if about to put the shoe on. It was almost too easy to guess. They held their pose for the requisite thirty seconds as the sound of pencils scratching filled the room.

Phillip glanced at Miss Brooke's elegant script *"Cinderella or The Little Glass Slipper."* She glanced up at him and he nodded his approval. How clever to use the full title of Perrault's story.

Phillip wondered how he would have portrayed the tale with Miss Brooke.

Undoubtedly the trying on of the glass slipper was the best scene but he would not have grasped her foot. The very idea made his hand tingle.

The time was called and their paper folded over the answer so they could not make changes.

Daniel leaned over Phillip to Miss Brooke. "You seemed very sure of your answer." Miss Brooke's only reply was a slight nod before she turned her attention back to the doorway. Mrs. Cooper and Miss Wilson had been called up.

Phillip held back his smile at the rebuff. They all closed their eyes as instructed. It took longer for the women to get in place and when Phillip opened his eyes, he didn't immediately understand the scene before him.

Miss Wilson was standing with the fireplace shovel poised over the floor as if she were digging. Her eyes were on Mrs. Cooper who was kneeling on the ground, holding a round object between her hands. She had a look of heartbreaking sadness.

Phillip was impressed by her ability to put such emotion into her performance but her expressive face did nothing to help him guess the story. A shovel could mean a farmer. There were several fairy tales and rhymes with farmers but that wouldn't explain Mrs. Cooper. Was she holding food? But then why was she so sad? A child, perhaps? Miss Brooke had not written anything down.

He leaned closer and whispered. "Is there some story about a farmer and some turnip or cabbage baby?" That seemed like a story he had heard though Phillip couldn't recall the particulars.

Miss Brooke shook her head and whispered back. The brush of her breath tickled his cheek. "I think it must be Hamlet in the graveyard."

He took a moment to compose himself before replying. "I believe you are right. Alas, poor Yorick." They shared a conspiratorial look before she hurriedly wrote the answer.

With the answer the scene was obvious, but he never would have guessed *Hamlet*. A glance around told him that others were also struggling. Beside him, Daniel craned his neck as if to see what Miss Brooke was writing. Phillip blocked his view. Miss Talbot shook her head with a half-smile and shrug as if Daniel's attempted cheating was to be expected.

Mrs. Brooke called the end of the round and, as the older ladies put away their props, asked for Lady Ashburn and Captain Hart to take their turn. Phillip shared a surprised look with his brother. It seemed neither of them had noticed she was playing. Miss Brooke showed no surprise and Phillip thought she was repressing a smile.

When Phillip opened his eyes again, he was pleased the tableau was not a love story.

Captain Hart stood with a cloak thrown about his front like a robe. He smiled as he looked at Mother. Mother stood beside the chaise, her hands wrapped around a fireplace poker that seemed to be stuck in the piece of furniture.

While others whispered, Phillip and Miss Brooke shared a knowing look. She quickly wrote down "King Arthur, *Le Morte D'Arthur.*"

She folded it before Daniel could try and cheat again. Phillip shot his brother a smug look.

Phillip turned back to the tableau. Captain Hart's smile was so broad and genuine that Phillip did not think it was merely acting. Phillip had given much thought to Miss Brooke's earlier words and his own observations. Did his mother return Captain Hart's admiration?

Their turn ended and, as Mother replaced the fireplace poker, Mrs. Brooke asked Daniel and Miss Talbot to the front. Daniel gave a mischievous grin. Phillip should have seen it as a warning.

When Phillip opened his eyes, he frowned. Why couldn't Daniel behave?

Miss Brooke took in a sharp breath. The room erupted in whispers.

Miss Talbot lay on the chaise, her eyes closed and hands folded over her breast. Daniel was on a knee beside her, his head bent over Miss Talbot, lips hovering above hers. Did Miss Talbot agree to him hovering so close as he paused in the act of kissing her? Was Daniel's look of loving adoration genuine or part of his act?

Phillip took in the reactions of others. Mrs. Talbot seemed pleased while Mr. Talbot frowned. There was no way to judge if the display had helped or hurt Daniel's chances with the parents. Farthing met his eye and shrugged as if to say, "what did you expect?" Miss Brooke had gone pale and though the answer was obvious, she had not written "*Sleeping Beauty.*"

In many ways, this was what Phillip had been working towards. Daniel showed clear partiality to Miss Talbot and Miss Brooke seemed to recognize it. But Phillip didn't feel triumph, just guilt. He wanted Daniel to marry Miss Talbot, but he hadn't considered how much it would hurt Miss Brooke.

The thirty seconds seemed to stretch for thirty minutes.

When Mrs. Brooke finally called time, her tone left no doubt of her disapproval. Daniel leaned away from Miss Talbot just as she was opening her eyes. She smiled shakily at the audience and her cheeks flushed while Daniel grinned beside her.

Phillip clenched his fist. He needed to get himself under control before he berated his brother in front of the company.

"Sir Phillip, Elaine, please come up." Mrs. Brooke's call meant that he could only give his brother a disapproving look as they exchanged places.

Once at the front, with everyone's eyes closed, Phillip focused on getting into the planned pose. They had chosen to depict the first part of the rhyme. He stood on the chaise, leaning his body forward and lifting one foot in the air as if struggling up a hill. Miss Brooke came beside him, holding the ashes pail she had retrieved from the fireplace. She copied his posture but with one foot on the ground and the other on the chaise.

She seemed far away, distracted, and sad. On impulse, he reached out his hand. She looked at it for a long moment before she moved. Her gloved hand was warm and small and seemed to fit perfectly in his. He smiled and squeezed her hand in reassurance. She returned a small, hesitant smile. Then he turned to Mrs. Brooke and gave her a nod to indicate they were ready.

"You may open your eyes."

Phillip couldn't see their audience but he suddenly felt their gazes upon them. He wondered what they saw as he schooled his body to keep still. Was their attention drawn, like his, to where their hands joined? Holding her hand was nothing to the display Daniel had just given. Surely none of them could tell that the simple act sent fire through him?

He had taken a lady's hand to help her out of a carriage or around an obstacle but never just held it. It was surprisingly disconcerting. Was it having the same effect on Miss Brooke? He wished he could look at her.

He wanted to break the pose.

He wanted to never let go.

He resolved to savor the experience.

Mrs. Brooke called the time.

Miss Brooke released his hand immediately. Obviously, she was not as reluctant as he to let go. He should have expected her reaction and yet it felt like a punch to his gut.

He straightened, stepped from the chaise, and avoided looking at her. Farthing was wrong. Miss Brooke was completely indifferent to him.

Chapter Fifteen

⚬Ↄ♥Ↄ⚬

T he road to Brightworth village was dustier than Elaine had anticipated. She was only halfway there and already the bottom of her dress had turned from pale blue to gray. She should have changed to a darker dress when Mama denied her the use of the donkey cart. It was her first meeting with Mr. Eden about the position as a teacher and she wanted to impress the vicar.

As she walked, Elaine tried to imagine how the conversation with Mr. Eden would go or what teaching would be like, but remembrances of the previous night kept intruding. Instead of conjuring her future, she was dwelling on the past.

The image that kept intruding was Daniel poised over Miss Talbot. The position itself was shocking but what caused Elaine's consternation was the look on his face. She did not think such tender affection was an act. Daniel's mask had finally been removed and his true feelings revealed. He cared deeply for Miss Talbot. He might even love her.

Surprisingly, this revelation had not broken Elaine's heart. She was shocked, confused, and somewhat angry but had remained dry-eyed. Perhaps the sadness would come later? She remembered how Penelope had wept when Mr. Aston abandoned her. She recalled how Mary would pine for her betrothed. If she loved Daniel, shouldn't she be desolate that he cared for Miss Talbot?

In *Le Morte D'Arthur*, Elaine of Astolat had died when her love for Lancelot went unrequited. Most of her life, Elaine had imagined Daniel in the role of Lancelot as she pined for him like her namesake. It had seemed tragically noble to love with no hope of return and imagine a life that could never be. But perhaps what she had felt for Daniel had never been real love? Not love like what her friends felt.

The sound of rapid hoofbeats interrupted Elaine's thoughts. She moved to the side of the road to let the rider pass, but the beats slowed instead. She turned and was pleased to see Miss Talbot coming up behind her. Her hair had escaped from its coiffure; her cheeks were red, her eyes bright. She looked far from the composed young woman Elaine knew.

"Miss Brooke, what luck. May I walk with you?" Her voice was calm and she didn't wait for a response as she gestured to her groom. Elaine waited while Miss Talbot dismounted and instructed her groom to take her horse and meet her in the village.

"You are going to Brightworth?" Miss Talbot asked as the groom rode away.

"Yes, to the church."

She nodded but asked no further questions.

"Do you ride alone this morning?" Elaine asked.

From the conversations at the hall, she understood that Miss Talbot rode in the mornings with the other guests with Daniel leading them.

"Yes, I am alone." She did not elaborate.

"Has your dress for the assembly arrived?" Elaine tried a different subject.

"Yes."

"Do you like it?"

"It will do."

Elaine gave up asking questions.

They walked in silence. How strange that Miss Talbot should stop to walk with her only to be so short in her replies.

"Miss Brooke, are we friends?"

The question flummoxed Elaine, but she was able to nod. "Of course."

"Then will you do me the favor, as my friend, of answering my questions?"

"I will do anything in my power to assist you."

"Even if the questions are impertinent?"

A knot of unease settled in Elaine's stomach. "Miss Talbot, please tell me what this is all about. You do not seem yourself."

"I do not feel myself." She shook her head. "You know Mr. Ashburn so well. Indeed, you seem such easy companions, that I feel. . . that is. . ." Miss Talbot sighed.

Elaine was not insensible to the implication. She carefully considered her reply.

"It is true we were close as children and I do find him easy to converse with. But then he speaks easily with everyone, does he not?"

"It's different with you. He is different."

"He is?"

A short time ago, she might have rejoiced in the thought but now it only confused her. He cared for Miss Talbot; Elaine was sure of it. She looked at the young woman beside her and saw silent tears streaking down her cheeks. Here was a young woman in the throes of passion. Elaine's heart went out to her.

"Miss Talbot, please tell me what troubles you. As your friend, I wish to be of some service."

"Oh Miss Brooke, but it is you that troubles me!"

"Me?"

"Please tell me, truthfully, is there an understanding between you and Mr. Ashburn?"

Elaine was stunned to silence. How had she come to such a conclusion? Was it merely her behavior with Daniel? The wild imaginings of a jealous heart? Or perhaps the loose tongues of gossips?

"Your silence speaks volumes," Miss Talbot said quietly.

"No, no! Miss Talbot, you misunderstand. I am silent because I am surprised. Dan—Mr. Ashburn has not made any offer. He has not even hinted at deeper feelings."

In saying it Elaine realized it was true. Daniel had flirted with her, he

149

had complimented her, but only a few times had he revealed a true, honest feeling. Indeed, she had had more genuine interactions with Mrs. Farthing.

"Truly?"

"I promise."

Miss Talbot wiped furiously at her eyes with a damp handkerchief. "Mr. Ashburn's behavior has been so perplexing. He speaks of you with inordinate fondness. I was going mad thinking Papa was right and that he was making love to both of us."

"But surely Mr. Ashburn has shown you favor?"

Elaine had keenly observed how Daniel partnered her for most dinners, spoke with her in the evenings, complimented her, and of course, there was the previous night.

"Oh yes," Miss Talbot agreed. "We were much in company in London and he was so attentive. I thought he would make an offer. Mama was sure he would. But we were both wrong. I think Papa was happy that it came to nothing until he saw how upset I was. My father has always hoped I would attract a title, but my happiness is paramount. He would not object to Mr. Ashburn if he felt there was true affection."

"Just when I had decided that I had imagined his attachment and resolved to forget Mr. Ashburn, we received the invitation to Ryder Hall. I began to hope again. Perhaps that was silly of me. So many women have lost their heart to him, but I reasoned that none had been invited to his family estate."

She sighed. "There are moments when I think he truly cares for me but then there are others, like this morning when he seems intent on avoiding me entirely." She paused as if remembering.

Elaine thought of the morning she met Daniel in the woods. Sir Phillip had accused him of hiding from the guests. Why would he behave in such a manner?

Was Sir Phillip right? Did Daniel think of nothing but his own pleasure? Was he toying with Miss Talbot's affections? Had he been toying with hers? A man of honor would never make a lady think he felt more than he did. He would not invite one woman for secret meetings only to stare at another adoringly. How had she been so blind to his true character?

"Miss Brooke, what am I to do?" Miss Talbot stopped and turned to her. Elaine was ill-equipped to advise her friend. They had almost reached the church and the sounds of life from the village filled the silence. She tried to think what Mrs. Piper would say in such a situation. The advice from her often-read letter seemed appropriate.

"There are far better men on which to fix your hopes."

Miss Talbot frowned. It was not the advice she wanted to hear. Elaine gripped her hand.

"If Mr. Ashburn is unwilling or unable to make his intentions clear, then you must guard your own feelings or you will go mad trying to understand his actions."

"Your advice is sound, but I do not know if I can do as you ask." Miss Talbot swallowed thickly.

Elaine heard what she did not say. Miss Talbot was in love with Daniel and Elaine was asking her to deny her heart. But it was the best way to keep Miss Talbot from avoiding the fate of a tragic heroine. She now understood Sir Phillip's frustration with his brother. Was Miss Talbot just the last in a long line of broken hearts?

"I promise I will do my best to help." Elaine clasped Miss Talbot's hand. Silently she determined to knock some sense into Daniel. "Tonight, during the musical performances, we shall sit together and tomorrow at the Old Priory, I will devise a way to ensure you are not alone."

Miss Talbot squeezed her hand. "Thank you, Miss Brooke."

"I think you should call me Elaine."

Miss Talbot smiled. "Then you should call me Freddie."

* * *

A half-hour later, Elaine's mind was no longer on Freddie and Daniel, but filled with her hopes and plans for the parish school. With Mr. Eden, she had thoroughly reviewed the curriculum, her use of the church as a schoolhouse, looked over supplies he had purchased, and discussed her schedule and pay. Mr. Eden was all affability and had not once glanced at the hem of her dress.

Last night she had discussed with Miss Wilson how rewarding teaching would be. Elaine could see herself standing before her students and helping them decipher words and tot up sums. They would look at her with round eyes and open minds. She would begin to collect their little gifts. The younger ones would hug her before they left. Like Miss Minerva, she would watch them grow and develop over the years.

Her daydream dissolved. Did she really wish to teach for years to come? She had happily agreed to Mr. Eden's stipulation that she commit to a year. There was no reason not to. She had no other prospects and no longer hoped that Daniel would offer for her. And if he did, she was not inclined to answer favorably. He was not the paragon she had always imagined.

"The pay is not a large sum," Mr. Eden's words brought her back to the matter at hand. "Indeed, Sir Phillip did not think we could find a teacher at so low an amount, but I knew the Lord would provide." He beamed as she murmured her agreement.

What had Sir Phillip said when Mr. Eden put her name forward?

The old church door groaned behind them. Elaine turned to see Sir Phillip framed in the doorway. She was not prepared for how her heart jumped at the sight of his tall, well-dressed form. Would she always be nervous around him? Last night as they held hands, her heart had been like a hummingbird in her chest.

"Ah, Sir Phillip, so glad you could join us." Mr. Eden moved down the aisle to welcome the baronet. Elaine trailed after him. Sir Phillip looked at her curiously before turning his attention to the vicar.

"Apologies for being late. I had a matter with a tenant. I can return later if you are busy."

"I am busy, but my business is the reason you are here." Mr. Eden turned with a smile that made his bulbous nose almost unnoticeable and beckoned Elaine forward. "May I present our new teacher?"

Elaine froze beside Mr. Eden. She thought Sir Phillip knew she was to be the teacher. Would he furiously declare that she was not suited for the job? That she was too brazen and outspoken?

"Miss Brooke wants to teach in the parish school?" He seemed incredulous.

His confused gaze met hers. He removed his hat and ran a hand through his hair.

"I knew you would be pleased," Mr. Eden said.

Sir Phillip blinked, then nodded. "Yes, certainly, I am pleased. That is, Miss Brooke is a perfect choice."

Elaine could hardly believe her ears. Did Sir Phillip actually approve of her?

"I just had not considered." He looked at her. "You do understand the contract is to be for a year?"

"I do, sir." She tried not to let her indignation show. Did he think she was inconstant?

"And you are prepared to teach for a year? Here?"

"As I have told Mr. Eden, I am settled now at the lodge and have no plans to quit it."

Sir Phillip looked as if he would ask another question but Mr. Eden spoke first. "We have talked over all the particulars and I am confident that she will do great work in the parish."

"Yes, yes of course. I have no doubt."

Elaine thought he might have many doubts, but she was happy he did not voice them in front of the clergyman. Sir Phillip had given no objections and though it wasn't approval, it wasn't rejection either. Why did she so deeply want his approval? Somehow, she had come to respect Sir Phillip's judgment, perhaps even desire his good opinion. A most unfortunate circumstance since Elaine was sure Sir Phillip thought her silly, improper, and opinionated.

Feeling uncomfortable, she tried to make her escape. "Mr. Eden, if there is nothing else, I should be returning home," she said.

"No, dear, I am satisfied. Sir Phillip, have you any questions?"

"No, I am sure you have taken care of everything." He opened the door and gestured to her. It had been her decision to leave, but he made her feel like she was being dismissed. She tamped down her annoyance.

"Thank you again for the opportunity." She smiled at Mr. Eden and took her leave.

As she strode past Sir Phillip, Elaine held her shoulders high and did not let her gaze stray to his face. When she was a few steps away, she let out her breath and congratulated herself for not saying anything untoward.

Sir Phillip was vexing. She did not understand him. Their conversations were rewarding when they didn't devolve into an argument. But he had wanted her to join the expedition to the priory. He had chosen to partner her in tableau vivant even when she told him he didn't have to. They had made a good team, sharing looks and whispering answers. It had been an unexpected and easy companionship. But the camaraderie had ceased after their tableau. He had become rigid and cold again.

She wasn't sure if the change was because of Daniel's display with Miss Talbot or Elaine's awkwardness. She had not quite known how to act after he took her hand. She still didn't know why he had done it, or why her hand had tingled while her heart raced. Elaine suspected Penelope could help her, but what would her friend think if she wrote asking for advice about a different Ashburn?

"Miss Brooke."

Elaine stopped halfway to the gate. Sir Phillip was walking towards her. She waited, though every part of her wanted to escape. His long strides soon brought him before her. He gave a slight bow before speaking quickly but precisely.

"I fear I did not express myself well in the church. I am pleased you will be teaching."

"You are?"

"Of course. You are intelligent, insightful, and patient. I cannot think of a better person." His blue eyes pierced her as much as his compliments. She looked down at the ground and her dirty hem. The sounds of the village filtered around them as neither spoke.

"I brought this for you."

She looked up. He was holding out a black leather book.

"I thought you didn't know I was the teacher?" Elaine looked from him to the book.

"I didn't. Yesterday you left the library without selecting something to read. I was going to bring this to the lodge but since you are here. . ."

"Thank you." Elaine reached for the book, careful not to brush his hand. She looked at the title. "*The Faerie Queene*," she read aloud.

"I thought you might appreciate it. There are lots of knights and quests."

Elaine was flattered by his attention and his choice. If he thought her equal to Spenser's prose, he must think her a capable reader.

She smiled. "I can't resist tales of daring. An excellent choice."

Sir Phillip smiled and ducked his head at her praise. She suddenly had no problem imagining him being a knight rescuing a lady from a dragon. "If you need more such tales, the library is at your disposal."

"You are too kind," she demurred.

"I am happy to share it with such a great reader."

"Thank you." The praise warmed her like hot soup on a cold day. Mama would wish her to protest further but she could not. "I have greatly missed books since I returned to the lodge. My father had a sizable library but. . ." Elaine stopped short of admitting they had been deemed a needless expense.

"I recall Mr. Brooke loved reading. My father often wrote of how he enjoyed discussing literature with him."

"He used to say that a good book could cure all ills."

"He sounds remarkably wise. I am sorry I never got to meet him," he said earnestly.

Elaine hugged the book to her chest as memories of Papa swept through her and threatened to pull her under. But she didn't wish to run away or change the subject, she wished to share her memories with Sir Phillip. Her recollections would be safe with him.

He would listen seriously, ask thoughtful questions, and not interrupt her. They might walk together for hours as she told stories. She yearned to make that dream a reality. The desire was almost frightening. When had she come to see Sir Phillip as a confidant?

* * *

That night at the hall, Elaine was no closer to answering her question and

Freddie prevented her from contemplating it. Her friend immediately came to her side when she arrived.

"Mr. Ashburn has been absent all day," Freddie whispered. "I am in such a state of anticipation. I have determined that I won't even look at him."

"And what will you do if he speaks to you?" Elaine whispered back.

"I shall say as little as required."

Elaine patted her hand. "And I will be by your side."

"Thank you, Elaine."

"And what are you two whispering about?"

They spun around to see Daniel had come up behind them. He was smiling broadly, ready to tease. Only a week ago it might have been an irresistible look, but recalling his treatment of her friend, Elaine was not charmed. She frowned and hoped Freddie was doing the same.

His eyes jumped between them; his smile flickered like a candle in a drafty hallway.

"Good evening, Mr. Ashburn," Freddie said coolly.

"Miss Talbot, Miss Brooke." He echoed her formality.

"Excuse us," Freddie said and turned away from him.

Elaine followed but not before she saw Daniel's face fall. Despite her frustration and determination to support Freddie, she pitied him. His actions were not clear but he was not indifferent. Should she tell Freddie?"

The other young woman let out a small sigh. "There, the worst is over."

"You did very well."

"How were his looks? I confess I averted my eyes as soon as I heard his voice. I do not think I could have walked away if I had truly seen him. His smiles always quell my anger."

Elaine was saved from an answer by the announcement of dinner.

Throughout the meal, she carefully observed Freddie and Daniel. They were seated on opposite sides of the table and both seemed intent on ignoring the other. Daniel gave no signs of distress and talked animatedly with the guests beside him. Freddie was more subdued, but still looked pleased with her companions. Anyone might think that the two of them were strangers.

Elaine glanced at Sir Phillip several times to gauge his reaction to this turn of events. He appeared relaxed. He even smiled and raised his drink to her, causing her heart to flutter and her thoughts to turn in a different direction.

After dinner, the party retired to the morning room. Chairs had been set up facing the doors that opened to the adjoining music room. The piano forte was framed in the doorway and several other instruments were on hand for the musical evening.

"What are you playing?" Freddie asked from beside her. "Mother insisted I play a concerto; she finds them elegant. I spent half the morning practicing. I am excessively glad I did not agree to a duet with Mr. Ashburn."

Elaine half-listened to Freddie's remarks. She should not have agreed to perform. She stretched her fingers, willing them to play without fault. Mr. Henry, her music master, would be appalled that she had not practiced in preparation for the event. But there was no piano at the lodge. She had been reduced to moving her fingers over a flat surface and hoping her memory was accurate.

Freddie went to sit by Mrs. Farthing, but Elaine begged their pardon and took a turn about the room. The piano always seemed to be in the corner of her eye, taunting her. She paused at the far window and turned her back on the instrument.

When her turn came, she would sit down and find she had forgotten how to play entirely. Or she might start only to get muddled in the middle and have to begin again. Her voice might break on the high note at the end. Everyone else would play flawlessly and pity her for her lack of instrument and talent. Sir Phillip would look disappointed as she stood. That thought increased her nerves more than the others.

Something brushed her shoulder and she turned to see Sir Phillip had come up beside her.

When had the men arrived?

His head was cocked as he studied her. How long had he been watching her? She met his blue eyes.

Noticing her attention, he leaned toward her and whispered. "My father always said that if you act with confidence, nobody will know you are scared."

"Is that what you do?"

He raised his eyebrows and his eyes danced.

"Truly?" she asked.

He flashed a quick smile and leaned away.

Sir Phillip got scared? She could hardly credit it. But he was a being of flesh and blood, of course he would have fears and anxieties. She hadn't expected him to admit to such things. First, he approved of her as a teacher and now this? Had she somehow won his good opinion? The thought was more overwhelming than her impending performance. Discomfited, she avoided his gaze and glanced again at the piano.

Captain Hart stood there with Lady Ashburn. Their looks were fond and their conversation animated. She thought again how well suited they seemed but dared not say it aloud. When she turned to Sir Phillip, he was also watching them, a thoughtful look upon his face.

"They do make a charming couple," he said.

How many times would he surprise her this evening?

His eyes cut to her. "I have shocked you."

"You must admit that you were once opposed to even a mention of the idea."

"It was not exactly opposition. I do want my mother to be happy."

"But it upset you when I mentioned Captain Hart might be the method of her gaining happiness. Why?"

He sighed and paused in thought. "I suppose it was a kind of fear. I feared the changes that might come if you were right. My mother has been my greatest support. I was not fit to be a baronet at nineteen and would have failed on my own. I cannot imagine this place without her. What will happen if she leaves? Or worse, what if she stays for my sake and is unhappy?"

"Have you spoken to her of this?" Elaine asked.

"I have only just understood my predicament." The look he gave her was unmistakably tender. "You have an uncanny ability to help me understand myself."

She had no ready reply.

"If everyone will please take their seats." Lady Ashburn called the room to order.

Sir Phillip accompanied Elaine to a seat beside Freddie and then withdrew to stand at the back.

Her mind was racing, so she was grateful for the distance. What did it mean that he gave her a book? That he sought to comfort her and shared his fears? If he were any other man, she would have dreamed several possibilities. But that Sir Phillip might care for her was beyond even her imagination.

Elaine sought the distraction of the performers. She was surprised by the talent on display. Mrs. Cooper played a haunting melody on the harp, Captain Hart livened the room with an Irish air on his violin, and the Farthings charmed everyone with their duet. As the notes of the duet faded, Elaine swallowed. It was her turn. Freddie squeezed her hand in support.

She stood and glanced at Sir Phillip.

"Confidence." He mouthed.

She lifted her chin, squared her shoulders, and strode forward. She sat at the instrument. With no sheet music to arrange, she gently laid her hands on the keys, took a deep breath, and repeated the word "confidence" in her mind.

Once she began, she felt easier, the music as comfortable as an old glove. When she opened her mouth to sing, she was no longer nervous. She made several errors but they did not ruin the performance. When she finished, the applause was gratifying. Her gaze went to Sir Phillip. He smiled and nodded. Her heart tripped. Why was his approval so much more important than the others?

Suddenly Daniel was beside her, offering an arm and showering her with praise. She could not refuse him in front of everyone and allowed herself to be led to a different seat. Daniel took the seat beside her as Freddie began to play. Her talent and practice was evident. Despite the difficulty of the piece, she played flawlessly. Elaine was glad she did not have to follow such perfection.

"I prefer your easy and lighthearted music," Daniel whispered.

Once she would have delighted in such a comparison to Miss Talbot. Now she was vexed. She gave him a quelling look and returned her attention to the performance. But he was not deterred and made several more remarks. She ignored him, but he didn't seem to care. He continued to smile.

Was he attempting to make Freddie jealous? Had his compliments to her always been about Freddie? But no, when they first met, there had been no audience but the birds in the trees. Knowing what had happened in London, Elaine saw that meeting differently now. How dejected Freddie must have felt to have him absent at her arrival. Did he not understand how hurtful his behavior was? Or did he not care? She could not believe the tender boy had grown into a callous man.

Elaine was beginning to understand why Sir Phillip was so frustrated with his brother. It was lowering to think how blind she had been to Daniel's faults, how ready to overlook and forgive. She would always be his friend, but she would not let him use her like a pawn.

Chapter Sixteen

P hillip rose early the morning of the excursion to the Old Priory. His agitation for the day was only slightly allayed by the blue sky and gentle, fluffy clouds. The source of his worry was not the comfort of his guests, nor the evident falling out between Miss Talbot and Daniel. He was worried about seeing Miss Brooke. Their interactions continued to be varied and it was becoming increasingly important that she think well of him. He didn't like to examine the reasons why.

Unable to sleep, Phillip attended to his correspondence but struggled to focus. His thoughts constantly strayed to recent events. While reading about a plan for a new canal he found himself remembering a conversation with Miss Brooke. When examining bills from London he couldn't help but recall the night before.

The musical evening had allowed the party entertainment and a chance to display. The Farthings, Mrs. Cooper, Captain Hart, and Miss Talbot had all displayed admirable skill. But it was Miss Brooke's performance that had captivated Phillip. She sang a ballad and though not technically perfect, he found it enchanting. Almost as enchanting as their conversation in the churchyard. Each memory brought on another and he was soon lost.

When Phillip finally managed to stop thinking of Miss Brooke and finish his letters, he found it was nearing the time for their departure for the ruins.

In haste, he made his way to the breakfast room.

He was surprised to find Mother and Captain Hart the only two at the table, sitting across from each other. There was nothing improper, but their plates were empty and neither looked up from their conversation when he entered.

Phillip went to the sideboard and began to fill a plate. Was she being a good hostess or was there something more between them? Was Miss Brooke right? Should he simply ask Mother her feelings? He did not know how to broach such a subject.

No longer hungry, Phillip took his half-filled plate to the table.

As he approached, Captain Hart looked up. "Good morning, Sir Phillip." Was the man nervous?

"Good morning, Captain, Mother," Phillip said as he took the empty seat between them.

"I thought you had already eaten." Mother gave him a questioning look.

"I was detained with business."

"But you are still going with the guests?"

"Yes, of course." Phillip turned to Captain Hart. "Are you sure you would not like to visit the ruins?"

"No, I thank you. I have been to them before."

"I didn't realize. Were you previously acquainted with the neighborhood?" He didn't know much of Captain Hart's background. The man was an old friend of the family, but Phillip didn't know how or when the friendship was formed.

The captain's eyes darted to Mother before he replied. "Tolerably acquainted."

"I am sure Captain Hart would much rather go shooting," Mother interjected. "There are only a few days left."

"Indeed," Captain Hart agreed. "In fact, I should go and change." The captain stood and took a quick leave.

Thoughtfully, Phillip watched his mother as her eyes followed Captain Hart. The conversation last night with Miss Brooke had renewed his determination to understand Mother's feelings. He did not spy any affection;

if anything, she looked vexed. They sat in silence as Phillip ate and Lady Ashburn stirred her chocolate. She stared out the large windows that overlooked the lake and the country beyond, wearing the same expression Miss Brooke often had when distracted. He was almost finished eating when she turned to him.

"I apologize for being so dull. Tell me, what business detained you?"

Phillip could hardly tell her what thoughts had actually preoccupied him and so said the first thing that came to mind. "Mr. Eden had questions about the parish school."

"I thought you were going to wait until next year?"

"That was because I believed I would need to wait until I could offer a higher salary, but Eden found a willing teacher."

Lady Ashburn raised an imperious eyebrow. "You never told me there was a problem with funding the school."

"It wasn't a problem. I simply didn't want to employ anyone if there was a chance of not having the funds. If there was an unexpected expense. . ." Phillip trailed off, unwilling to explain.

Mother nodded and reached for his hand. "Daniel is fortunate you are his older brother. I know this house party was not an expected expense and Daniel has not made your matchmaking easy."

Phillip chuckled wryly. "I think he deliberately tries to thwart me."

"I can't understand it," Mother said. "I thought their Sleeping Beauty tableau was a kind of declaration, but last night Miss Talbot seemed intent on avoiding him entirely. Do you think they quarreled?"

"It is very likely."

Phillip didn't know what had changed but it seemed Daniel had lost the favor of both Miss Talbot and Miss Brooke. Daniel was never out of favor for long; his charm would likely win them over again.

Lady Ashburn thought for a moment while she sipped her chocolate. "I will have a chat with Daniel."

"If you think it best."

Phillip was happy to let his mother try to untangle whatever was wrong between Miss Talbot and his brother. He could not muster his former interest in the scheme.

"It is time I talk with him. And furthermore, I want to help fund the school. I would have offered sooner if you had told me of the need."

Phillip tried to object but she raised her hand. "No, I insist. I have always had complete discretion with my funds and it will be no hardship. Since Miss Brooke finished school, I have had excess and this is a good cause."

"What do you mean since Miss Brooke finished school?" Phillip frowned in confusion.

"I paid for her schooling in Bath, you knew that."

Phillip shook his head. "No."

Mother hummed. "I suppose it was decided by your father while you were away at school, but I am sure we discussed it at some point."

"I assure you I would remember."

She shrugged. "Well, no matter. It was a good use of the money. She has turned into such a fine young woman. Such lively conversation and she sang beautifully last night."

"She did." Phillip tried not to smile at the memory. "But your investment was better than you know, for Miss Brooke is to be the new teacher."

Mother looked pleased. "Is she? How wonderful. Then I positively insist on helping to ensure she is well-compensated."

Mother's generosity was welcome. Miss Brooke deserved a much higher salary.

"With your permission, I will inform her today of the salary increase."

"I think that a fine idea. There is no need to tell her why it increased."

Phillip wasn't sure he deserved the approbation Miss Brooke would likely feel but he was excited to see her reaction to the information. He thanked Mother again and finished his breakfast quickly. His anticipation for the day was heightened by the good news he had to convey.

* * *

The walls of the Old Priory, though in places crumbling and mismatched, had stood for centuries; a window to the past and future. The ruins would continue long after Phillip was gone. Perhaps his great-grandchildren might visit them.

The white and yellow stone was speckled green with moss or in some places completely obscured by the plants growing around and from the walls, giving the picturesque effect so admired in London. His guests were satisfactorily awed as the carriages came to a stop beside a tumbled-down wall.

The party consisted of Daniel, the Farthings, Mrs. and Miss Talbot, Miss Wilson and Mrs. Cooper, and Miss Brooke. To Phillip's consternation, Daniel had fetched Miss Brooke in his phaeton and left him with Miss Wilson and Mrs. Cooper crammed into the gig. The ladies didn't seem to mind and kept up a lively dialogue about the priory, peppering Phillip with questions and waxing long on other ruins they had visited.

At any other time, Phillip would have enjoyed their conversation, but his mind kept wandering to Miss Brooke and Daniel at the back of their procession. What were they speaking of? Was Miss Brooke enjoying her time with him? Now that Miss Talbot was cold, had Daniel turned his sights back to their neighbor?

Phillip ground his teeth at the thought. They arrived at the priory and Phillip tried to focus on his duty, helping his passengers down from the gig and moving to the front of the party.

"Welcome to Ashford Priory," he gestured to the ruins. "It was established around 1250 by an Augustan order and dedicated to Saint Helen. Quite a small endeavor, it barely kept twelve monks at a time and was of course dissolved by Henry VIII."

"Oh, of course," Daniel said in what he probably thought was a whisper.

Phillip ignored him. "After the dissolution, we believe the church was used as a barn and much of the stone from the outbuildings was taken for new construction. Today the church is mostly intact while foundations and half walls are all that remain of other buildings. All the ruins are part of Priory Farm. They often graze sheep or cattle here so as you explore, do mind your step." All the ladies were wearing sensible half-boots but Phillip thought the warning necessary. "When you are done exploring, lunch will be available there." He indicated a grassy area nearby where the servants had already started to set up an awning and chairs.

"Let us hope the sheep haven't gathered there first," Daniel quipped.

Nobody laughed. Phillip had, of course, had the area cleared of any manure but he did not feel the need to say so. Miss Wilson and Mrs. Cooper thanked him and set off for the ruins with their heads turning every which way.

"The light is so perfect," Mrs. Farthing said. "I think I will paint now and explore later. What do you say, Miss Talbot?"

"Yes, I believe you are right."

"Excellent," Farthing said. "Let me show you the perfect prospect." He offered his arm.

"There is a better view than this?" His wife asked as she took it.

"Though I do not have your artist's eye, I believe you will prefer the view from the east."

Mrs. Farthing smiled affectionately. "I trust you. Miss Talbot?"

Miss Talbot smiled at the couple before looking to her mother.

"As long as there is shade, the sun is quite strong today," Mrs. Talbot said.

"The servants will bring a covering with the easels," Phillip assured her.

"Thank you, Sir Phillip, you are so thoughtful," Mrs. Talbot smiled at him before turning to Farthing. "Lead on."

It did not escape Phillip's notice that the Talbots ignored Daniel. Something had definitely changed in their opinion of him. Phillip was certain Daniel escorting Miss Brooke had not helped.

The group had only taken a few steps before Daniel turned to Miss Brooke. "I am so glad you are not painting. I could not abide having to sit by your side doing nothing." He spoke louder than necessary. The words were meant for more than just her ears.

"You forget, Mr. Ashburn. I have not asked you to stay beside me." Miss Brooke cast a quick glance at Phillip. "You are free to spend your afternoon as you wish."

"I wish for you to go driving with me." Daniel's smile was at its most charming, but Miss Brooke shook her head.

"We are here to explore the ruins."

"You have seen the priory countless times. You can't tell me you wish to wander around those old stones like we did as children?" Daniel was incredulous.

Miss Brooke stood firm. "Why would I have come if not to see these old stones?"

Phillip didn't even try hiding his smile as he stepped forward. "Miss Brooke, may I escort you?"

She looked up at him, her green eyes particularly fetching in the sun, but she did not take his arm. She looked at Daniel, who had an uncharacteristic frown, and for a moment Phillip thought she would choose to go driving after all. But her chin lifted and she met Phillip's eyes.

"No, thank you," she said gently. "I am quite capable of exploring on my own."

She walked away without a backward glance. Perplexed and hurt, Phillip watched her. Her words reminded him of their last meeting at the priory. Was she still upset at what he had said? Surely she knew how he regretted those words? Or did she prefer being alone to his company?

Daniel slapped Phillip on the shoulder. "I don't suppose you want to go driving with me?"

Phillip gave him a withering look.

"No, I thought not. No doubt you wish me to go sit at Miss Talbot's feet and fawn over her every brush stroke," Daniel spoke bitterly.

Phillip sighed. "I don't care what you do as long as you don't offend our guests." Without waiting for a reply, he began walking to the ruins, careful to veer to the west so that he would not encounter the painters or Miss Brooke. He had no desire to inflict his company on her when it was not wanted.

He wandered among the remaining foundations and half walls of the outbuildings. His mind turned to the morning he came upon Miss Brooke. At the time he had felt justified but now he was embarrassed by his conduct. She was fanciful, but not imprudent. Hardly an evening passed without her becoming lost in her thoughts. But it did not follow that she would meet a man in secret.

167

As he approached what remained of the church, he heard Miss Wilson and Mrs. Cooper talking. Their voices bounced off the mostly intact walls and drifted to him through the dramatic window arches. The windows were open to nature, the glass long gone, the ragged teeth of stone all that remained of once complicated ornamentation.

Through the window, he saw them in the middle of what remained of the building. Their heads were bent, examining a weathered statue on one of the columns. They were so engrossed that he did not think they noticed him. He was about to turn away and continue wandering the outbuildings when Mrs. Cooper called out.

"Sir Phillip, there you are. Perhaps you can settle our debate. Do you think this statue is of the Virgin Mary or Saint Helen?"

"Apologies, but I can't see it from here."

"Come and look." Miss Wilson beckoned impatiently.

Instead of walking around to an opening in the wall, Phillip placed his hands on the rough window frame and vaulted over it. In a few strides he was beside the ladies and the statue. He came up short when Miss Brooke appeared from behind the column, glancing nervously at him.

"So, what do you think?" Mrs. Cooper asked.

He turned his attention to the weathered carving. The years had worn it down to a robed figure with a smoothed face. It was clearly a woman, but which of the many female saints he could not be sure. Her arms, and whatever they held, had been lost to time. He reached out and touched her cheek. He had come to see the statues as kind friends with listening ears that kept a vigil over the once sacred space.

"I like to think it is Mary but I have no evidence."

Miss Wilson made a dismissive sound.

Mrs. Cooper smiled. "Now Genia, don't be upset that nobody agrees with you. And I, for one, find Miss Brooke's evidence compelling."

He looked at Miss Brooke but her eyes quickly moved to the statue. "It is hard to see, but here." She reached out and touched a place on the statue's chest. "It looks as if this might have been part of a blanket."

"How clever. I have never noticed that detail," Phillip said.

Miss Brooke met his eyes and pink suffused her cheeks. He quite liked it when she blushed.

"Margaret, come look, it is lady's smock." Miss Wilson's attention had wandered away from the conversation and was caught by the flowers that grew where the altar once stood.

"Really? A fairy flower on a Christian altar?" Mrs. Cooper followed her sister, leaving Phillip with Miss Brooke.

"Have you examined all the statues so thoroughly?" Phillip asked in an attempt to keep Miss Brooke from joining the other women.

She tilted her head. "I spent a lot of time here as a child making up stories and sometimes the statues became part of them."

"I played similar games. Although I am sure your stories were better than mine."

"By which you mean I am too fanciful."

"I did not say that."

She sighed. "But it is true. I'm always letting my thoughts run away from me."

"I can hardly condemn you for that. Especially given the presumptions I made the last time we were here."

She looked away. "I did give you reason to suspect."

"My actions were still unpardonable."

"Do you wish to argue over blame?"

"I do not wish to argue with you at all."

"Oh." She looked down at her hands.

Unsure of what to say, he turned his attention to their surroundings. Miss Wilson and Mrs. Cooper were picking flowers at the altar.

What remained of the church was Phillip's favorite part of the Old Priory. He loved the way the light came through the empty windows and illuminated the carpet of overgrown grass and wildflowers. Here pews once sat and worshippers sent petitions to heaven. The prayers seemed to still linger over the place, giving it a hushed and solemn air.

"I know it is not a great wonder of the world but I find it uniquely beautiful here," Miss Brooke said.

"The earth, and every common sight, to me did seem appareled in celestial light," Phillip quoted. Wordsworth's poem seemed appropriate. Without Miss Brooke's influence he would not have made time to read it. Miss Brooke was silent. Unsure, he turned to her.

"You are not quite what I thought," she said.

"Careful, Miss Brooke. I might think you are trying to compliment me." He smiled wryly.

"It is no compliment to my judgment but certainly a compliment to your character."

"If I had known quoting Wordsworth was all that was required to win your favor, I would have showered you with odes."

"My favor is not won so cheaply."

"No?" Phillip smiled. Seized with a roguish notion, he leaned toward her. "Tell me, Miss Brooke, how might one gain your favor?"

"You are teasing me," she frowned.

He sobered. He leaned away, feeling foolish and wishing he could take back his ill-advised words. "I—uh, I beg your pardon. You must be wishing me gone so you can rejoin Miss Wilson and Mrs. Cooper."

He gestured to the altar only to realize that the two sisters were no longer there. It was just him, Miss Brooke, and the birds fluttering between the pillars. Would that he could fly away. He gave a stiff bow and strode toward the entrance.

Phillip berated himself as he walked. What had possessed him? He was not Daniel to be flirting so outrageously with the woman who had rejected his company only a half hour before. Did Daniel ever land in such awkward situations? Phillip blamed Farthing for encouraging him and his own foolish heart for wishing Miss Brooke welcomed his attention.

Unwilling to risk another encounter, Phillip returned to where lunch was almost ready. He had hoped to have some problem to solve, but the servants were too efficient. The shades, tables, chairs, and food were all laid out.

Phillip sank into a chair and accepted the glass of lemonade Tom offered him. The cool morning had turned to a warm afternoon and he was grateful for the shade, though the heat beneath his skin had little to do with the sun.

The Farthings and Talbots soon joined him, speaking of their reluctance to leave their canvases. Shortly after, Miss Wilson and Mrs. Cooper appeared with Daniel between them as they talked animatedly of the ruins.

Phillip restrained himself from asking after Miss Brooke and was gratified when she finally appeared. Though he did not meet her eyes or speak to her, he caught Tom's eye and ensured she had a glass of lemonade the moment she stepped under the shade.

The conversation during lunch was lively as the painters and explorers exchanged information. Art, history, and other similar ruins were all discussed. Phillip was happy to listen without participating and managed several furtive looks at Miss Brooke. She sat beside Miss Talbot eating with a polite expression.

Miss Wilson drew him into the conversation. "Did you know, Sir Phillip, in Glastonbury Abbey they claim to have found the grave of King Arthur?"

"I had heard that."

"Sir Phillip enjoys King Arthur legends," Miss Wilson explained to the group.

"Doesn't everyone?" Daniel asked.

Miss Wilson sniffed and launched into an explanation of why she disliked chivalric romances. She seemed to take particular issue with Sir Lancelot. For a person who didn't like the legends, she certainly had a comprehensive knowledge of them.

Eventually Mrs. Cooper broke into the lecture. "Yes, sister, but many find them enjoyable." She gave Miss Wilson a long-suffering look.

"Right, of course." Miss Wilson smiled sheepishly and took a sip of her lemonade.

"Miss Brooke loves King Arthur," Daniel said. "Aren't you named for the mother of Sir Galahad?"

Phillip was annoyed by Daniel's secretive smile and the reminder of his brother's intimate knowledge of Miss Brooke.

"It is true, my father picked the name from the legends, but Galahad's mother was Elaine of Corbenic. I am named for Elaine of Astolat."

Phillip didn't hide his smile; perhaps Daniel didn't know Miss Brooke that well after all.

"Elaine of Astolat?" Miss Talbot asked. "I don't recall that story."

"There is no reason why you should. It is a very minor one compared to Elaine of Corbenic."

"Now, don't leave us in suspense," Farthing said.

"Yes, you must tell us her story," Jane Farthing added.

With all eyes on her, Miss Brooke had no choice but to speak.

Chapter Seventeen

⸙

T hough Elaine had often thought of the story of her namesake, she had no experience in sharing it. She could see her father as he told the story, smiling and pausing for dramatic effect, but such a performance did not seem proper for their gathering. She attempted to tell the tragic tale in as few words as possible.

"Elaine was the daughter of a baron and Sir Lancelot came to her family's lodge. She fell in love with the knight and even nursed him back to health after he was wounded. But Lancelot could not return her feelings because he was in love with Guinevere. When Lancelot was healed, he left the fair maiden of Astolat and returned to Camelot. Elaine's love was so great that she could not live without him and died. Her parents put her body in a boat and sent it down the Thames towards Camelot. When it was discovered how and why she died, Lancelot was devastated and buried her richly."

"I thought Guinevere was married to King Arthur?" Freddie asked.

"And so she was," Miss Wilson said primly. "These tales of courtly love." She shook her head.

"It seems to me," Farthing said, "that Sir Lancelot has a lot to answer for."

"Is it Lancelot's fault the lady developed feelings for him?" Daniel sounded as if Farthing had attacked his honor.

"No," Sir Phillip interjected. "But Lancelot encouraged the lady's feelings.

Miss Brooke didn't mention the part where Lancelot agreed to wear her favor, an honor he had not granted to any lady before. He created an expectation he had no intention of meeting and thus dishonored himself."

"Here, here," Mr. Farthing said.

Elaine was surprised by Sir Phillip's memory. Perhaps he had just read the story?

Mrs. Farthing broke in with soothing tones. "I think we can all agree that Elaine of Astolat's fate was tragic."

"Indeed," Mrs. Talbot said. "How strange your father should name you for her."

"My father was a singular man." Elaine didn't know what else to say.

"My father always spoke well of Mr. Brooke," Sir Phillip said with his unique gravity. And though Elaine had been avoiding looking at him, she met his eyes and gave him a grateful smile.

"I was named for my grandfather," Daniel said into the tense silence.

Everyone gladly took up the change in subject and began to share the origins of their names. Elaine was relieved to have their attention diverted. She had always been pleased with her namesake. When Papa told the story of the Fair Maid of Astolat, it had seemed beautiful and tragic; the ultimate expression of a love that outweighed all else. That the Lady Elaine's love for Lancelot was so all-consuming that it brought her to her grave had seemed an ideal to aspire to. She had come to consider herself like her namesake, pining for a man that did not return her feelings, who did not really see her.

Daniel's very indifference had seemed proof that her love for him was of the same epic type as Elaine and Lancelot. In retrospect, it seemed quite silly. Now Elaine agreed with the Farthings. It was tragic and Lancelot did have a lot to answer for.

Why had Papa enjoyed the story? Was his passion for Mama just as fierce? They had married against her parents' wishes; surely, they had had a great love. Even all these years later Mama had not remarried, had not so much as looked at a man. Despite all her imaginings and obsessing over Daniel, Elaine wasn't sure she loved him in that way. Returning home had allowed her to see him more clearly. Perhaps if the Lady Elaine had spent more time with Lancelot, she would have realized he wasn't worthy of her life?

Elaine loved Daniel, but if he married Freddie she would not pine away. Women could live full and happy lives even when they lost their great loves. Mrs. Piper and Mama were proof of that. If Elaine of Astolat had tried she could have found other things to live for, perhaps even a man that could have returned her love.

Her eyes sought Sir Phillip.

He was watching her, a question in his gaze. She was surprised to understand the question. He was worried. She smiled faintly to reassure him. He nodded to show he understood and then turned his attention to a footman.

How long had he been watching while she lapsed into a reverie? And what did his worry signify? Did he care for her? When he had asked how to gain her favor had he been in earnest? It seemed impossible but more likely than him casually teasing.

The party began to break up. Miss Wilson and Mrs. Cooper announced their desire to make sketches and detailed notes of the ruins.

"I am quite ready to continue admiring your canvas," Mr. Farthing said as he stood and offered his hand to his wife.

"I will be ready for your raptures when you wake from your nap," Mrs. Farthing returned.

Freddie and Elaine shared a smile as they also stood. Elaine thought she might accompany the painters, having explored enough.

"I did not realize we would be spending the entire day." Mrs. Talbot stayed seated, looking fatigued.

"Mama, if you wish to return to the hall, I am sure we might go." Freddie sat back down beside her mother.

"I do not wish to be a bother. I will just sit here under the shade until you are done."

Freddie bit her lip and looked at Elaine and the Farthings.

"I would gladly take you, Mrs. Talbot," Daniel said from across the table. "My phaeton is well-sprung and provides a capital view." His tone was light and persuasive as if he would like nothing more than to drive Mrs. Talbot.

"That is very considerate of you." Sir Phillip sounded surprised.

"Oh, well." Mrs. Talbot shared a look with her daughter. "If it is no trouble, then I really would prefer to go back."

"No trouble at all." Daniel offered his arm with a flourish.

"Thank you, Mr. Ashburn," Freddie said.

Elaine thought Daniel's smile grew wider as he assured her he was happy to oblige. Elaine wondered if it was the first kind word between them in two days. Freddie had been steadfast in ignoring Daniel though it was evident it pained them both.

Daniel and the Talbots moved to the carriages. Elaine waited for Freddie while the others departed for the ruins. Sir Phillip made no attempt to leave her or to speak. She avoided his gaze by looking at the carriages.

Their last encounter hung between them. She had been unprepared for him to apologize again. It discomfited her because the fault was not his alone. Then he had quoted Wordsworth and teased her. A week and a half ago, she would have thought that out of character, but she was beginning to realize she had misjudged him entirely, just as she had misjudged Daniel.

Just as she had misjudged her heart.

"Miss Brooke, I hope Mrs. Talbot's words did not injure you," Sir Phillip said carefully.

"I thank you for your concern, but I am not upset." She smiled at him. "It is natural she would find my namesake an odd one."

"I think Elaine is a beautiful name."

Her heart skittered at the compliment. She liked hearing her name in his baritone voice.

"Thank you."

They smiled at each other until a sound from the carriages drew their attention. Daniel was departing with Mrs. Talbot. Soon Freddie would join them. Elaine hoped her friend walked slowly.

"I have some business to attend to at Priory Farm," Sir Phillip said. "I will return before anyone is ready to leave. But if I am missed, will you please make my apologies and inform them where I went?"

"Yes, of course."

"You are not going to scold me for being unable to relax and enjoy the afternoon?"

Elaine held back a sigh. Would he always be suspecting her of censure? "I did not mean to imply that you should never attend to your duties. I honor the attention you pay to your many responsibilities."

His posture loosened and he looked as if he might say something further. He glanced at Freddie, who had just started back towards them before he spoke.

"I was hoping you might help me with one of my responsibilities."

"I would be happy to help in any way."

"You might not be so eager when you know what I ask." Sir Phillip ran a hand through his hair. Elaine had seen him do that before. Was he nervous? The great baronet nervous? A month ago, she would not have thought it possible.

"Miss Brooke, will you do me the honor of dancing the first set at the assembly?"

Never could she have expected such an invitation. But however unexpected the invitation, Elaine was pleased and did not hide it.

"Yes, I thank you. I would love to dance the first set with you."

He gave a broad smile that left Elaine breathless. There was no misunderstanding that look. Sir Phillip was elated with her acceptance.

Freddie reached them and he took a hasty leave. Elaine had no time to think of what had passed as she turned to her friend.

"That was so kind of Mr. Ashburn to drive Mama home," Freddie said.

"Yes, it was." Elaine was relieved not to talk of Sir Phillip. What would she say?

"Her health is not strong and I did not want her overtaxed. He seemed to know my thoughts on the matter and was quite willing to give up his own pleasure to assist."

Elaine could detect the thawing of Freddie's reserve in her warm tone.

"Such kindness is a good step toward regaining your favor." Elaine twined her arm into Miss Talbot's. She would not be a hypocrite. She would not tell Freddie to be practical or to control her heart. How could she when her own heart was creating havoc?

* * *

The next evening, Elaine's heart was still unruly as she dressed for the assembly. Her mind kept conjuring scenarios for the night ahead and she kept telling herself to be sensible. She had already imagined herself in love once. She did not wish to repeat the mistake.

When she entered the drawing room, Mama smiled warmly. "You look lovely. That shade of blue suits you. It was so kind of Miss Talbot to give you such a fine petticoat."

"Thank you, Mama."

The petticoat had been waiting when Elaine returned from the ruins. Freddie had left a note insisting that Elaine wear it to the assembly. She was touched by the gift and her pleasure only increased when she saw how lovely it looked underneath her Indian muslin.

Would Sir Phillip think it suited her?

"You will be one of the finest young women at the assembly," Mama said. "Were you rich, I daresay you would be swimming in suitors by the evening's end."

Elaine reached for her mother's hand. "Then I am happy to be poor, for I would not wish to drown in so much attention."

"You are a good girl." Mama patted her hand. "At least with Sir Phillip leading the way, you will not want for partners."

Elaine blushed.

"Such a kind and thoughtful neighbor to show you favor."

"Yes, very kind."

Since learning that Sir Phillip had asked for Elaine's first set, Mama had praised his kindness and condescension. It was enough to make Elaine question his motives. Had Sir Phillip asked her out of obligation? They had been speaking of his responsibilities so perhaps she had presumed too much. But what of his smile?

"And perhaps one of your partners will wish to become better acquainted?"

"Mama, please. I have no expectations of finding a husband tonight."

"You should at least be open to the possibility."

"Yes, Mama." Elaine gave a placating smile. How could she think of other men while Sir Phillip was in the room?

He would lead her to the top of the dance and take her hand. All eyes would be upon them, speculation would race about the room as they began their figures but Elaine would notice only the spark in his eyes. The music would begin and they would move together perfectly. Sir Phillip would smile and say—

Here Elaine's imagination failed her.

She did not know what he would say. She could not imagine him speaking of love or courtship nor could she imagine arguing with him. She understood him better now. He had agreed to let her teach at the school. Surely his opinion of her had changed as hers had. But how much?

Last night they had barely spoken, which only increased her anxiety.

The crunch of carriage wheels pulled Elaine from her thoughts. Mrs. Leigh had arrived to take them to Oakbury.

When they entered the Oakbury assembly rooms, the last rays of the setting sun shone through the tall window bouncing off the mirrors and draping the room in golden light. Soon the beeswax candles would be lit and transform the space with their twinkling. Elaine was glad they had arrived early enough to see it bathed in sunlight.

Elaine trailed after Mrs. Leigh and Mama as they made their way through the growing crowd. Every few steps, they stopped to greet someone. Over and over Elaine repeated how she was glad to be home and happy for the good weather. Her attention was not on the conversations but in scanning the room for Sir Phillip's tall form.

When her mother and Mrs. Leigh found seats, they immediately fell to talking behind their fans about those present.

"No doubt this crush is due to Sir Phillip's attendance," Mrs. Leigh said.

"I think people are equally curious about Miss Talbot and Mr. Ashburn," Mama replied.

Elaine did not blame her neighbors; she was also curious. Last night she had not found an opportunity for a private conversation with Freddie. But judging by her smiles, it appeared she was prepared to forgive Daniel. Elaine hoped they would reconcile. It was clear that Daniel truly cared for Freddie and he would be a fool if he did not use tonight to make amends.

"There are the Ashburns," Mrs. Leigh said.

All thoughts of Daniel and Miss Talbot fled as Elaine turned to catch sight of Sir Phillip. His evening dress was precisely fitted, his cravat hung in stylish waves, matching the brushed-back style of his hair. He looked every inch the baronet and Elaine was suddenly glad for her new petticoat. At least nobody would think her shabby next to him when they danced together.

A sea of people lay between them, yet Sir Phillip's blue eyes found hers. He leaned in to whisper something to Lady Ashburn and they began to move across the room, greeting people as they went.

Elaine's attention was diverted from the Ashburns by the approach of Mrs. and Miss Covington. While the older ladies made their greetings, Miss Covington sidled beside Elaine with a deadly sweet smile. She was dressed in the first stare of London fashion and looked out of place in the more modest Oakbury.

"And how do you find the assembly rooms, Miss Brooke? As fine as you expected?"

"I find them perfectly lovely," Elaine replied, unwilling to be goaded.

"I'm sure you do. I thought you were to be in Lady Ashburn's party?"

"Mrs. Leigh kindly offered her carriage."

"Yes, how fortunate to have such obliging friends."

"We have been very lucky in our friends." Elaine did not rise to the bait though she hated the reference to their poverty. What had she ever done to Miss Covington to deserve such barbed comments? Or was it the fact she was poor and thus unworthy of civility?

"Yes, the Ashburns have been very kind." Miss Covington fluttered her fan. "A pity their kindness does not extend to more permanent arrangements." Miss Covington's venom-tipped words were for Elaine's ears alone. "I understand Mr. Ashburn will soon be engaged to Miss Talbot."

Against her better judgment, Elaine replied. "When they marry, I will wish them happy. I desire nothing from Mr. Ashburn but honest friendship."

Miss Covington frowned and fluttered her fan, while Elaine turned back to the crowd in triumph. Though the words were ill-judged, Elaine would not take them back. It was the truth. She no longer wished for romantic love from Daniel Ashburn.

Mrs. Covington soon rose and they took their leave. Elaine wished she could avoid the Covingtons for the rest of her life, or at least the rest of the evening. Her frustration disappeared as Sir Phillip stepped through a gap in the crowd with Lady Ashburn on his arm.

As they greeted one another, she was warmed to her toes. She forgot all about Miss Covington as they exchanged inane pleasantries. Elaine hardly heard what was said. There were compliments to her dress, talk of the rooms, and a discussion of the weather. Then Lady Ashburn took a seat beside Mama just as Mr. Eden announced that the first dance was about to begin.

Sir Phillip offered his arm. "Shall we?"

Elaine gave him a shaky smile as she took it.

Just as she imagined, eyes and whispers followed them as they made their way to the top of the set. Elaine saw the jealousy and curiosity on her neighbors' faces. Sir Phillip was the most eligible man for miles and many had probably come to catch his attention, but he had bestowed it on his penniless neighbor. Did they, like Miss Covington, think it was pity? Would they all be waiting for her to misstep?

She was glad the minuet was no longer in fashion for she could not abide being the center of attention while performing such a complicated dance. They would only have to perform a few figures before being joined by the next couple in line.

The closer they got to the musicians, the more nervous Elaine became. Sir Phillip gave her hand a reassuring squeeze as they reached the top of the still-forming line. Elaine released Sir Phillip's arm and he turned to face her. She met his steady gaze; the ice blue of his eyes pierced her, but instead of freezing she was warmed.

He smiled and she knew that even if she danced abominably, he would not let anyone mock her. He was the baronet and leader of the neighborhood. As long as she had his favor, what did she care for others?

The music began and they moved into the figures. He took her hand and her heart fluttered out of time with the music. Soon she had forgotten all others, forgotten all her daydreams. She was focused only on the dance and the warm smiles of her partner.

Chapter Eighteen

Though Miss Brooke was not the most elegant nor the most precise of dancers, she was nevertheless the most enjoyable woman Phillip had ever partnered. He was so taken by her smiles, touches, and movement through the figures that they were halfway down the line before he remembered the necessity of polite conversation.

"It is quite the crush," he commented when they had a moment of peace.

"A compliment to you and the fine assembly rooms," Miss Brooke replied.

Phillip would not pretend to misunderstand her. It was hard not to notice all the eligible young ladies when he had been required to greet most of them on his way to claim Miss Brooke's hand.

Miss Brooke filled the silence. "I have not seen Captain Hart tonight. Did he decide to stay back with Mr. Poole and Mr. Evans?"

"No. I believe he came with the Talbots."

"I wonder if he will dance."

"Are you in need of a partner?" Phillip thought of volunteering to dance a second set with her. Now that would get the neighborhood gossips talking. The entire room had seemed to buzz like a hive as they had taken their place at the top of the set.

"I was not thinking of myself," she said.

Phillip followed her thoughts. "My mother?" Miss Brooke colored but

Phillip smirked. "Perhaps he will ask her. I have observed them carefully and I must confess you had the right of it. There is affection between them."

"They are a charming couple."

He laughed. Several eyes turned to them but he did not care.

They moved down the line and Phillip was surprised that the next couple was Daniel and Miss Talbot. He had been too preoccupied to notice. They were flushed and smiling, on much better terms than yesterday at the ruins. She was not immune to Daniel's charm after all.

As Daniel danced with Miss Brooke, they also smiled and laughed; she too was not immune. Phillip hated the jealousy that clawed at his throat and made his shoulders tense. When Miss Brooke returned to him, her eyes remained on Daniel. They took on that unfocused quality that he was coming to recognize. Did she still pine for Daniel? He had hoped her heart might be changing.

He wished to overturn her thoughts.

"And how goes your reading?" he asked.

"Hmm." Miss Brooke blinked and then returned her attention to him. "I'm sorry. Sir Phillip, I was not attending."

"Have you made more progress in *The Faerie Queene?*"

"Oh yes! It is wonderful. Spenser's writing is lyrical compared to Mallory. Are you still reading *Le Morte D'Arthur?*"

"I am. Though I confess I am enjoying it less than before."

"Really?"

They were separated by the dance. When they could speak again, Miss Brooke asked, "Why has your opinion changed?"

"After the discussion of Elaine of Astolat's tragic fate, I began to think differently of Sir Lancelot. He is not quite the hero I remembered."

"I have been thinking the same."

"Truly?" Phillip was surprised. When Miss Brooke had recounted the tale of Elaine of Astolat he had been sure she thought it admirable.

"I had not thought of the details in a long time. Telling the story to others made me see it very differently. Perhaps it is maturity or a change in taste but I could not quite approve of Lady Elaine or Lancelot."

They moved into the dance once more and Phillip was left in suspense of Miss Brooke's opinion. When they met again, they were at the bottom of the line and able to converse more easily.

"In what way has your opinion changed?" Sir Phillip asked as if no time had passed.

"My father always said Elaine of Astolat was a model of true love," Miss Brooke said. "But I wonder if she really loved Lancelot. She barely knew him." Miss Brooke bit her lip and Phillip waited. He did not want an ill-advised comment to stop her from sharing further. "I think she loved the idea of Lancelot or maybe the idea of being in love. I think if she had known Lancelot better, she might have realized he wasn't worth dying over. Especially since he didn't return her affections."

Was she speaking of fictional characters or of her own heart? Was it hope that made him think she no longer wished for Daniel's favor? If her heart was free, she might bestow it on a more worthy object. Did she think him worthy?

"I think. . ." he paused.

Was it wise to speak on love in this roundabout way? With any other woman he would not dare for fear of raising her hopes, but Miss Brooke wasn't any woman. Phillip wanted to raise her hopes. Farthing had said a woman could not reject what had not been offered.

"Sir Phillip, do not keep me in suspense," Miss Brooke teased. Her green eyes flashed impishly and his reserve loosened.

He began again but could not match her teasing tone. "I think you are right. Mutual affection is important in any match. My parents did not marry for love. I would not wish to marry someone who did not love me in return."

It felt an eternity while he waited for her reply. His heart beat loudly in his ears.

"I feel the same. I could not be mercenary in marriage."

Her answer pleased him. What more might he gain if he had the courage?

"If you want a model of true love," he said, "I admire Shakespeare's Beatrice and Benedick."

He did not name the play; he was sure she knew *Much Ado About Nothing.*
Miss Brooke's eyebrows rose. "They spend most of the play fighting."
"Yes, but that is because they are too wise to woo peaceably."
She smiled at his quotation. "So you wish to argue with your wife?"
"I wish for a partner in life. One who will challenge me and help me to
see when I am wrong." He held her gaze, forgetting the other couples that
surrounded them in his need to help her understand his meaning.

She blinked rapidly and looked away. They had reached the top of the line
and further conversation was impossible as they began to dance once more.

Phillip had not meant to speak so candidly. A noisy dance floor was no
place for such revelations. Had she understood his meaning? Did she see
how their own arguments had helped him to grow? How she had forced
him to look at his life and treatment of Daniel differently? He needed a wife
that would not bow to his whims and Miss Brooke certainly had no qualms
about speaking her mind. If she had thought his words forward, she would
not hesitate to tell him.

The second dance was more vigorous than the first and there was less
opportunity to speak as they were almost constantly in motion. Still, Phillip
tried to discern her feelings. She smiled as before, but her eyes seemed
less focused, her mind occasionally far away. More than once she missed a
step. He did not know if he should be encouraged or discouraged by her
distraction.

When the dance ended, he was at a loss at what to say. His chance to speak
was limited by the short time it would take to cross the room to where their
mothers waited.

"Your house party will soon be over."
"I am sorry for it. I think Mother has enjoyed the company."
"But you aren't sorry to have your home to yourself."
How well she understood him. "I will not miss running into guests around
every corner and worrying over everyone's comfort and entertainment."
"I must disagree with you," she said archly. "I have grown fond of your
guests and will miss the chance to talk daily with such interesting and varied
people."

"Since their loss is my fault, allow me to ensure you do not lack for good conversation," Phillip said trying to affect lightheartedness.

"And how will you accomplish such a feat?"

They were only steps away from the waiting chaperones and so Phillip spoke low and rapid. "Nothing so easy. I will call on you daily and we can talk and argue to our heart's content."

There, he had all but declared himself.

He leaned away as they arrived before their mothers. He hoped she understood his words as a promise. A promise to call, a promise of more.

Mrs. Brooke, Mrs. Leigh, and his mother all complimented their dancing. "You are so evenly matched," Mother said. "I have rarely had such pleasure in watching Phillip dance." For once he didn't mind his mother's matchmaking.

"I hope it is not the last time you have such pleasure, Mother," Phillip said.

Mother smiled while Mrs. Leigh and Mrs. Brooke exchanged significant looks. Phillip reluctantly took his leave. He needed to find Miss Wilson for the next set and there was no telling how long it would take to navigate the room.

As he walked away, his mind remained with Miss Brooke. He had revealed much of his intentions and she had seemed receptive, eager even. When he called upon her the next day, he would clearly state his desire to enter into a courtship. She must be expecting it; indeed, most of the neighborhood was likely speculating on the nature of their relationship. After their dance and conversation, he had every reason to hope that she welcomed his attentions.

The next day could not come fast enough.

Chapter Nineteen

s Sir Phillip walked away, Elaine's mind whirled with what he had said about marriage and his intentions to call on her. It felt like a dream. But no, even asleep she had not contemplated such a fantastical turn of events.

He had not danced with her out of obligation.

He wished to court her.

She was still struggling to believe the notion when Mr. Farthing claimed her hand for the next set. He talked easily as they walked but she was not attending. She glimpsed Sir Phillip as he began the figures with Miss Wilson. Unlike her sister, the woman still enjoyed dancing and performed with an unexpected vitality.

"I am sorry, Miss Brooke, that in partnering me you have been brought so far down." Mr. Farthing gestured to their position in the line. "But then after Sir Phillip, any partner is a step down." He grinned.

She could not stop the flush of her cheeks. What had Sir Phillip said to his friend?

"Mr. Farthing, I am honored to be your partner." She was pleased her voice had returned to normal. "You are a wonderful dancer. And I must confess I am happy to let others begin the dance."

"Most women love to be on display." Farthing tipped his head. "But I think you must be like my friend and avoid attention where you can. Of course, an eligible bachelor cannot hide in a ballroom."

It was true. She had noticed that everywhere Sir Phillip went, marriage-minded mamas and their daughters watched. She understood now how he had perfected his reserve. The choice of Miss Wilson had likely disappointed the gossips while thrilling those eager for his notice. Elaine selfishly hoped he would dance only with ladies of his party. She would not be jealous of Freddie or Mrs. Farthing. He did not care for either of them.

A doubting voice whispered that Sir Phillip might not care for her either. He had danced with her because he thought of her as a little sister. But he had not looked at her like a brother, had not spoken to her as a brother. That was surely not her imagination. She was fanciful but had not yet mistaken dreams for reality.

Sir Phillip and Miss Wilson were suddenly beside them as they came down the line. Elaine and Mr. Farthing joined them in the figures, weaving in and out, hands clasping. Elaine's heart skipped along with her feet when Sir Phillip's arm came around her.

"We meet again," Sir Phillip murmured.

Color rose to her cheeks. They had just danced an entire set together, so it was perfectly irrational to feel so much at that small contact. But everything was changed between them; every look spoke volumes. Though they were in a crowded ballroom, his smile was meant only for her, and then he was gone, moving on to the next couple.

Elaine moved through the rest of the dance with a kind of carefree joy she had not experienced since her first dances at the Assembly Rooms in Bath. Back then, she was naive enough to think herself in love with every partner and hopeful enough to think that they wouldn't care about her lack of fortune.

Perhaps she was still naive and hopeful, but her delight was such that she no longer cared. Sir Phillip had spoken in earnest about what he desired in a wife. His promise to continue to see her was heavy with meaning. Elaine was more than flattered that a man so honorable and kind wished to court her.

Was this love? A boundless joy that filled her from head to toe? It certainly seemed like what the poets described. In the swiftness of the dance, she could not examine it or fall into her imagination. She cherished the feeling, basked in it, as she spun through the figures.

When the dance brought her to Freddie, they exchanged smiles. Freddie was a marvelous dancer and was flushed with excitement. Her partner was a dashing young man in regimentals and when Elaine took his hand, she realized with a jolt that she recognized him. Colin Edgerton had certainly grown up.

"Mr. Edgerton, I almost did not recognize you," Elaine said as he took her through the dance.

"I believe much has changed since we last met, Miss Brooke." He emphasized her name as if amused that she was no longer a skinny girl throwing rocks at him.

"We are quite grown up now." She smiled at him.

"Quite." His eyes traveled over her figure and his mouth quirked.

Elaine did not reply and was relieved when the dance separated them. Colin Edgerton had certainly grown taller, but perhaps inside he was still the mean little boy that had teased her and tormented Daniel. What did Daniel think of Miss Talbot dancing with his old enemy? She had not encountered him on the dance floor.

A quick look about the room and she found him standing beside Lady Ashburn. He talked with the older seated ladies, including a smiling Mrs. Talbot. His posture seemed too stiff and it was strange that he would sit out the set. Elaine's good mood ebbed as she considered what might have happened to upset him. Perhaps Mr. Edgerton had been involved in some way?

When the first dance concluded, Elaine found herself near enough Freddie to speak and seized the opportunity before the line reformed. Elaine made the introduction of Mr. Edgerton to Mr. Farthing and once the two men began to discuss the shooting, she turned to Freddie.

"And how do you find our little assembly?" Elaine said.

"It is like a fairyland." Freddie looked about at the candles and couples.

"And your partners?" Elaine said in an undertone and cut her eyes to Mr. Edgerton.

Freddie flushed. "Mr. Edgerton is very attentive." She opened her fan and leaned in closer to Elaine so they could speak more freely. "Mr. Ashburn is not pleased that I am dancing with him. But he could not expect me to refuse a partner and sit out the rest of the night."

They both looked at Daniel only to find that he was watching them. He tipped his head and gave them a sardonic smile as if he knew the topic of their conversation. Elaine couldn't help rolling her eyes. The man was behaving like a child. Freddie seemed to share the sentiment as she frowned behind her fan and turned her back on Daniel. Elaine saw his shoulders slump and against her will, she was sorry for him.

"He has no right," Freddie muttered before blowing out a breath. "Exasperating man!"

Elaine gave a breathy laugh. "Yes, he is." They shared a conspiratorial smile before separating.

During the second dance, Elaine's mind was less pleasantly engaged. Despite Freddie's best efforts, it was clear her heart belonged to Daniel. He did not need to worry about Mr. Edgerton. And yet, it was clear that Daniel was jealous and insecure of Miss Talbot's affections. Though Elaine felt for Daniel, she was glad that she had not given him her own heart. She didn't know if he would have kept it safe.

When the dance ended, Mr. Farthing returned Elaine to her mother and Mrs. Leigh standing near the window. They welcomed her and complimented her dancing before continuing their conversation about Mrs. Edgerton's new carriage.

Elaine looked out the window at the full yellow moon just rising over Oakbury. Her reflection was mirrored beside it in the windowpane. Her cheeks were flushed and her eyes bright, the blue of her dress setting them to advantage. Behind her, the assembly room bustled with smiling and laughing people. Like an arrow to a target, her gaze found Sir Phillip. He was across the room with Lady Ashburn and the Talbots. Would he dance next with Freddie or Mrs. Farthing?

Wildly she imagined him crossing the room to ask her for another set. He would smile and run his hand through his hair. She would look to Mama for permission to dance another set and—

"Miss Brooke."

Elaine turned to see that Mr. Edgerton had approached without her noticing. Quite the feat given the brightness of his red coat.

"Mr. Edgerton." She did not keep the surprise from her voice.

His lips quirked. "Are you enjoying the evening?"

"Yes, thank you."

"I do not believe you have attended an assembly before."

"I have not attended here in Oakbury. But I have not been home much since I grew old enough to dance."

Elaine was aware that Mama and Mrs. Leigh had ceased their talking and were eyeing them as surreptitiously as possible as they strained for every word. No doubt Mama thought Colin Edgerton a fine catch for her daughter. For a second son of a mere gentleman, Mr. Edgerton had done well. The army had provided him with good pay and influential friends that would ensure his star would continue to rise.

"The neighborhood is better for your return," he said. "No one admitted to the privilege of seeing you dance could possibly feel different."

"I thank you, but I am sure there are many who are quite indifferent to my dancing."

Mr. Edgerton's next words would undoubtedly be an invitation to dance and she could think of no excuse. To spend the next half hour in his company would be torture.

As if conjured by her anxiety, Daniel appeared behind Mr. Edgerton.

"Mr. Ashburn," she said to forestall Mr. Edgerton.

"Miss Brooke, they are forming the set." Daniel ignored the other young man and offered his arm. Elaine took it with relief. Daniel had not actually asked her to dance but Mr. Edgerton didn't know that. She gave a polite smile to Mr. Edgerton as she murmured her goodbyes.

"Better luck next time, Edgerton," Daniel murmured with a triumphant look as he bore her away.

192

With a few short words, Daniel had transformed his rescue into a selfish contest. Her gratitude toward him soured.

"You did not even ask me to dance," she said curtly.

"But you would never refuse me." He gave his most charming grin. How much he reminded her of that little boy she knew. She shook her head.

"You, sir, are fortunate that our long acquaintance allows you liberties."

Daniel patted her hand. "You are right. I am very lucky to have you."

Despite herself, Elaine smiled back. She would always care for Daniel; she could not carve him from her heart. There was no question that her affection was familial, so different from what she felt for Sir Phillip.

"Thank you for saving me from Edgerton."

"Thank you for letting me save you," Daniel said bitterly.

She guessed the source of his discontent. "Do not be upset with her. You know Miss Talbot could not refuse him."

"I think we should join the Farthing's set." Daniel pretended he hadn't heard. "They are sure to be jolly and not censure us at every turn. Unlike others in the room."

Elaine held in a sigh as Daniel navigated to the Farthings. Daniel could be stubborn. If he was intent on talking nothing but nonsense that was his prerogative. She resigned herself to frivolous conversation. There would be no discussing Shakespeare or Spenser with him.

She looked for Sir Phillip. He was near the musicians with Freddie on his arm as they formed a group with Lady Ashburn and Captain Hart. She smiled to see her prediction had come true. What did Sir Phillip think of the development? Would that she could change places with her friend.

Daniel was in fine form as he bantered and teased throughout the dance. Elaine returned his smiles and tried not to let her worry show. She saw the way his smile did not meet his eyes and how his attention wandered to Freddie. But she was determined not to push him again. She wanted to help him remove his mask, but she would not rip it off him.

Elaine had spent half her life dreaming of a dance with Mr. Daniel Ashburn. Never had she imagined it would leave her annoyed and despondent. When the music ended, she felt like an out-of-tune piano.

The right keys had been struck, but the sound was all wrong. Dancing with Daniel had been exhausting. She struggled to maintain her cheerfulness when all she wanted was to shake some sense into him.

Chapter Twenty

P hillip was fortunate that his next partner was Miss Wilson. She enjoyed dancing and was able to carry on a conversation with little input from him. It gave him ample opportunity to observe and think of Miss Brooke. He reveled in the moments when they passed each other in the dance. Her welcoming smile made his hope burn brighter.

When the set was finished, Phillip brought Miss Wilson back to his mother. He was disappointed that Mrs. Brooke was no longer by her side. There would be no opportunity to speak with Miss Brooke between the sets.

"You are in fine form tonight." Daniel pushed away from the wall, waving his glass to indicate the room.

"Thank you. Did you not dance the last?"

Daniel shrugged. "There was no woman I wished to stand up with."

"You well know it is your duty to—"

"Yes, yes." Daniel waved off Phillip's censure. "I will be sure to dance the rest of the evening." Daniel finished off his drink. "Did you see that Colin Edgerton is here?"

"I did. That is not so strange. He is often in the neighborhood."

"He had the nerve to ask Miss Talbot to dance," Daniel said as if conveying a shocking piece of information.

"It is an assembly. I would think it strange if Miss Talbot was not asked to dance."

"I don't care if she dances. I just don't want her to dance with him."

Phillip frowned. Daniel sounded like a child that didn't want to share a favorite toy. "If it will ease your mind, I have claimed her next set and Farthing her last."

"That is comforting. There is at least no chance that she would prefer dancing with you."

"Yes, how could any woman possibly prefer me when you are around?" Phillip's caustic tone seemed to cheer Daniel and he smiled.

"Exactly! I am far more handsome and charming."

Phillip scoffed.

"You doubt but I will prove it." Daniel handed Phillip his glass and strode away. What fool idea did he have now?

Phillip soon learned his answer as he escorted Miss Talbot to the floor and spotted Daniel with a smiling Miss Brooke on his arm. Something in his gut twisted. Would she find Daniel the superior partner? Would her head be turned by his charm and flirtation?

Phillip had just chastised Daniel for irrational jealousy, but could not escape the same emotion. It was ridiculous to be jealous of her smiles. Phillip ignored the clenching of his heart and tried to pay attention to Miss Talbot.

The dance was a quadrille and since Daniel did not make up his set, Phillip could not hear what was being said between them. He could only look enviously on as Miss Brooke smiled and laughed. She had not laughed when they danced.

Phillip could not deny that they looked compatible. Alike in height and coloring, Miss Brooke's blue dress even complimented Daniel's blue waistcoat. He could never match his brother's carefree nature or banter. But certainly that was not what Miss Brooke wanted. Had she not said as much during their dance?

Consumed as he was with his own thoughts, it did not escape Phillip's notice that Miss Talbot was similarly distracted. He was not the only one who watched the couple and somehow that made his fears seem less outlandish. When the dance ended, Phillip turned to his partner.

"Miss Talbot, would you care for something to drink? There are only light refreshments but I think it will be restorative."

"Yes, I would enjoy that."

Phillip turned his back on the dancers, putting the object of his discontent out of sight if not out of mind. He escorted Miss Talbot to the small annex where a variety of drinks and sweetmeats were being served. They were not the only ones taking a respite and all around them conversation flowed, lubricated by the spirits and food.

Miss Talbot did not attempt to speak and Phillip was happy to stay silent as they retrieved their refreshment and retired to a spot near the balcony. The summer night was warm and the doors opened to those who wished to take in the air.

Miss Talbot made a comment about the food and Phillip managed a passable response. Voices from the balcony drifted towards them but Phillip didn't mark them until he caught the word "Brooke."

"She is making a complete cake of herself."

Phillip recognized Miss Covington's aggrieved tones.

"If she is trying to snare the baronet, then making up to the younger brother seems unwise," A male voice replied.

"You know she has always preferred Mr. Ashburn. When we were children, she was always declaring she would marry him. I am certain she only danced with Sir Phillip to make his brother jealous."

The man laughed. "A poor play. Ashburn is not stupid enough to be caught so easily or by one so poor."

"But he is already caught. They say his engagement to the heiress will be announced soon."

"Stuff and nonsense. I don't care how rich the girl may be. Ashburn has no intention of being leg shackled. Any woman is fool to try."

Miss Covington laughed. "Oh Edgerton, you are. . ." Their next words were inaudible, having moved too far from the doors.

Phillip was no longer hungry. Beside him, Miss Talbot looked pale and her hands shook. He had no doubt she had heard.

Phillip wanted to assure her that it was ugly gossip from mean-spirited people, but he did not want to acknowledge his own eavesdropping. And how could he refute their claims when he was unsure himself?

He did not think Miss Brooke would toy with his affections, but he could not deny that she had long preferred Daniel. Mother had said as much, and Phillip had assumed as much only a week ago. But as Benedick said the appetite doth alter. Miss Brooke had told him that her thoughts on love had matured. He thought that meant she no longer cared for Daniel, that she had begun to care for him. He had not imagined her smiles or her words.

Phillip downed his entire drink and ignored the burn in his throat. He looked at Miss Talbot and belatedly wondered at her thoughts. At the start of the house party, Phillip would have worried about the potential damage on Daniel's prospects for marrying Miss Talbot. But now all Phillip cared about was his own prospects. He would let his brother run as wild as he pleased if only he would leave Miss Brooke and her affections alone.

* * *

When the Oakbury assembly ended promptly a half hour before midnight, Phillip was relieved. Had the affair been in London or a private ball, he would have been forced to continue to stand up for hours while in misery and agitation. After listening to Miss Covington's poisonous words, he wanted to be anywhere but a crowded ballroom in sight of Daniel and Miss Brooke.

He avoided looking at her. The one time Phillip did meet her eyes she had smiled and it was almost enough to erase his doubts. But instead of returning her smile, he looked away.

When he climbed into the carriage behind Mother and Daniel, Phillip was weary in spirit, ill-equipped for company, and more than a little foxed. As the horses snapped into motion, Mother leaned against the cushions and gave a happy sigh.

"I can't recall a more pleasant evening."

Daniel chuckled. "I am glad you enjoyed yourself. I must remember to thank Captain Hart for standing up with you. It was good to see you dancing."

"Captain Hart was an excellent partner." Mother's smile grew but Daniel did not seem to notice. Had Miss Brooke shared her theories with him about Mother and Captain Hart? Phillip had thought the speculation was something secret between them, but that seemed a foolish notion now.

"Now Phillip," Mother turned to him, her hair shining in the moonlight. "You must admit it was not a punishing three and a half hours."

"It was an experience I have no wish to repeat."

"A pity," Daniel said. "For I have it on good authority that the neighborhood expects a repeat performance. They were not pleased that you danced only with those of your party."

"Nonsense." Mother swatted Daniel's shoulder with her fan. "Phillip was doing his duty to his guests. And he danced with Miss Brooke; she is from the neighborhood."

"Yes, the poor thing." Daniel's half-serious tone rankled.

Phillip only grunted in response.

"At least their strange pairing will keep the neighborhood gossips busy."

"Now Daniel, I thought Phillip and Miss Brooke looked perfectly charming together and I am sure if the gossips talk of anything it will be that."

"I rather think Daniel's antics are better gossip fodder." Phillip couldn't help the words from spilling out. The alcohol had made his lips faster than his self-control.

"My antics?"

"To openly flirt with every female may be acceptable in London, but here in the country it will cause talk."

"I did nothing but dance and make myself amiable. I can't help that the young ladies enjoy me more than any other partner. Nor can I help that others notice."

By the light of the full moon Phillip could make out Daniel crossing his arms and jutting out his chin. He looked like a child. And this is the kind of man Miss Brooke cared for?

Anger bubbled in him. "Are you saying that you don't care what Mrs.

Talbot, and indeed Miss Talbot, must be thinking?"

"They can think whatever they like, it is nothing to me."

"Nothing? Nothing! After all the trouble and expense of this house party, now it's nothing?" Phillip's voice rose with his astonishment.

Mother laid a restraining hand on his arm before turning to Daniel. "I am sure you do not mean that. If you and Miss Talbot have quarreled, then you must talk through it. You can make amends."

Daniel huffed. "Because of course, the fault must be mine."

"I did not say that."

"Good, because I did nothing wrong. I have made no promises to Miss Talbot and I daresay she expects none from me. I am sorry for the expense of the party, but I never asked for it. It was a vain hope to think I would come up to scratch. Miss Talbot and I do not suit." Daniel sighed and turned to the window.

Was Daniel saying that he had chosen Miss Brooke? The thought constricted Phillip's throat.

"Now don't be so hasty," Mother said patiently. "I do not think you should give up on Miss Talbot."

"You mean I shouldn't throw away my chance at a rich heiress, since I am not good for anything else."

"No," Mother returned. "What I mean is that one should never make big decisions after a ball. The party spirit and the refreshments cloud judgment."

"Or perhaps it merely reveals the truth," Phillip said. "It shows you a person's real character and feelings."

"For once, I agree with my brother."

"Stop it, the both of you. You are both soused. In the morning you will feel differently and I will be kind enough to forget this conversation ever happened. I imagine in your state you might do the same. Now, no more conversation." She spoke with the finality only a mother could manage, then sighed and turned to look out the window.

It had been a long time since Mother had treated him like a child. Shame crept over him for spoiling her evening. She had looked very happy on Captain Hart's arm.

He closed his eyes and pictured Miss Brooke beside him on the dance floor. He had not imagined the look in her eyes or the smiles she gave him. They had come far from that first morning at the Old Priory, but how far her feelings had changed, he could not say. But certainly, he should not trust overheard remarks at a ball. He hoped Mother was right and he would feel different after a good night's sleep.

* * *

Sleep eluded Phillip. Shortly after dawn, he was awake and asking for his horse. Riding fast and hard, he managed to avoid thinking of Miss Brooke and his misgivings. But when he approached his destination and slowed his pace, they all came rushing back. The Old Priory had always been a comfort but from the moment he saw the crumbling walls he could not avoid the new memories created there. He turned his horse before reaching them.

This was intolerable.

He forced his horse to a more respectable canter. When he came to the lane that led to Ryder Lodge, he paused. He needed to speak with Miss Brooke and make his wishes known. If she refused him, he would wish her well in life and do his best to meet her in society with equanimity. That is what a gentleman would do.

But he could not speak to her now. It was far too early, and he still had his pride. He would return later, when they were expecting callers. Though his mind was made up, he lingered. He sat there, staring at the spot through the trees where he could make out the chimney of the lodge.

Was Miss Brooke awake? Had her sleep been as troubled as his?

A rustling in the small bit of woods drew Phillip's attention. Miss Brooke emerged from the shadows of the trees. Had his sleep-addled mind conjured her? She looked like flesh and blood.

"Hello," he said to announce his presence.

She startled, her eyes coming up from the small woodland path. "Sir Phillip!"

Her eyes took him in for a long, torturous moment before she smiled. The smile was all the invitation he needed.

He dismounted. A true gentleman would wish her a good day and allow her to continue her morning walk, but Phillip would not waste such a providential meeting.

"May I join you?"

She blinked, glanced back toward the lodge. "That would be lovely. I had no fixed destination."

He nodded, not caring where they went. They walked in silence for a few steps, with only the sound of the horse's hooves and snuffling echoing in his ears. Now that he was beside her, he did not know how to approach the topic.

"Did you enjoy the assembly?" he finally asked.

"Very much."

"You enjoyed all your partners?" He glanced sidelong at her.

"Some more than others." She gave a small, secret smile.

Was he counted as one she enjoyed? Phillip wished he could ask with suave charm. Daniel would know just what to say.

"Pray, how is Dan—your brother?"

His heart dropped to his stomach at her almost using Daniel's name. "I imagine he is as well as ever."

"I'm sorry. I do not mean to pry. It is only that he was not himself at the assembly. I thought perhaps he might have spoken to you."

"If you wish to know Daniel's state of mind, perhaps you should ask him." Phillip could not hide his resentment.

"Yes, of course," Miss Brooke mumbled.

They were silent.

Inside Phillip raged. Miss Brooke thought nothing of him; he was only a means to learn more about Daniel. His brother had her heart and likely always had. Phillip never stood a chance. His blithe, useless brother did not even value the treasure he possessed.

"You know Daniel has no profession, no way to support himself." Phillip needed Miss Brooke to understand what a life with Daniel would mean.

She gave him a sidelong look. "You have said as much before. It is a shame, for I know he is capable. Perhaps with the right encouragement—"

"You think I have not tried to get him to choose a profession? I have done everything I can think of to get him to take responsibility for his life."

"Everything but allow him to choose his own path."

"I beg your pardon?" Phillip stopped walking and drew himself up. Clearly she still had a poor opinion of him. True to form, Miss Brooke did not shrink but met his eyes boldly as she spoke.

"When he was younger, he wanted to join the Navy and you refused him. He might be a captain now if you had let him."

"More like he would be in a watery grave, cut down by a French bullet or a tropical disease. My mother had just lost her husband. I was not about to send away her favorite son."

He vividly remembered the argument he had with Daniel over joining the Navy. His brother was only thirteen, just growing into his manhood, but he had fought fiercely for Phillip's permission. Daniel had only seen adventure and a dashing uniform; Phillip had imagined another coffin to bury beside his father. He did not want to be responsible for sending Daniel to his death. Phillip had refused and as the baronet, his word was final. Daniel had sullenly returned to school. That Miss Brooke knew such an intimate detail about Daniel spoke volumes.

Phillip stormed away, dragging a startled horse after him.

"Did you tell Daniel that you refused him in order to keep him safe?" she called after him.

He turned back to face her. "I did not need to give him a reason. I am head of the family."

She shook her head; she didn't need to speak for him to see her disapproval. She thought him a tyrant and Daniel a persecuted paragon. He had been a fool.

"It is clear, that in your eyes at least, that I can do no right and Daniel can do no wrong."

"No. That is not—I did not mean—" She let out a frustrated breath. "You think I am blinded by your brother's charm, but on the contrary, I see him quite clearly. He uses his charm and wit to hide his true feelings. You are wrong if you think he does not value your opinion."

"I see I have been mistaken in many things." Phillip could not stay beside her anymore. "I will take my leave. I am sure you have long been desiring my absence." He gave a stiff bow and turned to mount his horse.

"Please do not be angry with me." Miss Brooke followed, her hand reaching out as if she would physically stop him from leaving.

Even though she had censured him, even though she preferred his brother, Phillip's heart softened at her pleading tone. He paused and breathed deep. He refused to look at her for fear she would see the emotions written on his face.

"I must go. Good day."

Chapter Twenty-One

E laine sat in the study at her father's old desk, gazing out onto the small back garden but she barely saw it. Her pen was poised over the inkpot as she tried to decide what to write to Rosamund. Her last letter had been full of hopes about Daniel and excitement at being asked to eat dinner at the hall. She could not begin to explain how her thoughts and feelings had altered and yet she wanted nothing more than to pour out her confusion to her sensible, logical friend.

Her mind continued to review the looks and conversation of the night before and the argument of that morning. When she had come upon Sir Phillip on the village road, she had been a riot of emotions. She had hoped he would speak of his feelings, but instead, they argued about Daniel, again. How had that happened? Would he still call today? What would she say when he did?

Elaine longed to have Charity or Penelope or Mary or Rosamund beside her and not leagues away. She could pour out her heart, they would make her laugh, and give advice. She would be stronger and better with her friends surrounding her. Elaine tried to picture them, hear their voices and what they might say, but her imagination failed her. Her friends weren't there and any advice or comforting words would take days or weeks to arrive.

Loneliness hit Elaine like a fall from a tree. Sharing her concerns with

Rosamund seemed pointless. With a sigh, she grabbed a different sheet of paper. She would write to Mrs. Piper instead. She could tell her of the school and ask for teaching advice.

The letter took the better part of an hour; Elaine's mind kept wandering away. She had just finished when the sound of a carriage had her rushing to the drawing room. But it was only Mrs. Leigh. Elaine settled herself near the window and grabbed something at random from the workbasket so she would look busy.

Mrs. Leigh moved with energy that indicated she had gossip to share. She sat in her usual chair and dispensed with the usual pleasantries. "Well, my dear girl, do you know I have spoken to a half-dozen people this morning and not one of them can agree on what to make of you."

Elaine started. "Of me?"

"Why Augusta, what can you mean?" Mama looked at Elaine with as much puzzlement as she felt.

"I mean that the neighborhood cannot decide if you are interested in Sir Phillip or Mr. Ashburn and they are equally confused about the gentlemen's preferences."

Elaine's hands became slippery and her heart erratic as she pretended to look at her sewing.

"How absurd," Mama said. "All this because she danced with them?"

"Both gentlemen seemed to excessively enjoy their time with her," Mrs. Leigh replied.

"Surely no one thinks that my Elaine could possibly be trying to catch an Ashburn? She knows better than to presume so much."

"But you must admit that it would be a fine thing for her."

"Humph."

"Now Mary," Mrs. Leigh chided. "I understand your objections to Mr. Ashburn, but surely you agree that Sir Phillip would make a fine husband."

"Sir Phillip would be the best husband in all of England and if I thought him truly interested, I would indeed rejoice. But his attentions to Elaine are that of a good neighbor. There is no question of him wanting to court her and it does no good to pretend otherwise."

Mama's opinion was so fixed that Elaine couldn't help but doubt her own. The gossips were wrong about Daniel's interest, so they might also be wrong about Sir Phillip.

"I might agree with you, Mary, if the Ashburn carriage were not coming down your lane."

Elaine looked up from her sewing. Mrs. Leigh was right. The Ashburn carriage had arrived. Elaine's unsteady heart moved to her throat as the carriage came to a stop and the doors opened. Her heart dropped when Sir Phillip did not emerge.

"A shame it is only the ladies," Mrs. Leigh said. "Do not worry dear, I am sure Sir Phillip will call later on his own."

"Not a word," Mama said to Mrs. Leigh. A knowing look passed between them. Then the door opened and Rogers announced Lady Ashburn, Mrs. and Miss Talbot, and Mrs. Farthing.

The party was warmly greeted and seats found in the now full drawing room. Mrs. Farthing was all smiles as she joined Elaine near the window, but Freddie did not so much as glance in her direction. Elaine's stomach sank. What had her friend heard?

The conversation naturally turned to the assembly. The clothing, music, food, and guests were liberally discussed. Elaine gave up entirely on her sewing as she anxiously waited for mentions of Sir Phillip or for someone to ask her a question about Daniel.

"Mrs. Brooke," Mrs. Farthing said. "I was hoping to see your lovely garden."

"You are so kind." Mama looked at Elaine.

"I would be happy to show you," Elaine offered. "And anyone else who wishes to see it." She looked around the room. Freddie didn't meet her eye and the others demurred.

"Miss Talbot, will you come?" Mrs. Farthing made the invitation as they stood

"Yes, Freddie, go get some air, it will do you good," Mrs. Talbot said.

Freddie stood reluctantly and together they made their way through the back hall and into the garden. Elaine could guess at her change in manner.

Did her friend really think she had set her cap at Daniel?

"Here it is." Elaine gestured to the small expanse of lawn and the lone oak tree halfway between the house and the low stone wall.

"How picturesque," Mrs. Farthing said as they stepped out into the sun. She was eager to be pleased and exclaimed over the blooming hedge roses near the house and the neat rows of the kitchen garden. When they reached the stone wall and its wooden gate, they looked out at the brook gleaming in the late morning light.

"That is the same stream that runs in front of the hall?" Mrs. Farthing asked.

"Yes." Elaine pointed at the wooden footbridge. "Once you cross over, you are in the park."

"How very close you are," Freddie finally spoke with chilling tones.

"The park is very large," Elaine said. "It is still a half-mile of woodland and meadow before you come in sight of the hall."

"I must examine the bridge," Mrs. Farthing said. "But please continue walking without me. I will be looking with my artist's eye and my husband assures me it is very tedious."

She slipped through the gate before anyone could protest. Elaine turned and smiled at Freddie, but the other young woman glowered. They walked a few paces and the tension between them grew like a taut bow string.

Elaine could not stand the silence. "Mrs. Leigh conveyed some shocking rumors this morning, but people in the country are always talking nonsense. I hope you know better than to believe such—"

Freddie stopped walking. Elaine turned to her. Her friend's face was thunderous.

"Please stop. I know what you are now, Miss Brooke. What a fool I was to listen to advice from a viper! Think of other men, indeed! You didn't care about me, you only wished to drive a wedge between us. I thought you were my friend but you only wanted him for yourself."

"Freddie, that is not—"

"Please don't pretend that you haven't been in love with Mr. Ashburn since you were a child."

Elaine opened her mouth and then closed it. What reply could she possibly give?

"You do not deny it then?" Freddie's gray blue eyes shone. Her anger had burned itself out and left behind cold ashes of sorrow.

"I—" Elaine shook her head and took a few steps before turning back to Freddie. "I will not deny that there was a time when I wished to marry Daniel."

Freddie flinched away from the words. Elaine winced. Using his Christian name was not helping her cause.

"It was a juvenile crush that I have outgrown."

"I cannot believe that you are indifferent to Mr. Ashburn. I saw you both last night and the way you behave when together. . ."

"We are old friends." Elaine stepped closer and reached for Freddie's hand. "Please understand that our friendship is what allows us to be so free and easy in each other's company. We are more like siblings than anything else. Mr. Ashburn is charming and I will always count him a dear friend, but he is not the sort of man I wish to marry."

Saying the words out loud made it solid in her mind. Daniel would never be the man for her, not now. Miss Talbot must have felt the same truth because her lips turned up slightly.

"Truly?"

"I swear to you."

Freddie dashed at her tears. "Oh Elaine, I thought for sure that you had played me for a fool. You must understand I have been betrayed by other women, women I thought were my friends and I thought. . ." She shook her head. "Well, it doesn't matter."

"Freddie, I could never do such a thing and certainly not to my friend."

They embraced. Elaine realized how much she would have regretted losing Freddie's friendship. In their short time together, she had come to value her deeply. Though the conversation had been difficult, she was glad she had been given a chance to defend herself. When they pulled apart, Freddie wiped her eyes again.

"I am sorry that I thought ill of you. It's just that I was so confused. Mr.

Ashburn's behavior last night was hardly what I expected. And I heard. . . That is, I thought perhaps it could all be explained by an attachment to you."

"His only attachment to me is that of a brother to a sister."

Elaine remembered when Mr. Talbot had expressed a similar sentiment. She had been so upset by the idea. How much had changed.

Freddie sighed. "I have tried to think of other men, but it is no good. I don't care for anyone but him. Even with all his faults. Even though he is changeable and infuriating, I fear I would accept him if he made me an offer."

Elaine understood her feelings all too well. "He would be a fool not to offer for you."

Freddie smiled sadly. "He is a fool, and I am a fool. When we leave tomorrow, he will forget me and I will be left pining like the lady from your story. "

"If it is any consolation, I do not think he will forget you so easily."

"I hope he does not. At least then we will both be in pain."

Elaine smiled. Although she had plenty of suppositions on why he had acted strangely, she dared not offer any more speculation on Daniel's feelings. She suspected if he didn't ask for Miss Talbot's hand, he would regret it for the rest of his life.

They reached the oak tree and paused, looking up at its towering branches.

"I hope you don't waste away like the Lady of Astolat," Elaine said.

"I don't think I will." Freddie leaned against the tree. "I will just learn to live with my disappointment. In time I might find someone else I can love."

"He will be a fortunate man. I wish you every happiness."

"And I you."

They stood in peaceful silence. Elaine hoped she could have the same quiet fortitude as Freddie. She watched as Mrs. Farthing made her way back from the bridge. Had the older woman been giving them the chance to work out their differences? If so, Elaine was grateful. She would part with Freddie as friends. As they waited, they fell into easy conversation about travel. Mrs. Farthing joined them and sang the praises of the bridge.

"It is a pity I won't be able to paint it on this occasion."

"I hope you will return soon and spend an entire afternoon at the lodge."

Mrs. Farthing pressed Elaine's hand. "I will, and in the interim, you must write to me. I would love to continue our friendship."

"I would be honored," Elaine said.

"And you must write me as well," Freddie added. "I will not give up my first true friend."

Elaine readily agreed and they made their way back to the house. The visit had temporarily distracted Elaine from her worries, but once the visitors had left, her thoughts returned to Sir Phillip.

* * *

By the time the Ashburn carriage arrived to take the Brookes to dinner, Elaine was in a state. Sir Phillip had not come to call and she did not know why. Was he still angry with her? Had she imagined his interest just as she had with Daniel? Or had he heard the rumors and did not want to give them weight? Questions and anxieties swarmed in her mind and roiled her stomach.

When they arrived at Ryder Hall, she was more nervous than the first time. In the drawing room, she looked in vain for Sir Phillip before being pulled into conversation with Mrs. Cooper and Mrs. Farthing. It was the last night of the house party and Elaine tried her best to be cheerful. She would miss this interesting and varied company each evening. Unbidden, she recalled Sir Phillip promising to call on her regularly. Was he just being kind? Was Mama right that he was only being a good neighbor?

When they moved into dinner, Elaine was escorted by Mr. Poole and seated near Lady Ashburn. She caught her first sight of Sir Phillip at the opposite side of the table. As usual he was well dressed, but there was a tiredness about his eyes. Perhaps his day had been full of his responsibilities and that is why he hadn't called?

As she looked back up the table, she smiled at Freddie. She had been escorted by Captain Hart and was no nearer to Daniel than Elaine. Unlike his brother, Daniel was brimming with cheer, his laugh often interrupting conversation around the table. To her it sounded false, another mask he hid behind.

After an interminable dinner, Elaine was relieved to stand and follow Lady Ashburn to the drawing room. How long before the men joined them? Elaine hoped it was enough time to get advice from Mrs. Farthing or Freddie. She was in desperate need of their counsel.

She sought out Mrs. Farthing as soon as she entered the room. "Mrs. Farthing, might I talk with you?"

Mrs. Farthing's smile dimmed. "Yes, of course, whatever is the matter?"

Before Elaine could reply, her mother called for her. Elaine excused herself.

"I assure you she will pick something you will enjoy," Mama said as Elaine came to her side. "Elaine, Lady Ashburn would like you to read for us."

"If it is not too much trouble," Lady Ashburn hurried to add.

"I will read whatever you may like." She tried not to show her disappointment.

"I have no preference. You may go and choose something from the library."

"If you wish. I'll return directly." Elaine gave a slight curtsey before turning to leave. Her feet were leaden. There was little chance of speaking with Mrs. Farthing now.

Elaine waved off the footman's offer of assistance and carried a candelabra through the silent hall. In the library, the moonlight shone through the windows, turning the books silver. The pool of gold light she carried transformed them back to black as she approached the shelf. Thoughts of Sir Phillip intruded as she looked at the titles; talking with him in the library, discussing literature on the dance floor.

"If it helps, the poetry is on that shelf."

The candles guttered as Elaine spun around. "Daniel! What are you doing here?"

He sat slumped in a wingback chair next to the empty fireplace, the light throwing his face into harsh shadows, and for once, he did not affect a winsome smile. She set the candelabra down.

"You like me, don't you Elaine?" he asked bleakly.

"You are a dear friend."

"Do you think— That is, we rub along well and I think we might make a go of it."

"Make a go of it?" How much had Daniel had to drink? An empty glass sat on the table near the chair.

"You could marry me, if you want."

She could not believe her ears and laughed nervously.

He frowned.

She checked her laugh. "You are not serious."

"And why not?" Daniel sat up straighter.

How this offer might have affected her only a month before, she could not say, but now she was fondly frustrated. What kind of man asked someone to marry them in this manner?

"Tell me, if Miss Wilson had come to retrieve a book, would you have asked her instead?"

Daniel's lips twitched. Elaine felt that a good sign.

"Miss Wilson is a very interesting woman. Perhaps I will ask her."

"And Miss Talbot? What if she came to the library?"

Daniel scowled. "I know what Miss Talbot's answer would be."

"Have you asked her?"

"I do not need to ask her to know that I am not good enough for her."

"Not good enough?"

"I am not a fit prospect."

"A charming, intelligent, capable young man is not a fit prospect?"

Daniel leapt from the chair and began to pace. "I am a spendthrift second son with no profession and a reputation for intemperance. No, don't argue." He held up his hand to ward off any protest. "It is true and I know it. Phillip has listed my faults often enough. When I first courted Miss Talbot, I had no thought of anything like matrimony. I was certain she was far too intelligent to ever consider me seriously."

"That was very wrong of you." Elaine didn't have the heart to truly chastise him. "But surely your intentions have changed?"

"Oh, I am well and truly caught. She had my heart in London and I ran, only to have Phillip bring us together here." Daniel dragged his hand down his face. "But my feelings don't matter when I have nothing to offer her. When her father—" Daniel broke off. "I should not be telling you this."

Daniel was right they should not be speaking so but Elaine could not just walk away now. She would not leave her friend in such turmoil.

"Whatever Mr. Talbot said or thinks it doesn't matter. I know you are capable of anything you set your mind to. There is no reason you can't find a profession and reform your ways. And no reason to think Miss Talbot won't accept you as you are."

Daniel's too blue eyes sparkled in the candlelight as he looked up. "Do you honestly think so? You don't think she might prefer someone else? Like Edgerton?"

Elaine laughed and shook her head. "She doesn't care a fig for Edgerton. Ask her. I think her answer will be more favorable than mine."

"Truly?"

"If you apologize for your rudeness and ask her properly, I think you have every chance of happiness. Shall I send her to the library when I return to the drawing room?"

Daniel's face transformed as he smiled widely. "Elaine, would you?"

She nodded and he ran to her like a little boy. He took her in his arms and spun her around in his joy. "I am so glad you came home to save me from myself."

He stopped and steadied her as she regained her balance. "I think your brother deserves some of the credit. He has been trying to help you."

"Yes, well, I don't like to listen to him."

Elaine stepped back. "You should listen to him. He only wants what is best for you."

Daniel rolled his eyes. "You know, I had quite made up my mind to marry a penniless opera singer just to spite him."

"You decided being penniless was enough?"

"Yes, indeed, I am sorry about that." Daniel looked chagrined.

"As you should be. What if I was in love with you? Did you even think how heartbreaking such a proposal would be?"

"I did not think."

Elaine sighed. "I know. Now grab me that book of Wordsworth so I can return to the drawing room."

Daniel turned and went to a different shelf and came back with the book. "You will tell Miss Talbot to come meet me?"

"I will tell her."

"And she will come?"

"I believe she will happily come."

Daniel bounced on the balls of his feet. He reminded her so much of the little boy she had once played with. She hoped he never lost his exuberance, but she was glad he would not be her partner in life.

"Phillip will be unbearably smug when he learns that his scheme to get me married to Miss Talbot has been successful," Daniel said.

"You should thank him for his efforts to bring you together."

"Or perhaps I won't tell him." He smiled mischievously. "Don't look like that. Aren't secret engagements fashionable now? No, don't tell me, you must go before you are missed." He made a shooing motion with his hands.

Dutifully Elaine left the library, unable to stop smiling. She was still confused about Sir Phillip but seeing Daniel's happiness and knowing how elated Freddie would be made it easier to bear. If Daniel and Freddie could come together, despite all their disagreements and miscommunications, surely there was hope for her and Sir Phillip.

Chapter Twenty-Two

Phillip heard the low rumble of voices around the dinner table but he wasn't paying attention to what was being said. He had no mind for talk of canals, shooting, or crops; not tonight. He had spent the evening avoiding Miss Brooke, but he could not avoid her in his thoughts. It seemed she had permanently taken up residence there.

That morning, when he had the chance to speak with her, he had thought it fortunate. But it had been disastrous. His carefully composed questions were never asked, his declaration never made.

Now he did not know how to proceed. If Miss Brooke cared for Daniel, it did not follow that Daniel cared for her. Daniel might leave her heartbroken like Elaine of Astolat. Phillip did not want her unhappy. He hated the idea almost as much as he hated the thought that Daniel might offer for her.

Phillip took another drink. Farthing threw himself into the seat beside Phillip.

"It is a pity this is our last night," Farthing said and then chuckled at Phillip's frown. "But I see you are ready for some peace and quiet."

"It will be nice to attend to my affairs."

"Hmm, and might those affairs include ones of the heart?"

To avoid answering immediately, Phillip sipped at his drink. He wasn't sure he wanted to consult anyone about the tangled mess that was Miss

Brooke, Daniel, and his own feelings. Talking would solve nothing. If the lady had made her choice, there was little Phillip could do about it.

Farthing spoke again. "Don't look so sour. You need not speak on it if you don't wish. I only want you to be happy."

"Only that?" Phillip smiled mournfully.

Seeing the questioning light in Farthing's eye, Phillip decided he could not sit there drinking any longer. He stood. Taken by surprise, the other men began to move slowly to their feet. His brother was not among them. Where was Daniel? When had he left?

"Sit, drink a while longer," Phillip said. "I am in need of fresh air before joining the ladies."

"Take your time," Mr. Talbot said as he tipped his glass.

Without looking at Farthing, Phillip took his leave, not through the door that led to the drawing room but to the back exit of the house. The cool, evening air hit him as he swung open the door. He took the steps two at a time and strode straight out onto the lawn, thinking of nothing but putting space between himself and the house.

The exercise and air immediately began to clear his head. He chastised himself for his behavior at dinner and his maudlin attitude afterward. He was a baronet and master of the estate; he could not lose his head over a woman. Especially a woman who might love his brother. He sighed and turned back to look at the hall. The white façade was silver in the moonlight. The dining room windows blazed yellow, while only a faint glow came from other parts of the house.

He would need to return before he was missed. He had guests and it was their last night. Farthing was right, Phillip was looking forward to peace and quiet. Would Mother welcome it as well? Would she miss Captain Hart? He would miss seeing Miss Brooke each night. How lonely Ryder Hall would be if Mother married and left him alone. It was too large of a house for one person.

Someday there would be a wife and children, but tonight Phillip could not picture it. He only wanted Miss Brooke. Could she possibly want him? He recalled her many smiles and tried to hope. Hope that she held him in esteem. Hope that her feelings for Daniel were not love. Hope that she might come to care for him.

The breeze turned cold and he realized how foolish it was to be prowling the garden when the woman he cared for was inside. He could apologize for his harsh words that morning. They could reconcile. He could call on her tomorrow. All was not yet lost.

He strode back to the hall, feeling the stirrings of optimism. As he approached the house, a flickering yellow light caught his attention. Curious, he veered to the right. Who could possibly be in the library at this hour?

Through the window, he easily identified the figure of Miss Brooke standing beside the shelves. For a moment Phillip thought she was looking out the window. Did she see him? But then another figure paced in front of her. With horror, Phillip realized it was Daniel. Drawn like a moth to a flame, he moved closer.

He could not hear what was said but did not think it mattered since they were alone in a dark library. Miss Brooke laughed. Daniel stopped pacing and faced her. Phillip watched in mute distress. What was Daniel saying to make her mouth turn up and her eyes glow? Miss Brooke nodded and suddenly Daniel was rushing to her. He took Miss Brooke in his arms and spun her around.

Phillip could not breathe. It was like he had been kicked in the chest. How was he still standing when he felt this much pain?

Daniel had asked for her hand; they were engaged. There could be no other interpretation of what he just saw.

Sometime in the near future, she would be Mrs. Daniel Ashburn. Phillip stepped back from the window. Daniel put Miss Brooke down and they stood looking lovingly at each other. He turned away and fled. He did not want to see any more.

There was no question of returning to the house now. He could not hear them happily announcing their engagement or speak to anyone else. Duty forgotten, Phillip fled into the night.

He did not know how much time passed as he wandered in the darkness. When he finally returned to the house, an anxious Lennox greeted him.

"Sir, I am glad to see you. Lady Ashburn is quite worried. We did not know what had become of you."

Guilt filled him. He should not have left Mother alone, not on the final night of the party. It was childish and inconsiderate to disappear with not even informing his staff of his whereabouts.

"I will go to her directly," Phillip said, though he would rather be anywhere else.

"She has informed the guests you are unwell," Lennox said.

Phillip paused. Of course she had given a plausible explanation for his absence. And he could not appear in the drawing room now, his evening shoes and stockings damp, his hair askew, and eyes red rimmed.

"Thank you, Lennox. I will retire for the evening. Please extend my apologies and assure Lady Ashburn that I am well."

Phillip fled to his room and passed a fitful night. He rose early, guilt driving him to seek out Mother.

Once dressed for the day, Phillip went directly to his mother's room to make his excuses in person. He spoke vaguely of needing time to think over estate business and though Mother looked skeptical, she did not question him.

"I shall be in my study; please inform me when our guests depart."

He spent a long hour trying to focus on his affairs. His gaze kept straying to the library door and replaying what he had witnessed the night before. Any moment he expected Daniel to burst in and announce his betrothal. But his brother never appeared. Instead, a servant fetched him to see off his guests.

His goodbyes to Miss Wilson, Mrs. Cooper, Mr. Poole, and Mr. Evans were perfunctory. The parting with the Talbots was uncomfortable. Mother and Mrs. Talbot kept up a kind civility while Mr. Talbot seemed eager to depart. Miss Talbot and Daniel parted genially; there seemed to be no hard feelings between them.

Phillip wished he had never meddled, never planned a house party, never forced Daniel to return home. It had cost him greatly, in more ways than one.

As the Talbot's carriage pulled away, Daniel turned to Phillip. "If you have a moment, I would like to speak with you."

Phillip drew in a sharp breath; he was not ready for this conversation.

"I am busy at present." Phillip gestured to the Farthing's carriage thronged with servants as they prepared it for the journey.

"It won't take long," Daniel said.

"Here they are." Phillip turned to greet the Farthings as they made their way down the staircase. So much had changed since he had greeted them in this same place.

They exchanged pleasantries about the party and the road ahead, the kind of small talk Phillip usually abhorred but now tolerated to avoid Daniel.

"I do hope you will return for another visit," Mother said.

"We would like nothing more," Mrs. Farthing replied with real feeling.

Phillip shook Farthing's hand in farewell. His friend leaned in and whispered. "I expect to be invited to the wedding."

He froze. What could he say?

When Phillip didn't reply, Farthing chuckled and pulled away. Perhaps it was best he was leaving.

The door of the Farthing's landau had barely shut when Daniel turned to Phillip.

"Now may we speak?"

"When I return from my ride." Phillip left no opportunity for argument as he turned and strode to the stables.

He rode hard and far, too far. It was late afternoon when he returned to the hall. He had wasted another day. And it had been to no avail, for he was still heartsick and unequal to facing his brother. How long would this last? Could he even speak civilly to Daniel? And how could he face Miss Brooke?

It was fortunate he had not spoken more plainly at the ball. If he had declared himself out right and been rejected, life would be unbearable. At least now his feelings were known only to himself. The shame was his alone to bear.

When Phillip reached the stables, he considered trying to avoid Daniel. But his brother must have had a servant on lookout, for no sooner had

Phillip dismounted than he saw Daniel bounding toward him. When was the last time he had seen his brother so happy?

"We were beginning to wonder if you had fallen from your horse," Daniel called.

"I am perfectly fine."

Daniel was unruffled by Phillip's gruff reply and easily fell into step beside him. "It is fortunate you are hale and hearty for I fear I would make a poor baronet."

"You need not worry. Nobody will be calling you Sir Daniel in the near future."

Daniel laughed. "That is a relief. But perhaps it would be prudent for me to learn more about your duties."

"What?" Phillip did not follow. When would he announce his engagement?

"I want you to teach me how to run an estate. All those details about rents and crops and drainage, what have you."

This brought Phillip up short. He stopped and turned to get a good look at his brother. Daniel stood tall with a quiet confidence that Phillip did not recognize. He was in earnest.

"I have shocked you but you should not be so surprised. You have been urging me to find a profession and I have decided you are right."

Phillip blinked. "I—You have caught me off guard." At any other time, Phillip would have been thrilled with Daniel's change of heart.

"I expected a little more enthusiasm for the scheme. I am going to stop draining your coffers and support myself. Is that not what you wanted?"

"Yes, yes of course." Phillip continued walking and Daniel followed.

"Good, so you will teach me?"

"I—" It seemed becoming a husband was the motivation Daniel had always needed.

"Come Phillip, I know in the past I have not given you reason to trust my word, but I am determined. I can see my life unfolding before me and I know I must have some occupation. With your help, I think I might be a good landowner. I can think of no better teacher. Can you?"

Daniel's sincerity broke through Phillip's conflicted emotions. His younger brother was asking for help to improve himself. No matter the reason, Phillip would not deny him. Despite all that had passed, Phillip wanted Daniel to be successful.

"I will teach you."

Daniel grinned and pounded Phillip on the back. "I promise you, Phillip, you won't regret it. I will be a model student."

If Daniel became a successful landowner, Phillip would not regret his success. But he might always regret the reason Daniel had decided to get a profession.

Chapter Twenty-Three

$\sim\!\!\mathfrak{O}\!\!\mathfrak{X}\!\!\mathfrak{O}\!\!\sim$

I t was a beautiful Sunday morning. Elaine sat beside Mama in Mrs. Leigh's carriage. As they rolled toward Brightworth church, the widow gleefully recounted the latest neighborhood gossip.

"I thought that Miss Covington looked very pleased with Mr. Edgerton's attentions. And I must say I think it a very good match," Mrs. Leigh said.

Elaine silently agreed, the two of them were perfectly suited.

"I do not think Mrs. Covington is quite so eager," Mama said before sharing her own gossip.

Elaine barely attended. She did not care that Miss Covington had gone driving with Mr. Edgerton or what they bought in Oakbury. She only cared that the neighborhood had lost interest in her and the Ashburns. There was nothing to gossip about. Neither Sir Phillip nor Daniel had called at Ryder Lodge. She had not seen either of them in several long days.

Sir Phillip's absence was easily reasoned away. He could not be expected to call when he was feeling unwell. He must have been terribly ill to have neglected his guests on their last night. She had missed him that evening and every day since.

She missed his conversation, the way he would question her. He always seemed genuinely interested. She missed his insights on everything from farming to Shakespeare. She even missed arguing with him.

As they drew closer to Brightworth, her stomach twisted in anticipation of seeing him. Would they have an opportunity to talk? She desperately wanted to apologize for their last disagreement and discuss Daniel's engagement.

Elaine smiled thinking of Freddie's happiness when she returned from her conference with Daniel. There had not been enough privacy to share all the details, but Freddie had promised to write and tell Elaine all. Until then, she had amused herself trying to imagine what Daniel had said.

But often the scene would change and she would imagine herself in the library with Sir Phillip. She rehearsed what she might say if he declared himself. How she might share her own tender feelings. She imagined being held in his arms, kissing him.

"—and so, I said to Sir Phillip," Mrs. Leigh's words penetrated Elaine's daydream.

"Sir Phillip?" Elaine asked.

"Yes, he was at the Edgerton's dinner," Mrs. Leigh explained.

"I thought Sir Phillip was unwell?"

"Why would he be unwell?" Mrs. Leigh looked as confused as Elaine felt.

"No reason," Elaine murmured.

Mrs. Leigh gave her an exasperated look.

The carriage began to slow. "Are we here already?" Mrs. Leigh asked before craning her neck to look out the window.

Mama reached out and squeezed Elaine's hand. Had Mama known Sir Phillip wasn't sick? Had she guessed the reason for Elaine's listlessness?

"Augusta," Mama said, "have you made a decision regarding this winter?"

"Eh? Oh yes. I think Bath will do very well, very well indeed. It is a perfectly charming place and all my friends will be there."

For the last five years, Mrs. Leigh had spent her winters in Bath. She always insisted Mama spend some of the time with her. When Elaine was at school, this had meant instead of returning home for the holidays, she had simply moved a few streets away. In retrospect, Elaine wondered if Mama had arranged it so she did not encounter the irascible Mr. Ashburn.

"And of course, you and Elaine shall come with me," Mrs. Leigh said. "I simply hate to go alone and I am sure she has been missing the amusements of Bath."

"That is too generous," Mama demurred.

The carriage rocked to a halt, ending the conversation as they prepared to exit.

Only an hour before Elaine would have said she did not wish to go to Bath, did not wish to be parted from Sir Phillip. But he was not ill. There was no excuse for his absence. He had broken his promise to call. He did not spend his days dreaming of holding her. He likely did not think of her at all.

Elaine hoped Mama's prevarication was just a prelude to accepting the invitation to Bath. The streets of Bath seemed a sanctuary now. A return to a simpler time, before her friends all left, before the Ashburn brothers. Elaine would not be able to spend the whole winter; she still had her duty to the parish school. She would need to talk with Mr. Eden about the possibility.

From the moment they entered the chapel, Elaine's focus was on the Ashburn's empty pew. She sat nervously beside her mother and tried not to glance back every time someone entered. Her resolve was weaker than her need to look and she was rewarded when she turned to see Sir Phillip walking down the aisle.

He looked in good health, still handsome and elegantly dressed. His posture was impeccable, chin high, eyes forward as he hastened to the front. Lady Ashburn was on his arm and, as if to make up for her sullen son, had a smile for everyone. Elaine tried to return the smile, but found herself unequal to the task. Her eyes wandered again to Sir Phillip but his gaze did not so much as flicker in her direction as he walked by.

She pressed her lips together. Where was the man she had come to know and honor? She did not see him. He was a haughty baronet once more. Elaine let out her breath and trained her eyes on the pulpit, refusing to stare at the back of his head.

She sat quietly through the sermon but did not hear a word of it. Her mind was occupied imagining all the things she might say to Sir Phillip. She contemplated indignant tirades, coy rejoinders, and cold indifference, but nothing satisfied.

She was taken by surprise when everyone began to stand. Trailing after Mama as she exited and began talking to neighbors, Elaine had no interest in speaking to anyone. How she wished Freddie or Mrs. Farthing or Miss Wilson were still there.

When Mrs. Leigh began talking of going to Bath, Elaine was reminded of her resolution to speak with Mr. Eden. She looked about for the vicar, but he was not in the churchyard. Elaine left Mama and returned to the emptying church.

Mr. Eden was there, but Elaine hesitated. He was standing halfway down the aisle talking with Sir Phillip. She wanted to flee but Mr. Eden saw her and beckoned. She had no choice. She could not avoid Sir Phillip forever. Walking resolutely, she forced herself to smile while avoiding meeting Sir Phillip's gaze.

"Miss Brooke," Mr. Eden said. "I was just talking to Sir Phillip about the school."

"That is why I came to talk to you," Elaine said. She was proud of her calm tone. Her body was jittery with awareness of Sir Phillip.

"Yes," Sir Phillip said. "I was attempting to inform Mr. Eden that it would be best to find a different teacher." His tone was infuriatingly formal.

"Excuse me?" Elaine was not sure she understood.

Sir Phillip looked at her. "Given the circumstances, do you not think it best?"

What circumstances? Did he no longer trust her as a teacher? All because of their argument? Or did he think she would go back on her commitment in order to spend the winter in Bath? No matter the reason, it was clear he no longer wanted her to teach.

"I am very sorry to hear that there has been a change." Mr. Eden's sincerity helped Elaine swallow her resentment.

"I was looking forward to teaching," she said. "But Sir Phillip is right, under the circumstances I think it best you find a different teacher. I hope that you will find someone that will meet Sir Phillip's exacting standards."

Sir Phillip stirred beside her but she ignored him.

"I am sure with the Lord's help and the incentive of a higher salary, I will be successful." Mr. Eden gave a genial bow. "Now if you will excuse me, I should see to the rest of my flock."

Elaine turned to follow the vicar just as Sir Phillip did the same. He took a step back and gestured for her to precede him. When Elaine had imagined walking down a church aisle with Sir Phillip, it had been under very different circumstances. Her daydreams were not reality. How many times would she need to learn that lesson?

When they reached the door Sir Phillip finally spoke. "I didn't mean to speak out of turn. I know nothing has been officially said but—"

"It is your school, Sir Phillip, and you are right. I can hardly teach if I am not here."

He nodded curtly. On the other side of the thick wooden door there was a buzz of muffled conversations. She reached for the door, but Sir Phillip stayed her. Heat tingled where he grasped her arm. Startled, she looked up into the light blue eyes she had come to love. He was studying her in that thoughtful and careful way that she had once thought indicated a deeper emotion. Now she was unsure. He released her and pulled his hand behind his back.

"Miss Brooke, I wanted to make sure that you were not troubled by my words."

"Troubled?"

"At the assembly, I spoke unwisely. In the party spirit I may have implied. . . Indeed, you may have thought." Color stained his cheeks and he broke eye contact. "I want to assure you that my regard is familial and I am happy to call you sister." His tone was stiff and formal.

"Sister?" Elaine swallowed thickly, her emotions threatening to choke her. "Oh, yes, I see. Thank you for making that clear."

He did not wish to court her. She had been an utter fool and let her fancy rule her head. Worse, Sir Phillip knew of her expectations and had sought to crush them. What had come over her? A baronet offer for her? She must be mad.

She had to get away before he saw her tears. "I should go, my mother will be missing me." She did not look at him as she shoved at the door and escaped into the bright sunshine, fleeing the churchyard.

Taken by the party spirit? A sister?

The words bounced around her brain. He was happy to call her sister. He regretted his words at the assembly and had stayed away to lower her expectations. Had he heard the rumors and been mortified? Was he disgusted by the mere idea of their names being linked? She had gone from one folly to another. She left behind her childish infatuation with Daniel and replaced it with an affection for Sir Phillip.

Questions and recriminations swirled through her head with every step. Sir Phillip had never considered her anything but a sister; an annoying, argumentative sister. It was embarrassing to think how far she had erred in her judgment.

When she returned home, she was exhausted in body and spirit. She joined her mother in the drawing room.

They had been sitting in silence for some time, the crackling of the fire and the slow turning of a page the only sound echoing in the room. Elaine stared blankly down at her book, only to realize it was *The Faerie Queen* and tears had sprung to her eyes. Now she could only gaze at the page, unable to read without thinking of Sir Phillip.

Elaine looked up to find Mama watching her.

"So like your father." Mama gave a half-smile.

"You are forever saying that but I don't know what you mean," Elaine said, too tired to be cautious.

Mama sighed. "Your father was a man who struggled to live in the real world. A man who lived in his head as much as he lived in the physical world. I loved him for it but it was also his worst quality. He built castles in the air and when he died, they came crashing down and we paid dearly for it."

"Mama!" Elaine was surprised by this speech.

"I only speak what is true. Had your father not squandered away our money, we would not be in these reduced circumstances. You would have had a dowry, enough money to tempt a good man."

"A good man would love me without a dowry."

"Perhaps, but one can't live on love alone."

Elaine wondered if her lack of fortune had weighed with Sir Phillip. He was a practical man and had a responsibility to his estate and title. Perhaps even if he had cared for her, it would not matter; he would marry sensibly. But hadn't he claimed he wanted a love match?

"You are right. Too long I have harbored hopes of finding a man who would make all my problems go away. I had even hoped that—" Elaine stopped, embarrassment seizing her tongue.

"You hoped that one of the Ashburns might marry you?"

Mama really had seen more than Elaine thought. Elaine buried her face in her hands. "Mama, I am such a fool."

"My darling girl, we are all fools in love."

"But Sir Phillip does not love me."

"Perhaps not, but he certainly admires you and enjoys your company. All the neighborhood witnessed it at the assembly. I saw it every night we spent at the hall."

"But you did not say anything. You told Mrs. Leigh that he was being kind."

"Mrs. Leigh is a dear friend and gossip. I did not want her spreading tales. And I did not want to raise your hopes. But you are not a fool. That Sir Phillip does not wish to court you is a sign of his foolishness, not yours."

Elaine was surprised into laughing. She had never heard her mother speak ill of Sir Phillip.

"Now, let us speak of something more cheerful. Mrs. Leigh is most insistent that we accompany her to Bath. And I am minded to accept, but what of your position at the school?"

"Mr. Eden released me from the obligation." Elaine did not want to share any of the details.

"Then it seems there is no reason we should not go. What do you say?"

"I think I would rather be anywhere but here."

"I thought so." Elaine shared a smile with her mother. "Why don't you read that letter from Mrs. Piper and tell her of our plans? I am sure you will be happy to see her again."

Elaine looked at the pile of correspondence that she had ignored earlier. There was indeed a letter from Mrs. Piper on the top.

"Perhaps in the morning? I am fatigued."

Mama nodded with understanding. "Of course."

It was better to have everything in the open. She should have confided in her mother sooner. She resolved to spend less time daydreaming and more time living in the real world. She would be more like her mother and less like her father. It was time she accepted her lot. The sooner she accepted that she would not marry, the sooner she could start to build her own life.

Chapter Twenty-Four

"P hillip, are you listening?" Lady Ashburn asked.

"Apologies. What did you say?" Phillip refocused his attention.

Mother regarded him closely. They were sitting together in his study, the estate accounts before him on the desk, Mother across from him in a high wingback chair. They were meant to be discussing the household budget. Phillip chided himself for not listening.

"Are you quite all right?" she asked.

"Perfectly fine. I was just thinking about the school." It was not a lie. He had been thinking of his last conversation with Miss Brooke. It had been days since she had walked away from him but he could not stop recalling every detail of that moment.

His mother gave a low hum to express her disbelief. "Is there anything I should know about the school?"

"We are looking for a teacher," Phillip said flatly.

"I thought Miss Brooke was our teacher."

"She has decided it would not suit."

"Did you quarrel?" The concern in Mother's voice told Phillip he had been doing a poor job of hiding his feelings. Unlike Daniel, who had a great capacity for deception.

Phillip wished he could explain that Miss Brooke would soon be Mrs.

Ashburn and move to whatever estate Daniel chose to occupy. But, for reasons known only to Daniel and Miss Brooke, they were keeping their engagement a secret, even from their family. No doubt they thought it great fun to keep everyone in the dark. Phillip thought it immature.

"There was no argument. Miss Brooke's circumstances have changed."

Mother waited but Phillip would say no more. She sighed.

"It is a pity. I had such hopes for the partnership. But I suppose in time you might find someone else."

Phillip's insides twisted. He did not think Mother was talking about the school. Had Mother observed his partiality? Was she expecting a courtship? How surprised would she be when Daniel introduced his intended? It was bad enough that he had to deal with his feelings; he could not imagine the humiliation if Mother knew his secret. Phillip did not want sympathy or pitying looks.

He managed a small smile. "Do not worry," he said. "All will come right, eventually." He looked down at the account books. "Now, what were we speaking of?"

"I let Dolly go home to visit her sister."

The talk turned to servants and household management. Phillip was careful not to be distracted and managed to forget about Miss Brooke for almost twenty minutes. Then the conversation turned to the house party expenses. The cost was less than Phillip had expected.

"In every way, I believe the party was a success," Mother said.

"Except in the way that mattered," Phillip muttered.

"True, it did not result in the engagement you were hoping for."

Phillip scoffed. She did not know how true her words were.

"For that, I am sorry. I thought Daniel and Miss Talbot would have made an excellent couple. I don't know what that boy was thinking of letting her get away."

"Of himself."

Mother gave him a chiding look. "The party did result in Daniel finally taking on a profession. Surely you are happy with that result?"

"I will be happier when he is not constantly underfoot."

In the last week and a half, Daniel had rarely left Phillip's side. He was constantly asking questions as Phillip did his accounts, talked with tenants, or attended to other duties. It seemed that for once in his life, Daniel was taking things seriously.

Only a month ago such application would have overjoyed Phillip, but now his pride was tinged with bitterness. Miss Brooke had wrought this change; it was for her that Daniel strived to gain an income.

"Now Phillip, you don't mean that. He is not always with you."

"No, he does go for long rides." Phillip struggled to keep the bitterness from his voice. He strongly suspected that the rides were excuses for clandestine meetings with Miss Brooke.

"And it is not a permanent circumstance. Once Daniel finds a place to let, he will leave and you will miss him."

Phillip wasn't sure he would miss his brother, but he did dread the day Daniel found his own estate. When Daniel left, he would likely take Miss Brooke with him. Now he was in limbo, occasionally believing that the marriage would never happen, that there was still some chance it would all turn out differently. But that hope would be dashed when the betrothal was announced.

"I hope he won't find a suitable place for a good while yet," Mother said.

"I am not even sure what he can afford."

Phillip made a note to ask Daniel about his budget. He was sure that whatever place Daniel found, he would require help with the rent. Phillip tried not to resent the fact that he would still be financing Daniel's happily ever after.

Tried and failed.

"The house will feel much emptier when he goes."

Phillip was caught by her wistful tone. Was she unhappy? He had been so caught up in his own problems that he had not paid attention to Mother. Did she miss their guests? Did she miss one in particular? He did not know how to ask her about Captain Hart, so he settled on a more general question.

"Mother, are you happy here?"

"Happy?"

"Yes, here at the hall. Do you wish to travel or reside elsewhere, perhaps remarry. . . ?" Phillip paused when she frowned. "Whatever you might prefer I want you to know that I would support you. I'd even consent to more house parties."

She gave him a soft smile. "Thank you, Phillip. You are a thoughtful son. But I am quite content with my life here."

Phillip noted that content was not happy. He had long been content with his life before Miss Brooke showed him there was more. Phillip wanted his mother to be happy. She had been happy in the garden with Captain Hart and dancing with him at the assembly. But it seemed she did not wish to talk about it.

"Perhaps when you marry, I will wish to remove to London or Bath and give the new Lady Ashburn the run of the house."

"Rest assured, Mother, that day is far distant. And if that is all, then I should attend to this." Phillip gestured to his correspondence.

Mother gave him a long look before nodding. She stood. "Don't spend all day in this study. I don't want you working more than necessary."

"Yes, Mother," he said with his finest fake smile.

Once alone, Phillip did his best to throw himself into his accounts and correspondence. For a time, he was successful, but then he came to an invoice for a new copy of *The Faerie Queene*. He had ordered the book after deciding Miss Brooke should have her own copy.

Bitterly he considered if it was an appropriate wedding present.

Phillip leaned back in his chair and sighed. Would he always resent her choice? Would he always struggle to behave normally around her? Their conversation in the church had been stilted. He would have to get better, build up his walls higher so when she officially joined their family, he would be able to meet her with indifference.

He had said he would be happy to call Miss Brooke sister. How long before it was true? How long before his desire to tell her all his thoughts and opinions disappeared? How long before he didn't want to kiss her?

He hoped they would marry soon and leave the neighborhood. Time and distance were needed before he could conquer his emotions. Once she was gone, he could take his feelings and lock them behind a heavy door in his mind. Only then could he reconcile himself to being her brother.

Muffled voices reached Phillip through the door that led to the library. Eager for an excuse to stop his work, Phillip stood and crossed to the door. Nothing could have prepared him for what he saw when he entered.

Daniel sat with Miss Brooke, cozy as an old married couple, in the chairs next to the fireplace. Mother and Father had often sat in those very chairs as they talked over their day. They were a tableau of domesticity. They weren't touching and the door was open, but he was clearly intruding on something intimate, though not quite as intimate as the scene he had observed days ago.

Phillip thought wildly of making excuses and departing but that would only raise their suspicions. This was his first test. He must treat her as nothing but his brother's intended.

Feeling ridiculous on the threshold, he took a few steps into the room. Daniel spoke but Phillip wasn't really attending. His eyes kept flitting to Miss Brooke; she wasn't looking at him. Did that mean anything?

"So will you?" Daniel asked.

"Will I what?" Phillip frowned.

Daniel rolled his eyes. "You see what I mean?" he said to Miss Brooke before turning back to Phillip. "Will you assure Miss Brooke that I am becoming an excellent landowner?"

"You are certainly applying yourself to the task."

Daniel chuckled. "Faint praise, but I guess I should be satisfied with any kind words from you."

"I did not mean—"

"To praise me? It's too late," Daniel teased.

Miss Brooke had once accused Phillip of having too harsh an opinion of Daniel. She had asked him to encourage his brother. It was not fair to take out his frustrations when Daniel was truly trying. And it would ease Miss Brooke's mind to know her future husband would be able to provide for her.

"You are a quick learner," Phillip said. "I have no doubt you will be able to apply the lessons to your own estate. If you work half so hard on your own land, I am sure it will prosper,"

Daniel flushed and looked away. He had no ready quip.

"You asked for his opinion," Miss Brooke chided.

"I did not think it would be so favorable."

"That is unfair to your brother." Miss Brooke's eyes darted to Phillip.

"You must allow me to be surprised but I have rarely met with his approval."

"Perhaps you should have tried harder to earn it."

"You do not understand." Daniel waved his hand. "Everyone always approves of you."

"Not everyone approves of me." Miss Brooke's cheeks colored.

Though they were talking of Phillip, it was like they had forgotten he was standing there. He was the spectator to their little scene. Would this be his life, always on the outside watching their happiness? The idea pierced his heart.

"Who does not approve of you?" Daniel feigned shock. "Phillip, do you know of anyone who does not approve of Miss Brooke?"

Phillip was unable to avoid looking at her now. She wore her familiar plain walking dress with the shawl that set off the green in her eyes. Her hair was not quite contained; she had probably walked to the hall. She was loveliness itself. Phillip turned back to Daniel.

"I cannot speak for everyone, but I certainly approve of Miss Brooke," Phillip said.

"Two compliments in one conversation? That must be some kind of record."

Daniel's high spirits grated on Phillip.

"I should go." Miss Brooke stood.

Daniel stood with her. "Really? I thought you came to borrow a book?"

She shook her head. "No. I wanted to return one." She glanced at her hands and for the first time, Phillip noticed she held *The Faerie Queene*.

"I am sorry you did not enjoy it," Phillip said.

"Oh, no I enjoyed it very much," Miss Brooke said earnestly. "But I have finished it."

"That tome?" Daniel said.

Miss Brooke shrugged. "When I enjoy a book, I can't help but read it quickly."

"But doesn't that shorten the experience?" Phillip asked. "Wouldn't it be better to draw it out and savor the story?"

"I guess I am impatient." Miss Brooke met his eyes and the shock that went through him was proof that he was far from indifferent to her. If this was a test, he was failing.

"Impatience is a trait we share," Daniel said. "Shall I walk you home?"

"I don't want to take you from your work with Sir Phillip."

"Yes, we should go over the expenses from the house party."

Phillip hoped his obvious desire to keep them apart was not evident. It was silly when they were to be married, but he couldn't help it.

Miss Brooke stepped forward and offered the book. He waved her away. "You should keep it. I certainly won't have time to read it."

She looked like she might argue but her eyes darted to Daniel. She nodded. "Thank you." She hugged the book to her chest.

As she took her leave, Phillip suddenly wanted to beg her to stay. He wanted Daniel to leave. He wanted to speak with her about the book and so much else. He wanted to ask why she chose his brother and why they were keeping it a secret. He wanted the awkwardness between them to disappear. But he could not have what he wanted. There was no returning to how they were before.

He bowed.

"Goodbye, Miss Brooke."

Chapter Twenty-Five

S ir Phillip's goodbye echoed in Elaine's mind as she entered the woods. The pain was acute, worse than anything before. He had barely glanced at her. He was entirely indifferent. But then, why had he given her the book? Might it be evidence of his affection?

Oh, why was it so difficult to govern her heart? Despite her resolution to put away her childish dreams, Elaine found herself still hoping.

Since their conversation in the church, she had walked to the Old Priory several times. She told herself she only wanted to see the ruins, but when she returned home disappointed, she had to admit to her hopes of encountering Sir Phillip. Each time she heard a carriage in the drive her heart jumped. Despite his rejection, she still wished to see him.

Using the book as an excuse to visit Ryder Hall was more evidence that she still lived in a fantasy. She had reasoned that even if he thought of her as a sister, they might still talk of literature. But it had gone all wrong.

Daniel had discovered her as she approached the hall and insisted on accompanying her. He had spoken of nothing but Freddie and his plans to acquire his own estate. She was happy for them, but it was difficult to sit and listen to his raptures. It had become impossible when Sir Phillip arrived.

She started when the stream and its wooden bridge appeared before her, scarcely remembering how she had gotten through the woods. Sighing, she hugged the book to her chest. How could she continue to live in the same neighborhood as Sir Phillip?

She wished it was winter, that she was already in Bath. When she did not live in constant expectation of meeting him, then she could rid herself of her fancies.

As she entered the lodge, Perkins greeted her with a broad smile and offer of fresh bread. Elaine accepted.

"You have a new letter, miss," Perkins said as she placed the bread before Elaine.

"Thank you."

Elaine did not wish to read any letters from her friends for fear of what they might say about Sir Phillip. But when she looked at the small square of paper, she was surprised to see Mrs. Piper's handwriting. Elaine had not yet replied to her last letter. Curious, she opened it.

Dear Elaine,

I apologize for the brevity of this letter. I am presently quite overrun. I was pleased to hear of your plans to teach and happy my advice to seek occupation was heeded. But I must urge you to reconsider your plan. First, because the salary is too low, and second, because I would like to offer you better. I am in great need of a teacher here at Pembray House. Knowing your temperament and intelligence, I can confidently say that you would be suited for the work. You can begin immediately. If you are amenable, please reply post haste.

Affectionately,
  Honoria Piper

She reread it to ensure she had not dreamed its contents. Relief washed over her. She did not need to wait for winter; she could escape to Bath immediately. Standing, she went in search of Mama.

"Well?" Elaine asked after reading the letter aloud.

"I think working for Mrs. Piper will be a fine thing. And you like Bath."

Elaine nodded. "I do."

"It would be better than pining away here."

Elaine was glad Mama understood. She could not live so close to Sir Phillip. It was too confusing, too painful. And it would only get worse. Someday Sir Phillip would marry, likely a rich, accomplished lady from London. Elaine would be forced to smile and attend parties with them. While Sir Phillip led a young Lady Ashburn to the dining room, Elaine would trail bitterly at the end. If she stayed at the lodge, Elaine would never be able to escape conversations about them. She would never be able to escape him.

"And if you find a husband, then all the better." Mama broke through Elaine's distraction with her teasing tone.

Elaine smiled. "Yes, let us pray I find a rich, kind widower."

"With a large house and no children," Mama added.

Elaine shook her head. She couldn't honestly think of any man with her heart in tatters. She would not go to Bath only to repeat her folly.

"Do you really wish for me to marry? Even without love?"

"Oh, Elaine, I don't want you to spend your life scrimping and always living off the charity of others. I married for love. I wish better for you. A kind and respectable man with enough money to keep you comfortable would be a fine thing. But if you can earn your living as a teacher, so much the better. Then you need only rely on yourself."

Elaine liked the idea of being an independent spinster and not ever letting a man close enough to break her heart again. Her choice was simple.

"I shall accept Mrs. Piper's offer immediately."

Mama smiled. "I will miss you, but I think you will be very happy in Bath."

"Thank you, Mama. And we won't be parted for long. You will come with Mrs. Leigh and we shall see each other frequently." Elaine pulled out a small sheet of paper.

"Speaking of Mrs. Leigh, she is taking me to Oakbury this afternoon. Would you like me to post your letter?"

"That would be wonderful, thank you."

As Elaine wrote, a weight lifted from her shoulders. Bath would be a good change. Even without her friends, there was Mrs. Piper and the safety of knowing where she fit. She would have a purpose there. She would not fall into misery like the fair maiden of Astolat. She would make new plans; she would forget Sir Phillip.

She was not running away, she was seizing an opportunity.

When Mama returned from Oakbury, she brought the news that Mrs. Leigh had declared she would take Elaine to Bath. The widow was going to look at lodgings and insisted it was no trouble.

* * *

In two short days, Elaine was looking through a carriage window as the glowing white marble of the town came into sight. She breathed out a sigh and smiled. The sleepless nights and rush to pack slipped away from her.

Bath was home. A welcome familiarity surrounded her as they clattered through the streets. Warm memories filled her as Pembray House drew closer. She had made the right decision. Sir Phillip would become a distant memory and she would recapture the happiness of her school days. She was determined to make it so.

As the carriage slowed, Elaine turned to Mrs. Leigh. The widow had slept the majority of the six-hour ride.

"Thank you for your assistance."

Mrs. Leigh smiled. "I was happy to have a companion. Please give my regrets to your Mrs. Piper. Another time, when I am at my leisure, I will come and call."

"Yes, of course."

The carriage stopped and Elaine thanked her again before exiting.

As she was handed out, Elaine instinctively looked up to the drawing room window. Two young faces quickly disappeared. She smiled, wondering which girls were peeking. Elaine and her friends had spied out the window often. They would check who was arriving and then report to the rest of the room. Sometimes Miss Minerva would censure them, but more often she was thankful for the intelligence. It was strange to think that soon she would be the teacher and not the girl looking through the window.

How did she look to those girls? The elegant carriage must have occasioned excitement only to be dashed when nobody of consequence descended. Did they see an old school fellow or a stranger? Elaine was so different from the person that had left only months ago but the differences were not visible. Even her traveling dress was one she had worn while in school.

The door opened and Brimley greeted her with the smallest of smiles.

"Welcome back, Miss Brooke."

Elaine greeted the serious butler warmly.

"Would you like to freshen up or meet with Mrs. Piper?" Brimley asked as he took her hat and gloves. Elaine was calmed by his familiar, deep baritone.

"I would be happy to meet her now," Elaine said as she handed over her traveling coat. She had no desire to be alone a moment longer. Mrs. Piper would not mind if she was a bit travel worn.

Brimley led the way to Mrs. Piper's private sitting room. As a child, Elaine had only gone to the study when being disciplined, mostly for not paying attention to her teachers. How strange to be walking down the familiar hall with no trepidation. Brimley announced her and then turned and gave her a lightning-fast wink before retreating. It was so out of character, that Elaine was surprised into a smile.

"My dear, you are here! And how are you?" Mrs. Piper stood from her writing desk.

The headmistress was as tall as Elaine remembered. Her light brown hair was pulled back in a simple bun and her expression welcoming. She moved with grace as she crossed the room and reached for Elaine. Elaine was astonished; Mrs. Piper had never been demonstrative. After the worry, lack of sleep, and day in the carriage, the kindness proved too much.

Elaine promptly burst into tears.

Sometime later Elaine was ensconced in a comfortable chair, an empty teacup beside her. Her eyes were dry but her handkerchief damp.

"I am sorry," Elaine said. "I don't know what came over me." Wasn't she supposed to be happier in Bath?

"There is no need to apologize; it is quite understandable, given the circumstances."

It had taken little prompting for Elaine to lay bare her recent history. She poured out her heart as Mrs. Piper listened stoically. How many other young ladies had brought their troubles to this very room? How many others had Mrs. Piper counseled with her shrewd and practical advice?

"I expected trouble of this kind," Mrs. Piper said as she set down her teacup.

"You did?"

"Though I thought Mr. Ashburn the likely source of any heartbreak."

"Not an unreasonable assumption." Elaine smiled wanly. Would everyone always think she cared for Daniel?

"The heart is fickle. Which is why I find it best to ignore it whenever possible."

"I begin to see the wisdom in such an approach."

"Good." Mrs. Piper pressed her lips into a firm line, every bit the strict schoolmistress.

Elaine straightened, unconsciously preparing herself for the pending lecture.

"Now I will say this once and then we will speak no more on the subject. You have always been prone to flights of fancy, but I do not think you imagined this baronet's interest. It is clear to me from his actions that he was not indifferent to you. That he chose not to pursue the relationship speaks only of his cowardice and shortsightedness. Any man who cannot see your worth does not deserve your time or attention."

Elaine ducked her head while twisting her handkerchief. She wanted to object but knew better than to interrupt.

"I honor you for not wasting away, hoping for his notice. That you have come here is another mark of your sense and resilience. I think you will be an excellent teacher. But I warn you that I will not have a watering pot. This must be the last of your public displays. No heartache was ever mended with tears, only hard work and clear purpose can do that."

Elaine nodded. "I understand."

"Good." Mrs. Piper reached out and took Elaine's hand. "It will get easier with time, you will see."

Her soft, sympathetic tone was so at odds with her prior pragmatic attitude that Elaine's eyes filled again. Mrs. Piper truly understood. Did it come from personal experience or wisdom gleaned from helping other young women? Elaine suspected it was both.

"Now," Mrs. Piper said, returning to business. "You go and rest. I have put you in the blue room. I will send up a tray for dinner. Tomorrow we will go over the curriculum and you shall meet your students. There will be many familiar faces but plenty of new ones."

They stood. "Thank you, Mrs. Piper. I am so very glad to be here."

Chapter Twenty-Six

A s August ended, the days grew subtly colder. Harvest would soon be upon them. After the meeting in the library, Phillip worked hard at mastering his emotions. He must learn to be indifferent, to forget his attachment. But thoughts of her continued to intrude. At the oddest times the sound of her laugh, the flash of her eyes, the feel of her hand in his, would plague him. And while he refused to dwell on the memories, he could not escape them.

Reminders of their conversations were ever present. When he was about the countryside, he thought of their ride and how she listened and asked questions. When in the drawing room, he was reminded of her deep knowledge of many topics and her penchant for argument. At dinner, he missed simply seeing her face at the table.

He avoided the library and Old Priory entirely. He avoided any mention of the Brookes in conversation.

His only solace was also his torment; he had not seen her since the library. He did not count his dreams. She invaded them every night, causing him to rise late.

"Phillip," Mother called to him as he was passing the breakfast room.

Phillip reluctantly slowed and entered the room. "Yes?"

"Are you not eating this morning?"

"I'm not hungry."

"But you must be, you did not have dinner."

"I had a tray in my study." Food had been brought to him, though he had not eaten much.

Mother pursed her lips. "Phillip, I wish you would tell me what is wrong. And don't say nothing. I know you better than that."

Phillip could not deny her allegations but neither could he explain. "I am sorry I have not been myself. It will soon pass."

"Perhaps if you just spoke to the lady, you might resolve your problems?"

Heat raced up his neck. "I do not know what you mean."

Mother scoffed.

"Believe me, Mother, if a simple conversation was all that was needed, I would not hesitate to speak to her." Phillip snapped his mouth closed. He had said too much. "Now you will excuse me." He fled from Mother and her knowing eyes.

He needed to get farther away. That morning he contrived urgent business to London and left that afternoon. Thus, he was able to avoid both his mother and attending church in Brightworth. He was not equal to seeing Miss Brooke again. For the first time in his life, Phillip preferred London to Ryder Hall. But a change in location did not change his heart or his responsibilities and only a few days passed before he returned.

It was late in the afternoon when Phillip arrived. Though travel weary, he went straight to his study. Instead of a quiet sanctuary, he found Daniel ensconced behind the desk.

"You are back! Excellent." Daniel grinned wide.

"I see you have made yourself at home," Phillip said as he strode into the room.

"Don't worry Phillip, I am not trying to steal your title. Though I must say that in your absence, I have executed the duties admirably."

"I am sure."

Phillip hated to admit it but Daniel had all the makings of a good landowner. If he continued to apply himself, Miss Brooke would be in safe hands.

"I am happy to relinquish your chair, but first, you must congratulate me."

His mouth went dry as his heart plummeted to his knees. Here it was, the words that would seal his fate. As long as the engagement was secret, he had retained some hope that Miss Brooke would come to her senses and cry off.

"Phillip?"

"What am I to congratulate you on?" He was being curt but couldn't help it.

Daniel picked up a paper from the desk and waved it. "My solicitor has found me the perfect estate. I am of the mind to settle on it, but of course wanted your approval of the scheme."

Phillip reached for the paper, trying not to let his relief show on his face. He read through the details quickly. The solicitor sketched out the merits and drawbacks of the estate in plain language. It was close enough to London for Daniel's tastes and far enough away from Ryder Hall to suit Phillip.

"The hunting lands seem to be particularly appealing," Daniel said.

Phillip looked up from the letter and realized Daniel was pacing anxiously. It seemed his brother felt the weight of his decision.

"They are a definite asset," Phillip said.

Daniel nodded. "Good, I am glad to hear you think so."

It occurred to Phillip as he returned to reading that Daniel was anxious not just for his opinion, but his approval. Phillip had not stopped to consider what a daunting task it was to acquire a profession, an estate, and a wife in such a short time. Despite his jealousy, Phillip wanted Daniel to be successful.

"The rent is a bit high," Daniel said. "But I think it is well worth it."

"It is an excellent establishment and I will provide any assistance you may need."

"Phillip, you don't need to—"

"No, I insist. You are a good investment."

Daniel's eyes grew wide. "Do you really believe that?"

Phillip had never thought Daniel lacked self-confidence but it seemed encouragement was in order. "I think you will be a fine landowner; the neighborhood will be lucky to have you."

Daniel smiled. "Yes, they will be. I shall write immediately and accept it."

"Accept what?" Mother stood in the doorway.

Daniel danced over to her. "I have found an estate that even Phillip approves of."

Phillip sank into his leather chair as Daniel spun Mother in a circle. Phillip could easily see Daniel doing the same to Miss Brooke when he brought her the news. How long until the business was all settled? He was tired of living in limbo.

When they stopped spinning Mother was laughing. "And now that your home is secured, will you be making another announcement?"

Phillip sat up straighter.

"Now Mother, what are you implying?" Daniel asked with false innocence.

"It is quite obvious to anyone with sense that you are turning from your bachelor ways," Mother said sternly.

"Is it?"

"And there is the small fact of this," Mother held out a small letter, still sealed but bearing the unmistakable mark of a woman's hand.

Why would Miss Brooke risk a letter?

Daniel laughed. "You have found me out. I confess, I asked the lady and she accepted."

Though Phillip knew it, had seen it with his own eyes, it was different hearing Daniel admit it. Now was the time for him to offer his approval but Phillip could not find words.

Mother had no such impediment. "Daniel, that is wonderful! But when did it happen and why did you keep it a secret? You know we would welcome her with joy."

"I was accepted on the last night of the house party. We wanted to wait until all was in order with an estate. I have not yet spoken to her father."

"Her father?" Surprise gave Phillip his voice. "However do you intend to talk to him?"

"I was going to write, unless you think I should go in person?" Daniel asked.

"Her father is dead," Phillip murmured more to himself than his brother. A chill ran through him as his heart tried to accept what his brain had already worked out.

"Good God! Mr. Talbot is dead? Did you hear that in London?" Daniel's face went white as he reached for the letter Mother held.

"Talbot?" Phillip stood. "Talbot isn't dead."

"What? Why would you say that he was—?" Daniel sounded truly angry.

"Daniel," Mother intervened. "Let us be clear. You are to marry Miss Talbot."

"Yes, of course Miss Talbot."

Phillip had guessed the truth, but the words felled him. He sank back into his chair. Daniel was betrothed to Miss Talbot. Miss Brooke was not promised to Daniel.

"You should be happy. Was not the entire point of the house party to get me to offer for Freddie?" Daniel looked between Mother and Phillip.

"No. . . yes. . . I mean. . ." Phillip ran a hand through his hair. He could not focus on his brother as his mind whirred like a trapped bee. He had seen them. In the library he had seen them embrace. A horrible thought raced through his mind. Had Daniel made promises to Miss Brooke? Promises he did not intend to keep?

Phillip clenched his fists. "Daniel, you can't dally with one woman and marry another."

"What? What do you take me for?" Daniel was indignant. "I may flirt but I would never dishonor a woman." He turned to Mother. "I swear it."

"Of course not, Daniel," Mother placed a calming hand on his arm.

"I saw you," Phillip growled as he stood. "I saw you and Miss Brooke in the library." He couldn't continue, couldn't recount how he watched them embrace.

"Miss Brooke is my very good friend, nothing more."

"And does she know that? Does she know you are secretly engaged to Miss Talbot?"

"Yes!"

"She does?" Mother broke into the conversation. "You told Miss Brooke before you told your own family?"

Daniel ducked his head. "It wasn't like that. I asked Elaine to marry me first."

"You what?"

"Phillip, let him explain." Mother held up her hand to forestall him.

His head was spinning.

Daniel continued. "I was quite dejected. I was sure Freddie would not have me. In my despair, I realized that Elaine would be an excellent alternative. I thought we would rub along quite well but she refused me. Didn't even consider the idea and told me that I needed to ask Freddie. She was right."

Mother said something but Phillip didn't hear. Miss Brooke had rejected Daniel? She wasn't marrying his brother? How had he been so wrong?

In a rush, their conversation in the church came back to him. After practically declaring himself at the assembly he had told her he thought of her as a sister. That his affection was only familial.

What must she think of him?

He needed to see her, he needed to explain. Phillip moved to the door and was surprised that Daniel and Mother were still standing at the threshold.

"Pardon me," he said as he tried to move past.

"No, you are not leaving now," Mother replied. She turned to Daniel. "I need to speak with your brother."

Daniel looked between them. "I think I should be a part of this conversation."

"I don't want to talk. I need to go and see—" Phillip swallowed. "I need to go."

"Miss Brooke is in Bath," Mother said.

This did what nothing else could and brought Phillip to a standstill.

"I knew it," Daniel crowed. "You care for Miss Brooke."

"You knew no such thing," Mother said.

"I suspected. He paid her particular attention and frowned less around her." Daniel's lips twitched. "And what's more, I think the feelings are mutual."

Phillip's heart jumped. Was Daniel speaking the truth? Had she said something to him?

"I think Daniel is right," Mother said. "I believe Miss Brooke is partial to you."

"She may have been," Phillip replied. "But I have made a horrible mistake. I have treated her. . ." He shook his head. "What must she think of me?"

"I do not know what has passed between you, but the only way to know her mind is to speak with her," Mother said.

"Miss Brooke's advice for my proposal was to apologize for my rudeness and ask properly," Daniel added with an encouraging pat on Phillip's shoulder.

"How long will she be in Bath?" Phillip asked.

"She isn't coming back," Mother said. "I understand she took a position as a teacher at her old school."

Miss Brooke had left. She had left without saying goodbye. She wasn't engaged to Daniel, but she didn't want Phillip either. If there had been any spark of tender feeling, his inconstancy had surely doused it before it could become a flame.

Phillip's shoulders slumped. He took a deep breath. For the first time in his life, he was at a loss on how to proceed.

Daniel clapped him on the back. "My advice, dear brother, is to go to her, make your apology, and hope she will forgive you."

For once Phillip agreed with his brother. He could not stay here. He needed to see her, know how she felt, ask her if she could consider forgiving him.

"Phillip," Mother must have understood his intention. "If you must go, then I insist you take a carriage. You can't possibly ride in your state. You only just returned from London."

"So he won't need to pack." Daniel grinned. "What are you waiting for?" He stepped away from the door and swung his arm invitingly.

"Yes. Yes." Phillip rushed forward.

"Phillip."

He stopped and turned to his mother.

"She is at Pembray House, Queen's Square."

"Thank you."

Without another word, he hurried from the room and set out for Bath.

Chapter Twenty-Seven

Mrs. Piper was true to her word and Elaine spent the next day in nervous preparation for her new role as teacher. On her second day, she stood in front of a half dozen girls ages ten to fourteen. They looked so young, Elaine could hardly believe she had once been their age and sat in those same chairs.

"This is Miss Brooke," Mrs. Piper introduced her. "Many of you remember her as a student here. But she is no longer a student and you must treat her with the same respect as the other teachers."

Elaine looked at their expectant faces and was surprised to see several new ones. It seemed even at Pembray House, things did not stay the same.

"Thank you, Mrs. Piper," Elaine said. "I am very pleased to be here."

After admonishing the students to be on their best behavior, Mrs. Piper left and Elaine was alone. For a moment, fear seized her. Then she took a deep breath and smiled. It was not her first time teaching and she was prepared.

"Today we will be discussing how best to manage your income."

The smallest girl, with raven black hair and striking green eyes, raised her hand.

"Yes?"

"Miss Brooke, I don't have an income." A few other girls smirked.

"Not now, but certainly you have pin money."

"Yes, but it's not much." The girl glanced down.

"I never had much pin money either, but that just made it easier to manage. You should pity those that have to balance all those purchases."

Some of the girls smiled, but one, Miss Turner, frowned.

"I don't see why she should pity me. I always have more money than I know what to do with. I never need to worry about managing my purchases."

Elaine was acquainted with Miss Turner. From her arrival at the age of eleven, she had been sure to inform everyone that her father had "heaps and heaps of money." Though she was now fourteen and more woman than child, it seemed she had not grown out of that unfortunate habit.

Elaine held back a sigh. How was she to get all the girls to understand the importance of this lesson? She had derived much benefit from the lesson when Miss Minerva had taught it.

"Learning to manage your money is helpful no matter the amount in your possession. And you must remember that fortunes change. Today you are only keeping track of your pin money, but in a few years, you may be responsible for a large household. Then you will be glad you know how to manage, save, and balance sums."

Miss Turner scoffed. "I would never marry a man so poor that I would need to watch my expenses."

"I would not be so sure of your future, Miss Turner. Life can change suddenly and if you were to find yourself in reduced circumstances you would be grateful for this knowledge."

"You might become an orphan and have a wicked stepmother," one of the younger girls said solemnly.

"Nonsense." Miss Turner tossed her head. "You read too many novels, Eliza."

"Of course, life is not a novel," Elaine interjected before the girls could begin to bicker in earnest. "We should be so lucky, for in novels the heroine gets a happy ending. In real life, there is no such guarantee. You might marry a wonderful and rich man, only to see him die young and your home entailed away to a cruel relative. Your betrothed might die and leave you devastated with no desire to marry another. You might be left an orphan and have to make your own way in the world with paltry funds."

Elaine looked over the young girls, trying to make them understand what she hadn't. "These are not just tragic tales from novels. I know a woman who was deceived by a man and now must maintain herself. I know a woman whose father died and they discovered he had gambled away everything. Misfortune strikes every day. Do not think you will be spared."

Elaine paused. There was no need to cast a pall over their first lesson. They would think her full of doom and gloom.

She had not abandoned her former optimism; she still believed she could be content. There were many of her acquaintance who had found happiness outside of a husband. Mrs. Piper had carved out a life of service and meaning, Lady Ashburn's arranged marriage brought her two sons and made her the leader of a neighborhood. And Mama had created her own island of enjoyment despite the disappointed hopes of her youth and small income.

"What I mean to say girls, is that you can't rely on anyone else to give you a happy ending or think that happiness only comes at the end of a story. You must grab hold of your life and find happiness."

The truth of her words hit Elaine. She was disappointed and heartsick now, but in time she would find happiness. She must.

"Now no more distractions, please get out your slates."

The rest of the lesson went smoothly and at the end, she was bursting with pride. Helping to teach these girls was good and useful work. She would learn to be cheerful here. She would not be like Elaine of Astolat and die from a broken heart. All she needed was time.

* * *

Trying to follow her own advice, Elaine attempted to be content with her situation. The schedule at Pembray House was familiar. The only change was that she now taught the lessons and supervised the girls with their other masters.

When she became distracted there was no scolding, only the giggling of her girls. She was no longer surrounded by her friends, but at night, after the girls had gone to bed, she spent an hour in tea and conversation with Mrs. Piper and Mrs. Ford, the current teacher of the older students. Elaine was not yet happy but she was carving out a new life, a quieter life than the one she imagined. It suited her current temperament. She had no interest in expanding her social circle.

Before she went to sleep, Elaine's mind would wander to Ryder Hall and its inscrutable owner. Replaying conversations and imagining different outcomes was pointless but she couldn't help herself. Night was also when she allowed herself to cry. It was then that she felt most like Elaine of Astolat. She would not die from her broken heart, but that did not stop the pain.

Elaine woke early most mornings. In need of exercise, she would sheepishly ask for a maid to accompany her on a walk to Crescent Fields. She wished Mrs. Ford was partial to walks so she might have a real companion. Miss Minerva had been partial to long walks and often supervised Elaine and her friends through Bath. But, like everyone else, Miss Minerva had moved on with her life. Elaine would just need to do the same.

On her fifth day at the school, Elaine found Mrs. Piper waiting for her at the door.

"I thought I would accompany you this morning."

"That would be most agreeable." Elaine was happy for the company.

The morning was chilly and a light fog hung over the streets, a harbinger of the coming winter. Elaine did not have her pelisse but welcomed the invigorating cold. She set out for the nearby Crescent Fields and Mrs. Piper made no objections. They walked in comfortable silence until they reached the relatively empty gravel walk.

"And how are you finding the life of a teacher?"

"I have been surprised by how different it is from being a student and yet so familiar."

Mrs. Piper regarded her for a long moment before she spoke. "When I first started the school, I was much like you, lost, missing a man that did not deserve my affection. You will never feel like the girl you once were. You have changed and there is nothing wrong with that."

Elaine wondered again about Mrs. Piper's past. One day, when they knew each other better, she hoped she would hear the full story.

"How long does it take? To feel like you belong? To forge a new home?"

Mrs. Piper gave her a knowing look. "It takes as long as it takes."

Elaine was surprised into a small laugh and Mrs. Piper smiled.

Their talk turned to discussing the girls. Mrs. Piper asked for Elaine's honest assessment of their abilities and how they might improve shortcomings. Elaine took to the topic and soon found herself eager to implement the new ideas. Helping Eliza with her penmanship or trying to temper Miss Turner's pride were easier problems to focus on.

In the midst of the conversation, Elaine suddenly found herself wishing to talk over her plans with Sir Phillip. What would he think of their strategies? What insights might he have? She pushed the imaginary conversation with him away and tried to concentrate on Mrs. Piper's words.

"I think we should be going back," Mrs. Piper said.

Elaine nodded though she would have preferred to continue; they had only just passed the Royal Crescent. As they turned toward Pembray House, they resumed the conversation. When they had come again to the gravel walk, Mrs. Piper pulled her closer.

"I don't like the look of that fellow."

Elaine followed her gaze to a man approaching from the opposite direction. She gasped and stopped walking. At first, she could not credit what she saw. Surely she had conjured him with her mind? She blinked several times, but the image did not change. It was Sir Phillip.

Elaine could understand Mrs. Piper's trepidation. He looked far from the composed and impeccably dressed baronet. His great coat was crumpled, his cheeks covered in stubble, his head hatless and hair wild. He held his hat in his hand and slapped it against his thigh as he walked, oblivious to the world around him. He was staring at the path ahead as his lips moved silently.

"I am sorry to have worried you," Mrs. Piper said. "I am sure he is harmless."

Elaine's eyes were fixed on Sir Phillip and she did not answer. How had he come to be here? Would they forever be meeting unexpectedly on morning walks? It was almost enough to put her off the habit.

He was drawing closer but had not looked up. When he did, would he acknowledge her? Speak to her? Possibilities whirled in her mind but before she could imagine a scenario he looked up and saw her.

He stopped short and stared, looking as surprised as she felt.

"Do you know him?" Mrs. Piper asked.

Elaine could only nod.

He strode forward. Elaine's heart was pounding so loud she thought Mrs. Piper must be able to hear it.

He reached them and made a deep bow. "Miss Brooke," he said huskily.

As she rose from her curtsey, she turned to Mrs. Piper. "Mrs. Piper, may I present Sir Phillip Ashburn."

Mrs. Piper's eyebrows rose but she allowed the introduction.

"It is such a pleasure to meet you," Sir Phillip said. "Miss Brooke has spoken often of her time in your excellent school." Sir Phillip's eyes darted to Elaine.

"That is gratifying to hear," Mrs. Piper said flatly. "Now if you will excuse us, we must be getting back to my school."

Elaine was reluctant to move.

"May I walk with you?" Sir Phillip looked at her hopefully.

Elaine wanted to say yes. She wanted to say no. What was he doing in Bath?

"Thank you, sir, but we know the way." Mrs. Piper's tone was icy.

Sir Phillip swallowed and nodded. He looked down at his hat, as if suddenly realizing he wasn't wearing it. He looked up with determination in his eyes.

"Then may I call on you?"

Elaine had not the heart to refuse him but she turned to Mrs. Piper for permission. The older lady was frowning but gave a slight nod.

"You may call," Elaine said.

"But not for long," Mrs. Piper added. "She has responsibilities to attend to."

"As you wish, madam." Sir Phillip gave a hesitant smile.

Mrs. Piper took her leave and pulled Elaine with her. They didn't speak, or at least Elaine didn't hear anything that Mrs. Piper might have said. Even as they moved away, Elaine's mind remained with Sir Phillip.

Had he come to see her? If she had walked with him, would he have confessed his love? He would take her hand and—Elaine cut off the thought. She would not make the same mistake, not again.

She must keep hold of her hopes and fancy. She would not imagine that Sir Phillip felt anything for her. He might be in Bath on business. He could be calling as a mere courtesy. She would make no speculations, imagine no fantasies. She would wait for him to call and until then she would not think of him at all.

It seemed an eternity away, but came all too soon.

Chapter Twenty-Eight

W ith more hope than he had any right to feel, Phillip watched Miss Brooke walk away. He would prefer to be walking with her but was satisfied with permission to call. He had spent much of the carriage ride worried that he would not be allowed even that.

The full moon had allowed him to travel through the night. He slept briefly, the bouncing carriage and his nerves keeping him awake. The sun was just beginning to paint the sky pink as they found Pembray House. When Phillip climbed from the carriage and looked at the white townhouse gleaming in the early morning light, he became all too aware that it would be hours before it would be proper to call.

Providence, or mere stubbornness, drew Phillip to instruct his servants to meet him at the inn while he stretched his legs with a walk. He was deep in thought, rehearsing what he would say to Miss Brooke when she appeared before him.

In his distraction, he had forgotten her penchant for early morning walks. But unlike their previous encounters, Miss Brooke was not alone and there had been no chance to truly speak.

Mrs. Piper had clearly not approved of him.

Phillip looked down at his disheveled appearance. He didn't blame her; he looked a sight. Hardly in a fit state to be making declarations of love to a woman. Exercise forgotten, Phillip strode purposely to his lodgings. Once his valet shaved and dressed him, perhaps Mrs. Piper would not look so forbidding at him.

Hours later, he looked considerably more like a baronet as he once again approached the door of Pembray House. Above, he saw a curtain flicker and caught a flash of dark hair; someone above was spying. The door opened and a swarthy, middle-aged butler ushered him into the house.

Above, Phillip could hear giggling from an open door. How many girls were in the school? Would he have to sit before all of them? How would he talk to Miss Brooke then? He had been spoiled in the country with all the opportunities to speak with her alone.

The butler gave him a stern look. Phillip shifted his weight, his stomach was in a riot, his palms sweaty, and he hadn't even seen Miss Brooke yet. Instead of leading him upstairs, the butler ushered him down the hall and glared him into the room. Phillip felt like he should apologize to the man but he didn't know for what.

"The ladies will join you presently."

"Thank you."

The room was small and cozy, not a formal drawing room. He didn't know if that was a good sign, but he was happy not to be facing a room full of girls. He looked at the chairs but could not sit. He paced the length of the room instead, his anxiety growing with each step.

Daniel had told him to make a dashing proposal, but Phillip did not think himself capable of properly talking about his feelings. No, he would take the advice Miss Brooke had given Daniel. He would apologize first for his rudeness and then ask her if he had some hope of earning her favor.

The door opened. Phillip turned but Miss Brooke was not there, only the tall and stern Mrs. Piper. He had imagined Mrs. Piper to be his mother's age but she was a much younger woman. He greeted her formally. His change in appearance did not dispel the coldness in her gaze.

"Sir Phillip, I confess that I am allowing you to see Miss Brooke against my better judgment."

"Oh." Phillip did not know what to say to such a blunt assessment. Would she deny him?

"You have ten minutes and then I will return. Unless Miss Brooke speaks for you, I will then bar you from this house."

"I understand. I would not wish to stay where I was not wanted."

He hoped ten minutes would be enough. After a long assessing look, Mrs. Piper departed. It seemed an eternity before Miss Brooke appeared.

They greeted each other and then fell into a brief silence. Neither sat.

"Do you have business in Bath?" she asked.

"Not everything in my life is about business."

"I did not say it was." Miss Brooke sounded wounded. This would never do.

Phillip looked down and took a deep breath. "My sole purpose in coming here was to see you." When she didn't reply he looked up. Her eyes were full of questions. "I came to ask you. That is, I know I have not behaved as I should. But if you would consider. . ."

The words would not come. How could he possibly say all that he felt? He met her eyes. The bright green stood out more than he could remember. The words came in a rush.

"Can you possibly forgive me for my arrogant assumptions? For my stupidity? I should have spoken that morning, after the assembly."

"We did speak," she said.

"We argued. It was not what I intended."

"What you intended does not matter, only your actions."

She was right and had every reason to resent him. "I traveled all night so I could be here and ask for your forgiveness."

"To what end? Why come all this way to apologize to your penniless neighbor?"

"I didn't come just to apologize. I came to tell you I love you." The words were out, said with less grace and more anger than he intended, but he had said them.

She blinked at him in disbelief, tears dropped from her brimming eyes. "You love me?"

He was fairly certain a woman was not supposed to cry when you confessed your feelings. Chastened, he ducked his head.

"And how long before your feelings are overpowered by your reason?" Miss Brooke asked bitterly.

"I beg your pardon?"

"No doubt the consideration of my fortune prevented you from speaking before. What has changed?"

"It was not your fortune that deterred me, but your relationship with my brother. I was jealous and behaved irrationally."

"Jealous? Sir Phillip of Ryder Hall was jealous?"

"Yes. I thought that you. . ." Phillip shook his head. It seemed ridiculous now that he knew the full truth. "I devised the house party as a means to get Daniel to marry Miss Talbot. But then you were there and one look, one conversation, and it was clear Daniel would be a complete fool not to prefer you. I did my best to keep you apart."

She frowned. "The drive about the estate, the conversations at dinner, dancing with me, was all to keep me away from Daniel?"

"No! That is, it started that way, but it was not long before I thought more of you than him. I came to enjoy our time together, to look forward to our conversations. But it seemed you still cared for Daniel, still wanted him."

Miss Brooke shook her head. "But I don't. I don't care for him in that way."

"But you did. You cannot deny that at one time Daniel was your ideal man."

He shouldn't push but a part of him still wondered if all her tender feelings for Daniel were truly gone.

"I was a child. What did I know of men or love? Of course, when I saw him again, I did think. . . but that seems so long ago. My desires have greatly altered." Her eyes became unfocused as she thought. Hope stirred in him for the first time since she walked into the room. He wanted to reach for her and for once, he gave into the impulse.

He took her hand in his and when she met his eyes, her cheeks were still wet. He reached up and brushed the remnants of her tears away.

"My desires have also changed since that first day. I now wish for nothing but to have you by my side, always."

A quick intake of breath was followed by a small smile. "Are you saying you don't think of me as a sister?"

He pursed his lips. Could she not answer him?

"Pray forget I ever said such a thing. I was driven by the belief that you were engaged to Daniel. I was convinced I had no choice but to regard you as a sister."

Her smile grew. "Engaged? I thought I was the one prone to wild fancies. How could you think such a thing? Surely you know he loves Miss Talbot."

"I know that now! But I saw you in the library that night." Phillip could not meet her eyes while he recounted his foolishness. "You were smiling and he held you in his arms. I thought he had just asked for your hand. What conclusion was I meant to draw?"

Miss Brooke's hand came to his chin and gently raised it until their gazes met. Her eyes danced with merriment as she smirked.

"If I was to accept an offer from a man, this is how I would treat him." Then she drew her face to his and he only had time to catch his breath before their lips were touching. It was brief, a tantalizing promise of things to come. She pulled away, blushing furiously but smiling.

Pure elation filled him. She was not indifferent. She had accepted his offer. He pulled her into his arms. This time the kiss was longer, firmer, and a promise of the life before them. They broke apart only at Mrs. Piper's voice.

"Well, it seems ten minutes was too long."

Sheepishly, Phillip pulled away from Miss Brooke but kept firm possession of her hand.

They had much to speak on, much to decide together, but he wasn't afraid. He was eager for their future.

Epilogue

The cold air and frost made the Old Priory sparkle in the midday sun. Beams of light streamed through the windows, turning the dusting of snow into a carpet of diamonds. Elaine did not mark the chill because she was enveloped in her husband's arms.

She pulled away from their kiss and breathed deeply, the cold biting her lungs. She smiled at him.

Phillip grinned as he tucked a stray hair under her bonnet. Four months ago, Elaine could not have imagined seeing Sir Phillip Ashburn grin so often and so freely. She was happy her imagination had been so lacking. He wrapped his arms around her, pulling her closer. She snuggled into his shoulder while he put his chin on her head.

"So, has the priory worked its magic?" His voice rumbled against her cheek.

"I do feel a little more relaxed. Though that might be the company," she said into his coat.

He chuckled and rubbed a soothing circle along her lower back. Elaine wished they could stay away from the hall all day, but their responsibilities could not be ignored. They had a house full of guests and Twelfth Night was fast approaching. When Phillip had grabbed her hand and told her they were going for a drive, she should have guessed the destination.

The Old Priory was fast becoming their sanctuary. Away from the servants, responsibilities, and the expectations of the neighborhood, she felt more like herself. Being among the ancient stones always gave Elaine perspective and peace. She had needed both in her first month as Lady Ashburn.

She sighed again. "I just keep thinking that something will go wrong and the whole neighborhood will blame me for spoiling the ball," she confessed.

Phillip pulled away so he could meet her eyes. "What could possibly go wrong?"

"I could mess up the figures of the opening dance."

"You dance beautifully. I have yet to see you misstep."

"The food and drink might not be to anyone's liking."

"It's the same menu we always serve."

"There might be a storm and nobody can come or they do come and then get stranded at the hall."

"That would hardly be your fault and we would manage. It would not be the first time winter weather trapped guests."

"A game of snapdragon might get out of hand and the curtains could catch fire. The entire hall might burn down."

Phillip cocked his head and his lips twitched.

"It might happen," Elaine insisted.

"While I love your ability to imagine all kinds of possibilities, I think your talent might be better served by contemplating all the ways the ball will be a success."

"Perhaps."

"You will charm everyone with your manner and your smile. They will all remark how marriage suits me. Everyone will enjoy the night so thoroughly they won't want to leave. Even the Covingtons will be forced to admit that you make a marvelous Lady Ashburn."

She liked his version of the ball better than her doom-filled fancies.

"And if there is snow or a fire, I am confident you will handle it with grace, just as you have handled all your new duties."

The weight of being Lady Ashburn was heavier than Elaine had imagined. And after Phillip came to Bath, she had had ample time to imagine their life together.

They had not married immediately. She still had her obligation to teach and he had a busy harvest to oversee. They had written letters and had occasional visits. It was the longest two months of her life. Finally, in November, they had married at Brightworth church.

Becoming Phillip's wife had been easy compared to becoming Lady Ashburn. She would never regret marrying him, but she sometimes wished the house wasn't quite so grand or the servants so numerous. His mother had patiently helped her and even done most of the work for the Twelfth Night ball. The older woman kept assuring her that she would grow into the role. She better understood now how daunting becoming the baronet must have been for Phillip and it made her love him more.

She slid her hand into his silky hair and pulled him down for another kiss. Their responsibilities could wait a little longer.

* * *

The next few days flew by and the night of the ball came all too soon. Elaine was standing in the ballroom, fussing with some decorations. All around her, the servants went about their jobs with admirable efficiency.

"Elaine dear," the Dowager Lady Ashburn appeared beside her. "I told you to go and rest. It will be a long night."

"I just wanted to see how the decorations were coming. As a young girl, that was my favorite part of the ball."

The dowager grabbed her hands and Elaine was forced to stop what she was doing. She looked up at her mother-in-law as she tried to quell her tears.

"Elaine, I promise you all will be well. You have done splendidly and nobody worth knowing will find fault. Your true friends will congratulate you on your success and the rest can go hang."

Elaine giggled. Lady Ashburn had never spoken quite so plainly. The dowager often reminded her that part of being the leader of the neighborhood was knowing which connections were worth cultivating. She might never gain acceptance from the Covingtons or Edgertons, but there were many other families who had warmly received her.

"You are right," Elaine said. "I am so glad you are here to guide me. I don't know where I would be without your help."

"Nonsense. Your Mrs. Piper taught you well. You are more than capable. Next year, you won't even miss my help."

Elaine furrowed her brow. The dowager often implied that she would not be staying at the hall. Elaine always meant to ask her about her plans but the timing was never right. In her heart, she hoped a certain naval captain had something to do with these references.

When Elaine had proposed inviting Captain Hart for the holidays, Phillip had smiled and not raised an objection. Over the last week, it was clear there was something between Captain Hart and the dowager, but Elaine tried not to get carried away in her assumptions.

"It is utterly transformed!"

They turned to see Daniel and Freddie joining them. Freddie was looking about the room with wide eyes. Elaine appreciated the praise, even though it was Freddie's first Twelfth Night at Ryder Hall so she had no comparison.

Daniel watched his wife with a fond smile. He was as handsome as ever, yet Elaine felt nothing but a sisterly affection when she looked at him.

"I can't wait to throw a ball at our home," Freddie said.

Though Daniel and Freddie had married in September, they had only just returned from their marriage trip. They had not yet moved into their new estate, but spent much of the time discussing their plans for it. Daniel was still quick with a jest but when it came to his new responsibilities, he was all seriousness.

As Freddie continued her raptures, Phillip leaning in the doorway caught Elaine's attention. Her heart skittered. Though she had seen him at breakfast, she was struck by how attractive he looked in his blue coat. He watched her closely with the stare that used to unnerve her but now filled her with warmth.

Freddie soon noticed her distraction and turned to follow her gaze. Phillip pushed off the doorframe and strode to them.

"Phillip, there you are," his mother said. "Come, we were admiring your wife's work."

"I think he was just admiring his wife," Daniel said in an undertone.

Elaine blushed but Phillip smiled. "You are right, that was exactly what I was doing." He clapped Daniel on the back. "Does not Lady Ashburn look remarkably pretty?"

Daniel smiled. "Her beauty is surpassed only by the ravishing Mrs. Ashburn."

Freddie and Elaine exchanged an exasperated look. The two brothers delighted in dispensing dueling compliments. Elaine enjoyed this dulled version of their old bickering. It matched the change in their relationship. Now that Phillip no longer resented his brother and Daniel didn't feel stifled, they were becoming something like friends.

"I think we can all agree that you both married women too sensible to want to be in competition," the dowager said.

"My thoughts exactly," Freddie agreed.

Elaine nodded. She was happy to call Freddie her sister.

"I agree there is no competition." Phillip smirked. "Now, if you will excuse me, I need Lady Ashburn for something important." He spoke in an authoritative tone he rarely used with her.

"What has happened?" she asked, suddenly worried something had gone wrong. "Did the food spoil? Is there snow falling?"

"No, nothing like that," Phillip assured her.

"Have the footmen all come down with colds? Did everyone change their mind about coming?"

"I promise it is not so dire. Just come with me."

"Phillip, you best tell me now."

Daniel laughed. "My dear sister, I believe what your husband wishes to communicate is best done in private."

The tips of Phillip's ears grew red and understanding dawned on Elaine. Daniel put his hands on her shoulder and propelled her toward his brother. She took his arm with all the dignity she could muster through her embarrassment. She was Lady Ashburn, after all.

Wordlessly, he led her to the stairs. He glanced up and down the corridor before dipping his head and kissing her swiftly.

"I hate to admit when Daniel is right, but I do have several important things to say to you in private."

She giggled and allowed herself to be led up the stairs to their chambers.

When the door closed, he took her in his arms. He did not kiss her right away but stared into her eyes. She had once thought his eyes dull and incapable of sparkling like Daniel's. How wrong she had been.

There was a time when she did not know what his stares meant or what he was thinking. She would exhaust her imagination trying to understand him. But now she didn't need her imagination; his eyes were so full of love that it took her breath away.

"You know, even if every single thing went wrong tonight, it would not change how I feel about you."

"Oh?" She arched an eyebrow. "I seem to recall you once said that you regarded me as a sister."

Phillip groaned. "Will I never live that down?"

"Hmmm, perhaps you should show me how you feel. Just so there are no misunderstandings."

Her husband needed no further promptings and swiftly dipped his lips to hers. His kisses left her senseless. When he pulled away, she sighed.

He pulled her towards the bed and gently pushed her down. "Enough, you must rest," he said. "Twelfth Night will require all of your stamina."

She frowned at him. "Must you always be so managing?"

He did not rise to the bait but leaned down and kissed her forehead. "It will be a wonderful night, trust me."

She nodded and laid down. He looked at her for a long moment before turning for the door. After tossing and turning with all the worries in her head, she eventually managed to rest.

In the end, Phillip's predictions came true and her worries were for naught. There was no snow. The guests all arrived in good time. Everyone she greeted smiled and praised her, even the Covingtons. When it came time to open the dance, she was still nervous, until Phillip whispered in her ear.

"Confidence."

Then she lifted her chin and fancied herself as noble as Queen Guinevere.

As she twirled and spun about the room, she felt giddy with her triumph. Daniel and Freddie danced beside them and they shared jests and smiles throughout the set. When the music faded, she was standing beside Daniel.

He nudged her. "Look there."

She followed his gaze and spotted two small faces pressed against the glass.

"Remember when we used to watch from the windows?" he asked.

Elaine nodded. It was from that window she had watched Daniel and dreamed of one day being his wife. Phillip came to her side, his smile wide and his eyes dancing. Her heart swelled as she took his arm.

In all her daydreams, Elaine had never imagined she would find such perfect happiness. She was glad her reality had turned out far better than her dreams.

* * *

Enjoyed the book? You can make a difference!

In a world full of excellent entertainment, reviews are a powerful way to find readers. I'm a new author so every review counts. Honest reviews help others find my books. And the more readers I have the more books I will be able to write!

If you enjoyed *The Imagined Attachment* I would be very grateful if you could spend a few minutes leaving a review. It can be as short as you like and it would mean the world to me. Find the book here: **https://books2read.co m/Imagined**

Want more? Join the Newsletter and get an exclusive short story featuring the beginning of Daniel and Freddie's courtship

The best part of being a writer is getting to connect with readers. I send occasional newsletters with updates on my writing, details on new releases, and fun freebies. No spam. Ever.

Sign-Up at: **https://tinyurl.com/hjsubscribe**

About the Author

Holli Jo is a country girl who joined the Army and became a Captain before leaving the service to travel and pursue writing. She enjoys all genres as long as they have some romance. Holli Jo has survived live nerve agent training, deployed to Afghanistan, climbed Kilimanjaro, backpacked around the world, and SCUBA dived in Bali so she knows that sometimes staying home with a book is the best adventure of all.

You can connect with me on:

🌐 https://hollijomonroe.com

📘 https://www.facebook.com/AuthorHollijo

🔗 https://www.instagram.com/hollijo.writes

Subscribe to my newsletter:

✉ https://tinyurl.com/hjsubscribe